The Cowboy's Outlaw Bride

By Cora Seton

Author's Note

The Cowboy's Outlaw Bride is the second volume in the Turners v. Coopers series. To find out more, look for the rest of the books in the series, including:

The Cowboy's Secret Bride (Volume 1)
The Cowboy's Hidden Bride (Volume 3)
The Cowboy's Stolen Bride (Volume 4)
The Cowboy's Forbidden Bride (Volume 5)

Also, don't miss Cora Seton's Chance Creek series, the Cowboys of Chance Creek, the Heroes of Chance Creek, the Brides of Chance Creek, and the SEALs of Chance Creek:

The Cowboys of Chance Creek Series:

The Cowboy Inherits a Bride (Volume 0)
The Cowboy's E-Mail Order Bride (Volume 1)
The Cowboy Wins a Bride (Volume 2)
The Cowboy Imports a Bride (Volume 3)
The Cowgirl Ropes a Billionaire (Volume 4)
The Sheriff Catches a Bride (Volume 5)
The Cowboy Lassos a Bride (Volume 6)
The Cowboy Rescues a Bride (Volume 7)
The Cowboy Earns a Bride (Volume 8)
The Cowboy's Christmas Bride (Volume 9)

The Heroes of Chance Creek Series:

The Navy SEAL's E-Mail Order Bride (Volume 1)
The Soldier's E-Mail Order Bride (Volume 2)
The Marine's E-Mail Order Bride (Volume 3)
The Navy SEAL's Christmas Bride (Volume 4)
The Airman's E-Mail Order Bride (Volume 5)

The Brides of Chance Creek Series:

Issued to the Bride One Navy SEAL
Issued to the Bride One Airman
Issued to the Bride One Sniper
Issued to the Bride One Marine
Issued to the Bride One Soldier

The SEALs of Chance Creek Series:

A SEAL's Oath
A SEAL's Vow
A SEAL's Pledge
A SEAL's Consent
A SEAL's Purpose
A SEAL's Resolve
A SEAL's Devotion
A SEAL's Desire
A SEAL's Struggle
A SEAL's Triumph

Visit Cora's website at www.coraseton.com
Find Cora on Facebook at facebook.com/CoraSeton
Sign up for my newsletter HERE.
www.coraseton.com/sign-up-for-my-newsletter

Chapter One

I T WOULD BE a miracle if this wedding didn't end with a fistfight.

Noah Turner watched Carl Whitfield waltz with his new bride, Camila, alone on the temporary dance floor built in the front yard of the Whitfields' new ranch. Surrounded by friends and family, it was clear they saw no one but each other. They deserved their happiness as far as Noah was concerned, but judging by the sour expression on his uncle Jed's face—and the looks and attitudes of the rest of the Turners and Coopers present—not everyone wished Carl and Camila well.

Carl had made the mistake of living for three years on Cooper land, renting a cabin from them at Thorn Hill, their extensive ranch. Camila had rented a cabin on Turner land at the Flying W for just as long. As far as Noah's uncle was concerned, Carl could be a Cooper himself, which made his marriage to Camila, an honorary Turner in Jed's mind, insupportable.

It would be funny if everyone wasn't taking it so damn seriously. Noah was keeping an especially close eye on his brother, Liam, who was glaring across the dance floor at Lance Cooper. Those two were apt to throw down whenever they met up. Noah wished they'd get over whatever had caused all that animosity between them, but the feud had stood between the Turners and Coopers for over a hundred years, and it obviously wasn't going to end tonight.

Which made it impossible for him to ask Olivia Cooper to dance.

He wanted to, though. Badly enough it took all his strength to stay where he was.

Olivia looked beautiful tonight in a short, light-blue off-the-shoulder dress. Her long legs were encased in cowboy boots. Her blonde hair done up in a twist. She looked sassy and sexy, and Noah couldn't keep his eyes off her.

No surprise: he could never look away when Olivia was around.

Everything had conspired to make this night a wonderful celebration for the newlyweds. The air was soft and warm. The evening sky glowed with an early June sunset. Stars were beginning to light up overhead one by one. The murmur of the other guests and the sweet melody of the string quartet provided a backdrop for the swaying couple. Noah wished he could relax and enjoy the occasion, but happy endings belonged to people like Carl and Camila, not people like him. Carl was a millionaire, and every inch of his new ranch oozed prosperity.

The Flying W didn't look half as good these days. Noah's family had fallen on hard times, and no matter how hard he worked, he couldn't seem to get them out from under their bills. He envied Carl the partner he'd gained in this wedding, too. Camila wasn't wealthy, but she had a good head on her shoulders, worked hard and obviously loved her new husband. What would it be like to have someone to share your life with? Someone on your side the way Camila seemed committed to Carl?

His own parents' marriage hadn't worked out, and that's when the fortunes of his family had turned. His mother had decamped to Ohio. His father died a few years back. Now Noah, the oldest of his siblings, was left in charge.

He was making a mess of the job. How could he expect any woman to want to be with him if he couldn't get it together?

His gaze slid to Olivia again. She was talking with her great-aunt Virginia on the other side of the dance floor, a stern old woman with upright bearing who carried an old black umbrella wherever she went. It was in her hand now. It was closed, and she was using it like a cane, leaning on it for support. She looked frustrated—or maybe *thwarted* was a better word. She didn't approve of this wedding any more than Noah's uncle Jed did.

Olivia was far more animated, talking rapidly, gesturing at the dancing couple. Trying to convince her aunt of something. Noah sighed, shoving his hands in the pockets of his good jeans. Much as he was attracted to Olivia, if he married someday, it couldn't be to her.

The Coopers had been his family's enemies since 1882, when Ernestine Harris jilted Olivia's great, great,

great, great-grandfather, Slade Cooper, and married Noah's great, great, great, great-grandfather, Zeke Turner, instead. The feud between their families had been renewed when Virginia and Jed had a falling out in their early twenties. Then there was the trouble thirteen years ago...

Noah didn't like to think about that. He still wasn't sure exactly what had happened, except Olivia's father, Dale, had landed in jail, and her mother, Enid, had taken her and her siblings to Idaho for nearly a decade, leaving them with her sister when she ran off with a man and settled in New Mexico.

His own mother, Mary, had left home soon after Dale was arrested. Sometimes the disintegration of his and Olivia's families seemed linked in his mind, but it was only coincidence that it happened at the same time. Olivia's dad didn't live long enough to serve out his term. Noah's own father, William, died soon after. Even though the family rivalry hadn't caused this set of problems, the old feud was still in effect. His great-uncle Jed constantly bickered with Olivia's great-aunt Virginia at the Prairie Garden assisted living facility where they both lived. His brother, Liam, got into fisticuffs with Olivia's brother Lance with depressing regularity.

Thank goodness her sister, Tory, had decamped for Seattle years ago, or who knew what kind of arguments she'd have with his sister Stella. As for his youngest sister, Maya, who was near to Olivia's age, she and Olivia pretended each other didn't exist.

They were like Capulets and Montagues, Crips and

Bloods… or, more apt, Hatfields and McCoys.

Which made it damn awkward he couldn't seem to get Olivia off his mind these days.

What did she think about him?

Did she ever think about him at all?

Noah settled his hat more firmly on his head. Probably not. Hell, he'd caught Olivia breaking and entering into his own house just a couple of weeks ago. She wouldn't do that if she liked him, would she?

He suppressed a smile. Actually, when he'd caught her she hadn't been in too much of a hurry to get away. In fact, she'd almost let him drive her to the Spring Fling Fair, except his family had arrived and all hell had broken loose.

Maybe she did like him a little bit.

But that didn't make their situation any better.

She clearly wasn't pleased with whatever her great-aunt was saying now. Noah edged sideways to get a better look. Virginia stood tapping the ground with her umbrella, giving Olivia what-for. As Noah watched, Olivia rolled her eyes and crossed her arms over her chest. Noah wondered what had riled up those two.

Not that it took much to rile a Cooper.

"What do you think that's about?" Maya appeared at his elbow and offered him a plate that held several kinds of dessert. Noah waved it off, and she shrugged, scooping up a bite of cake with her fork. Almost a foot shorter than him, with light brown hair and a pert nose, she stood on tiptoe to try to see. It was obvious she'd been watching the Coopers, too. She might ignore

Olivia in public, but privately she seemed awfully interested in what Olivia got up to.

"Who knows?" He didn't want Maya to catch on that he was awfully interested, too.

"Life would be a whole lot more peaceful if they hadn't come back to town." She stabbed her fork into the cake again.

"Don't say that."

"Why not?"

Noah thought fast. "Thorn Hill is their home, just like the Flying W is ours. Must have been hard enough for them to stay away as long as they did."

What would Maya say if she knew who'd kept the lights on at Thorn Hill the whole time the Coopers were away? It sure had been a surprise to him when Lucas Maynard, the family's solicitor, took him aside after his father's death to explain the job his father had passed on to him. Noah still didn't understand why William was caught up in Cooper affairs.

This wasn't the time for that conversation, though. His father had wished to keep the arrangement a secret, and it was all done now—the Coopers were back at Thorn Hill, running it themselves. He'd keep his mouth shut and spend the rest of his life wondering what had happened thirteen years ago to make partners of two men who'd spent their lives on opposite sides of a family feud.

"You're always so fair," Maya chided him. "Anyway, it doesn't matter what we think about it. They're here now."

"Yes, they are." Noah wasn't sure whether to thank God or curse Him for that. Olivia had gotten under his skin good these past few years, and he couldn't shake her off. She kept him up nights. Kept him prowling the Dancing Boot, running errands with the hope of seeing her in town, riding down to their western pastures with the hopes of catching a glimpse of her across Pittance Creek.

He was acting like a teenager. Hell, he was certainly as frustrated as one.

"They're going to win the Founder's Prize, too, with that school renovation project they're spearheading," Maya said. "Them or the Washingtons, with their reforestation project on the edge of town. Wish we'd thought of that. I know Uncle Jed thinks we can run off with the Ridley property because we donated the high school a hundred years ago, but he's wrong. I think we need to make a plan."

Noah thought Jed was wrong, too. "What kind of plan?" The Ridley property was a huge, abandoned ranch that abutted the Flying W—and Thorn Hill. It straddled Pittance Creek. Whoever won the Founder's Prize would take possession of that ranch—and control the flow of water to both the downstream ranches and beyond.

"A good one."

Across the room, Olivia rolled her eyes at her aunt again and shook her head. Noah could almost read her lips as she spoke: "I'll take care of it."

Take care of what?

Virginia said something sharp back and walked away. Olivia scanned the crowd, her mouth tilting into a private smile. Then she turned and headed around the house toward the driveway.

What was she up to?

"I'll think about it," Noah told Maya. "Gotta go."

"Go where? Noah!"

He didn't answer. Didn't look back, either. He couldn't be seen trailing Olivia, so he made a wide arc through the crowd around the dance floor and waited until he'd turned the corner of the Whitfields' large house before he broke into a run. He caught the red glow of taillights as Olivia backed out of her parking space and drove away. He dashed across the parking lot, hopped in his Ram pickup, and quickly followed.

Once out on the country highway, he hung back, not wanting to spook her, but Olivia kept a steady pace and drove in a straight line toward her destination. She must have thought she'd gotten away clean, or—more likely—she simply hadn't given a thought to being followed. She was probably going home, he told himself, and here he was acting like a stalker. But something about that smile made him think she might have another plan....

Noah straightened when they got to the turnoff. If she wanted to go to her family's ranch, she needed to turn left. Instead she went straight.

Toward the Flying W.

Noah shook his head as he followed her slowly, still hanging back. Just as he'd suspected: she was going to try to complete the robbery he'd foiled about a month ago. He'd caught her creeping into his house in the middle of the day, crossing to the living room and lifting their grandmother clock off the fireplace mantel—the one Ernestine had kept over a hundred years ago when she married Zeke instead of Slade.

Did Olivia really think she could steal it tonight?

Not if he could help it.

Noah knew why Olivia thought the clock belonged to the Coopers, and rationally he had to admit there was a case for it, but nothing about the relationship between the Coopers and Turners was rational. It never had been.

Back in 1882, the scandal had split the town, with most people taking the Coopers' side, until Slade diverted Pittance Creek and left the Flying W without its water for an entire summer. In the end he saw reason—at the barrel of a loaded gun wielded by Zeke, some said—and Pittance Creek ran true to its course again.

Things hadn't gone easy between the Coopers and Turners since then. And the Turners had never relinquished that clock—figuring it was payment for their trouble that long, dry summer.

In 1951, when his uncle Jed was courting Virginia Cooper, rumor had it he might return the clock to the Coopers when they married, but they never got that far. He stood Virginia up on the day of the Founder's Ball and went with Maybelle Wright instead. Virginia refused to listen when he came to apologize the next day. They never dated again. Neither of them ever married, either.

Jed kept the clock, and it remained with the Turners to this day.

Noah suspected Virginia had just ordered Olivia to steal it. He couldn't blame Olivia for wanting to please her aunt, but there was a line.

He waited several minutes before turning in after her, but first he dimmed his headlights so as not to give his presence away. The moon had risen, and it gave off plenty of light to steer by. Besides, he knew this terrain like the back of his hand.

Which meant he shouldn't slip up and fall for Olivia Cooper.

Except he already had.

He parked several hundred yards from the house on a bend in the driveway where trees and brush blocked his truck from view, then ran noiselessly the rest of the way until he could see the front door.

Like most folks in these parts, his family didn't lock the place when they left. This was a small town. Everyone knew each other.

Maybe they'd better start.

The door was partway open, probably the better to slip out of if Olivia surprised someone at home. Noah knew there wasn't anyone to surprise, however. They were all at the Whitfields' wedding. He slipped inside as quietly as he could, took a moment to let his eyes adjust to the dimness inside the unlit hall and held his breath.

There. In the living room.

He heard a footstep. A scraping sound of wood sliding over wood.

Olivia was taking the clock right now.

He stepped lightly to the entrance of the living room and eased around the corner.

Olivia's slim, shapely form was lit by the moonlight sliding through the wide windows at the back of the house, framing her in front of the large fireplace. Her arms upraised, in the act of lifting down the clock, her every curve was evident. He couldn't help feeling connected to Olivia, even while she was stealing his clock. She was trying to please her aunt, the same way he was always trying to do what was best for his family. Olivia deserved far more than she'd gotten from life, and he wished he could be the one to make up for all the difficulties she'd known.

He remembered the girl she'd once been before the latest round of trouble had torn apart their families. Olivia was five years younger than him, so they hadn't been in high school together. She was just a cute preteen he used to stumble over in the stacks of the Chance Creek public library now and then when he was doing research for some high school class. He knew she volunteered there, but what he remembered most was her library cart half-full of the books she was supposed to reshelve, and Olivia sitting cross-legged on the ground, so buried in a novel she didn't look up when he passed. Noah had been raised to think of Coopers as thieves and ne'er-do-wells—his great-uncle's term for them. *Some ne'er-do-well,* he used to tell himself with a grin whenever he spotted Olivia like that. She was just a little girl.

Now she was grown up, and she was… stunning.

He still remembered the first time he'd bumped into her when she'd come back to town three years ago. He'd stopped at the hardware store to pick up a few things. Outside, a kid had a box full of puppies he was trying to give away to good homes. Noah had spotted an unfamiliar blonde crouching down by the box, picking up and cuddling first one and then another of the puppies, until she'd given each of them an equal amount of love. When she straightened and turned around, she'd been familiar, but he couldn't place her face at first.

"You want to take a picture, cowboy?" she'd drawled at him.

Then he'd remembered.

"Olivia? Is that you?" he'd asked, too flummoxed to pretend he hadn't been ogling her.

"It's me." She'd grinned at him, as if she wasn't a Cooper and he wasn't a Turner. As if they were merely a man and a woman—and were allowed to flirt.

He wasn't allowed to flirt with Olivia Cooper, but he'd wanted to ever since. He wanted to pull her close. Touch those curves. Wanted to explore her body with his hands—his mouth—

He dragged his thoughts back to the present. Olivia's family was about to steal the Founder's Prize away from his. If the Coopers were allowed to take possession of the Ridley property, they'd control the creek. Which meant just like their forebears, they could divert the water and leave the Flying W dry.

He couldn't let that happen.

Couldn't let a Cooper steal their clock, either. Even a really cute Cooper.

Noah stepped into the living room. "Drop it!"

Olivia shrieked and nearly did so, just stopping the clock's fall with a shove back onto the mantel. She whirled to face him. "Noah—what are you doing here?"

"It's my house. What are you doing here?" He blocked the door so she couldn't escape.

"Retrieving my clock." Olivia squared her shoulders and turned back to gather it up again. "I'll be out of your way in a jiffy."

"Like hell." Noah crossed the room and grabbed it.

Olivia held on. "Give it to me. Noah, I'm warning you—don't try to stop me."

"Warning me? What are you going to do?" He gripped the clock tighter and lifted it up, nearly pulling her off her feet.

Olivia tried to wrench it back out of his arms. "I swear to God, Noah. Don't push me!"

"I'm not pushing you." Quite the opposite; he was dragging her across the living room now, her high heels unable to get any leverage against the slippery hardwood floor.

She dug those heels in, though, yanked back, slipped, lost her grip on the clock—and her balance—and went down hard with another shriek. Something ripped as she fell.

Noah nearly dropped the damn clock. "You okay?" He set it on the mantel and reached to help Olivia up.

That rip—it had to be fabric, right? Not a tendon tearing.

"I'm fine. Go away." Olivia scrambled to her knees but refused to meet his eyes.

"Let me help." He tried to take her hand, but she dodged him and managed to get to her feet on her own. She clutched the hem of her dress in one hand. Where a small slit used to expose an inch or two of her right thigh, now a much bigger tear exposed far more.

Noah's gaze traced the path of that slit up her leg. Her skirt was barely decent now.

In a minute he wasn't going to be decent, either.

He wrenched his gaze to her face, realized she'd seen him staring and shifted his stance. "We should get back to the wedding."

"Like this?" Olivia pinched her lips together. "I don't think so. This night is a bust."

Not entirely, Noah thought. At least he'd gotten a few minutes alone with her. This close he could see the rise and fall of her chest as she breathed. Her full mouth enticed him, and her gray eyes made him want to keep her here all night. Ask her a million questions.

Kiss her.

Hell, he could kiss her now. Despite himself, he leaned in.

Olivia stiffened, but she didn't move away. She seemed mesmerized by his approach. Waiting.

Watching him.

Noah moved closer still. They were alone. They'd witnessed a wedding. No one could blame them for letting the moment take over.

"Noah." Olivia's whisper felt somewhere between a warning and a plea.

He decided it was a plea. He closed the distance between them and brushed his mouth over hers.

So sweet.

So—

Noah jumped when something vibrated against his leg.

Olivia jumped, too, reached for the tiny blue purse hanging from an equally tiny strap over her shoulder and pulled out a phone. She sighed. "Hold that thought." Turning her back, she answered the call. "Virginia? What's wrong?"

Noah tried to get himself under control. He'd kissed a Cooper. And she'd let him. She'd told him to hold that thought when they were interrupted.

Did she want to pick up where they left off when she finished her call?

Noah ran a hand through his short hair. What the hell was he doing? He wasn't supposed to kiss Olivia. Couldn't get involved with an enemy.

Was it Olivia's fault she'd been born into the wrong family, though? She wasn't the one who—

His phone buzzed in his pocket, and he slapped a hand over it, startled all over again. He pulled it out reluctantly. It was his uncle Jed calling.

"Jed, what's up?"

"Get your ass over here, and get me out of this hellhole!" Jed shouted down the line.

"Hellhole? You still at the wedding?"

"Liam dropped me here at the Prairie Garden ten minutes ago. Took off back to the wedding like his ass was on fire."

"Probably didn't want to miss the fun."

"Fun? Watching Camila betray us and marry that wannabe Cooper? More like getting stretched on the rack, if you ask me."

"So what's wrong now?" His uncle had moved to the assisted living facility several years back, and for the most part he liked it, especially since women outnumbered the men there. He hadn't been doted on like that for years. He was able to call the shots, with a bevy of ladies oohing and aahing over his prowess. The only thing he disliked about the Prairie Garden was Virginia's presence.

"I've been kicked out! Can you believe it? Kicked out when I pay damn good money to be here! I've got twenty-four hours to vacate my room."

"That can't be right." Even if he'd misbehaved, wasn't there a whole mediation process to go through?

"Kicked out!" Jed repeated. Noah heard a crash on the other end of the phone. Someone screeched. "Get out of my room, you harpy!" Jed shouted back.

"Virginia? Virginia, what's going on?" Olivia cried behind Noah. "Who's that shouting at you?"

Another crash. Jed hooted. "Nice try! You couldn't hit the side of a barn!"

"Virginia, did you drop something?" Olivia cried, just as Noah hollered, "Jed, who's throwing things at you?"

Olivia turned to face him, and Noah replayed in his mind what they'd both just said.

"Well, shit," Noah told her. "Your great-aunt is beating up my great-uncle!"

"I'm pretty sure it's the other way around!"

Noah wasn't sure about that at all. Virginia might be eighty-four, but she was a tough customer. "Jed's been thrown out. He's got to leave tomorrow."

"I've got to leave tonight," Jed hollered into his ear. "You come get me right now. I'm not spending another second in this swamp!"

By the sounds of it, Virginia was giving Olivia an earful, too. "She's been kicked out as well," Olivia confirmed. "Damn it, Noah—what did your uncle do to make this happen?"

"How do you know Jed started it? Maybe it was your aunt!"

"Who are you talking to?" Jed demanded.

Noah hung up on him. "Leave the clock where it is, and go get in your truck," he told Olivia. "I'm going to lock up, and then I'll follow you. We'd better sort this out."

"Fine!" Olivia blew out a frustrated breath. "I'll pick up my clock another day." She followed him to the front door and waited on the stoop for him to lock it behind him.

Noah realized he'd just lost his moment alone with Olivia, which was far more important than who should own the damn clock. Who knew when he'd get another chance to be with her.

What the hell, he thought. Make hay while the sun shines. Or the moon, as it happened. He bent down, pulled Olivia in tight and kissed her.

NOAH TURNER HAD just kissed her—twice.

Olivia struggled to keep her eyes on the road as she drove to the Prairie Garden, all too aware that the handsome cowboy was following close behind her. Noah had been on her radar since she'd moved back to town. They'd had a couple of run-ins, and she enjoyed flirting with him. The fact that he was a Turner added a little zing to the back and forth. Still, she'd never thought things would go this far.

Never thought a man like Noah would even notice a woman like her.

Though, if pressed, she had to admit she was pretty sure she was his type. Noah was a practical guy, but when she got near him, he got a certain look in his eye. A look that told her he might abandon his careful way of thinking things through if it meant he got to be with her.

Like tonight.

She was pretty sure he'd made a conscious decision to throw caution to the wind when he kissed her, but Noah wasn't one to let his emotions rule the day. That innate caution would return, and that would be the end of that.

Disappointment coursed through her at the thought, but that was the kind of day it had been, she reasoned.

Virginia had been in high form since this morning, furious at Carl for betraying the Coopers and marrying Camila. She'd insisted Olivia steal the clock today, and Olivia had thought she had a good chance of managing it during the wedding reception. She'd meant to place it on the mantel at Thorn Hill and wait for everyone to come home and see it.

Thwarted again.

But Noah had kissed her.

God, he looked good today. His black jeans snug in all the right places. Dress shirt showcasing his strong body. Casual jacket making his shoulders look a mile wide. What would it be like to be with a man like that? Someone so secure with his standing? Someone who always did the right thing? Noah Turner was an upstanding citizen, respected in Chance Creek. A man who was going places.

If they were together, could she turn around the mess she always made of things? Break the pattern of bad luck that always kept her family down?

She glanced in the rearview mirror. Noah's headlights bumped and flashed behind her as they traveled the old country highway.

She probably wouldn't get the chance to find out.

Not only was Noah an upright, solid citizen, but he was a parole officer, too. She'd never broken the law herself—but her father's time in prison tainted everyone in her family. Noah might have slipped up and stolen a kiss or two just now, but tomorrow he'd pretend it had never happened, and he'd be one more person to avoid when she went to town.

"Ready for this?" Noah asked when she met him at the front door of the Prairie Garden some minutes later.

"As ready as I'll ever be, I guess." She hardly allowed herself to look at him. She had to stay strong. *He's your enemy*, she told herself. *Pull yourself together.*

Inside, the receptionist looked about as unenthusiastic as Olivia felt.

"You come to get your crazy relatives?" she asked.

"You're not supposed to talk about people that way," Noah told her.

"If they really had psychological problems, I wouldn't," the receptionist retorted. "Your uncle and your aunt, however, are completely sane, which means they don't have any business causing this kind of trouble. They've each had more than their share of warnings already. Get them out of here."

"Warnings?" Olivia asked, surprised.

"First I'm hearing of it," Noah said.

The receptionist shrugged. "You taking them or what?"

"That's why we're here." Noah was clearly irritated, but Olivia couldn't blame the woman for her bad attitude. Virginia was always cantankerous. She'd probably created her share of difficulties here.

They paced down the corridors, then split up, Olivia turning right, Noah going left.

"Good luck," Noah said.

"Sure. You, too." She waited for him to say something about that kiss. When he didn't, she gave up and went to find her aunt, knocking twice on her door and calling out, "Virginia? You in there?"

"I'm here. For now." Virginia was sitting on her throne, as Olivia liked to call the stiff, decorative chair her aunt had always favored. She liked it because sitting upright helped her back, but she looked for all the world like a diminutive queen sitting in state on the formal piece of furniture.

"What's all this trouble you're in?"

"It's not my fault that man's so touchy. Just told him he'd missed a spot or two when he was shaving today. You'd think I'd pointed out how ugly he is."

"Virginia." Olivia assumed she was talking about Jed Turner. Who else? Jed was the only person Virginia mentioned on a regular basis even though Olivia knew Virginia spoke to everyone else at the Prairie Garden. Interrogated them, more like it. Virginia liked to keep her finger on the pulse, and she terrorized all the other residents into coughing up their secrets.

"Called me an old bag," Virginia complained. "Maybe I lost my temper after that."

"I just bet you did."

"Don't get snippy with me, young lady. You aren't any saint yourself, are you? All our family's troubles start with you. Look at you, dressed like a harlot. You going out to make some money after taking me home?"

Olivia counted to ten. She didn't need this tonight. "Virginia, pack a bag. I'm taking you to Thorn Hill for now. We'll find you a new place tomorrow."

"Oh no, you won't. From now on I'll stay at Thorn

Hill, where I belong. And I'm not leaving here without my things. All of them. This place is chockablock with thieves."

"I don't think that's true."

"I don't care what you think. Start packing. All of it." Virginia waved a hand.

Olivia sighed. "We would need boxes—"

"I've got boxes." The receptionist appeared as if by magic and handed over a stack. "I've got tape and a marker, too. You can label them. Pack her belongings. We can send the furniture later, if necessary."

"You're not keeping a stick of it!" Virginia called after her as the receptionist slipped away again.

It was going to be a long night, Olivia thought, but there was nothing for it but to get to work. Once Virginia's mind was made up, there was little chance of changing it. "Pack your clothing in your suitcases," she told her aunt. "I'll get busy on the knickknacks."

An hour later they'd barely made headway, but a stack of boxes was making it difficult to move around the small apartment. Olivia decided to haul them to her truck. It was getting late. The wedding should be winding down. When she was outside she'd call her brothers and get them to come and help.

Not for the first time, she envied Tory, who'd left all this behind and never looked back. Maybe she had the right idea…

Olivia picked up the box nearest the door and began the trek to the facility's front door.

"Damn it, Jed, I'm doing the best I can," she heard

Noah yell when she was halfway there. He appeared around a corner hauling a large box. Maybe the receptionist had supplied him with a stack, too.

"Well, your best is pretty pathetic, isn't it? What have you got to show for yourself? A man your age. No wife. No girlfriend, even. When are you going to grow up and settle down?"

Noah kept walking even as Jed pursued him, easily putting distance between himself and his uncle. He didn't point out Jed had never married, either. When he got close to Olivia, he made a face she found all too easy to interpret. He was putting up with Jed, just like she was putting up with Virginia, because they were family and that's what one did.

"That looks too heavy for you," Noah murmured to her.

"I've got it," she assured him. They both turned for the front door. The receptionist scuttled out from behind her desk and rushed to open it for them.

"That's what I like to see," she said. "Keep it going."

"Jesus," Noah muttered under his breath.

Olivia bit back a laugh. Outside, after the door swung closed behind them, they stopped, having left their respective relatives far enough behind to get a moment to themselves.

"Great night, huh?" Noah said, shifting the box in his arms.

"Pretty sweet," she agreed sarcastically.

"Well, it was for a minute there. Olivia—"

Another truck pulled into the parking lot, followed by a second and then a third. Olivia watched helplessly as her brothers parked and made their way toward her, followed by the rest of Noah's family. What would Noah have said if they hadn't been interrupted? Was he actually interested in her?

Her oldest brother, Steel, strode over and grabbed the box from her arms. "Heard there was trouble with Virginia."

"You got that right." She followed him to his vehicle without another glance at Noah, figuring he'd understand and approve. No sense stirring up another fight between their clans; things were bad enough already. She wished they'd been able to finish their conversation, though. "She's moving home. Isn't that wonderful?"

Steel whistled. "Perfect."

A commotion back at the door had them both swinging around. Steel cursed and dropped the box in the bed of his truck, then loped toward the building, where Jed and Virginia had exited and seemed to be coming to blows. Olivia stood back as Steel and Liam Turner managed to separate the octogenarians. Steel hustled Virginia to Olivia's truck.

"Get her out of here," he said.

"What about my things?" Virginia demanded.

"We'll get them home, don't you worry." He tucked her into the truck and shut the door. "Seriously, Olivia. Take her straight home, and don't let her cause any more problems tonight. Can you do that?"

Stung at his tone, she said, "Yeah, I can do that."

Steel sighed. "Hell. Didn't mean to take anything out on you. This is all we need, though. We were just making headway."

Olivia knew what he meant. As soon as the Founder's Prize had been announced at the Chance Creek Spring Fling Fair, Virginia had pounced and strong-armed Carl Whitfield into helping her fund a renovation and technological upgrade to Chance Creek High. The renovation was going to be fantastic. The old run-down building would be a high-tech palace by the time it was done and would feature a robotics program open to all its students to participate in. Carl had gotten donations from all kinds of major tech companies, and she was pretty sure he'd thrown in some of his own money to boot.

The Coopers' fortunes had taken a turn in the town. Suddenly they weren't just troublemakers. They were troublemakers who made a difference. Troublemakers who might just win that prize—and the Ridley property. If Virginia kept this up, though, soon enough they'd go back to just being trouble.

"Did you at least get my clock tonight?" Virginia demanded when Olivia got behind the wheel. "I told you it was the perfect time when everyone else was at the reception."

"Noah followed me. Caught me in the act," Olivia said matter-of-factly and braced herself for Virginia's response.

"Huh. You probably blurted out all our secrets the

minute he walked through the door. Never could hold your tongue."

Count to ten. Count to ten, Olivia told herself. Every time she saw Virginia, her aunt managed to slip in a dig or two about the past. Repetition didn't take away the sting, though. Nor the feeling her aunt was right.

"Your father would be alive, and your mother would still live in Chance Creek if—"

"Virginia!" Olivia exploded. Caught herself. "Virginia," she started again in a calmer tone. "If you know what's good for you, don't push me tonight. I'm tired. I've had a long day. I'm liable to pull over and make you walk."

"Ingrate." Virginia crossed her arms and stared out the window, mercifully holding her tongue—for a minute. "What the hell happened to your dress?"

THE NEXT DAY Noah entered the house after his early chores to find Jed sitting at the kitchen table nursing a cup of coffee and reading the newspaper.

"Morning," Noah said, eager to get past him and on with his business. He needed to leave for town in a minute.

"Morning, yourself. You seen this nonsense?" Jed ruffled the paper and began to read aloud. "'Coopers to Bring Chance Creek High into the Twenty-First Century.' What a load of baloney."

"Can't blame the school board for voting to accept their proposal. They're going to update all the wiring and bring in high-tech equipment. Teach the kids computer programming and robotics. Things that'll be useful to them."

"Useful? Who needs computers? And those robots are just waiting to kill us. You know it's true."

"Maybe. Maybe not. But if they're coming after us, maybe it would be smart to train a passel of kids to stop them, don't you think?"

Jed glared at him. "It'll be funny right up to the minute one of those machines breaks you in half."

"Whatever, Uncle Jed. I've got to get to work." Noah crossed to the sink, poured himself a glass of water and took a long drink. Ranching was a dusty business, and there hadn't been rain in weeks.

Jed snorted. "That's what you're calling your day job? Lotta work it takes to jaw for half an hour now and then with your criminal friends."

"I'm not *jawing*. I'm supervising parolees. It's an important job." Not to mention somebody had to keep the Flying W afloat. "I help make sure they get a chance to reintegrate with society. Or do you think we should just kick them to the curb when they've served their time?"

Ironic, Noah thought, that he was rebuilding the Turners' finances by helping people bounce back from their mistakes. His father's decision to help the Coopers bounce back from the ones they'd made had helped drain their coffers in the first place.

Not that any of the Coopers showed a whit of gratitude for that.

Noah forced himself to take a deep breath. He was being unfair. As far as he knew, none of the Coopers were aware of what he'd done, and paying Thorn Hill's bills for the few months it stood unoccupied during the years they were away really wasn't the crux of the Flying W's money problems. He'd made a few mistakes the first years he'd taken over the operation. He was trying to set that right.

"No one's helping me with my life," Jed declared.

"Are you serious?" Noah waited, but Jed didn't qualify his statement, and Noah wondered why he'd bothered spending half the night moving Jed's things home. He set the glass on the counter and readied to go.

"Hold up there," Jed said. "I've got a job for you."

"You just said—" Noah gave up. "What job?"

"If we let those Coopers get away with their plan, they're going to win the Founder's Prize, which means they're going to leave us high and dry."

"You said we'd win it just because we're Turners. Because we built the high school in the first place, and because you served on the council all those years."

"We *should* win the prize for what we've done. I'm not on the council anymore, though, and people these days have short memories. You need to think of something that outshines what the Coopers have done. Something to fix or build or... something."

"Like what?"

"You figure that out. I don't get around as fast as I used to. You'll have to be my eyes and ears on the ground. Go into town, ask around. What do people need that they don't have? That's what we'll build."

"We don't have a lot of extra cash—"

"Stop making excuses and get it done. Meanwhile, I'll figure out our strategy for blocking the Coopers. A project as big as theirs can have all kinds of things happen."

Noah checked the time on his phone. He was late and didn't have time to argue, even though he didn't like his great-uncle's train of thought. "I'll get back to you on that," he promised Jed. "But only if you leave that school alone. If I figure out you've been interfering, there'll be consequences."

"I'm shaking in my boots." Jed scowled. "Think fast. Those Coopers already have a big head start."

Maybe Chance Creek needed a bigger jail, Noah thought as he headed for his truck. One with an extension on the back of it—housing for ornery relatives.

Fifteen minutes later he slid into one of the rear booths at Linda's Diner, where he and Brandon Sykes could have a quiet chat. He liked to meet his clients in public rather than in his shared office at the sheriff's department. It was less intimidating. Parolees were more likely to open up when you treated them like human beings.

Noah had only worked this job for a couple of years, and he was aware he had a lot to learn. Men—and women—leaving the system entered civilian life like farmed fish thrown into the ocean. They were often caught off guard by unexpected currents. Easy prey for the same predators who'd influenced their decisions before they were incarcerated. Jumpy. A little lost.

He'd learned he had to work fast to establish a connection with his clients before their other, less helpful friends and acquaintances established one first. He was amazed how often first-time offenders ended up back in prison within months—even weeks—of being released.

Brandon arrived on time, Noah was happy to note. He had high hopes for the twenty-five-year-old man who'd gone to jail for tampering with an ATM machine. Brandon had gotten drunk at a family barbecue one weekend and let an older cousin with a long history of bank robbery and other offenses convince him to help out with the job. Thankfully, Brandon broke off his relationship with his cousin when he went to jail. If he kept away from him, Noah thought the young man had a good chance of making something of himself. He was smart and seemed truly sorry for what he'd done—not like some habitual offenders who gloried in the lifestyle.

"Coffee?" Noah asked.

"Sure. Thanks."

"Hi, Noah." A waitress hustled up to their table.

"Hi, Christie. How's it going?"

"Same as ever," she answered with a smile. A cheerful brunette with her hair pulled up into a messy ponytail, she held up her notepad. "What can I get you?"

Noah placed their order, and she went off to fetch it. When he turned back, he noticed Brandon watching the waitress walk away.

"Any luck with your job hunt?" Noah prompted him.

Brandon shook his head ruefully. "I've applied to

everything. No one ever calls me back. Why would they? They all know what I did."

"You'll find something. It takes patience." Noah nudged the salt shaker until it lined up with the pepper shaker in the middle of the table. He picked up a packet of sugar substitute and added it to the line. He knew Brandon was going to have a rough time finding someone to hire him, but this was part of the process: he had to experience the search and the eventual success. Sooner or later some rancher would need an extra hand, and there would be Brandon, ready to help.

"Waiting around is driving me nuts. I need money. My folks don't want me back home. I'm twenty-five, for God's sake."

"Lots of people live with their folks a lot longer than that. I did." He wished his folks were still around to share the ranch now.

"Yeah, well, we're not getting along."

"Tell me about that."

They paused while Christie delivered their coffee. "Anything else?" she asked.

"No, thanks," Noah told her. He turned back to Brandon. "Well? What are you and your folks arguing about?"

"My mom's always on me. Clean your room. Do your laundry. It's like I'm a kid again."

"Why do you think that is?"

Brandon scraped a hand over his face. "I don't know—because I'm acting like one?"

"Are you?" Noah took a sip of coffee and noticed

Christie hovering nearby. "We're good," he told her. She nodded and left. "Friend of yours?"

Brandon turned to see who he meant. Frowned. "Christie? I guess I know her from high school. She was a couple of years behind me. She's grown up a bunch, though." He shrugged.

Noah made a note to keep an eye on the situation. Christie wouldn't be the first bored small-town girl to take on a project like Brandon to make life more interesting.

"So how can you act more like a grown-up?" he asked Brandon.

The other man sighed heavily. "Get a job and get my own place," he growled. "Which I'm trying to do, but it's not working."

"How about seeing your parents as allies rather than as wardens, huh? Think about it." Noah set his coffee cup down in line with the shakers. Added a fork to the lineup. "They're your bridge to the community. Your parents are respected. They have jobs. They meet other people with jobs. People who might need new employees. You act like a kid at home, give them a hard time, throw your dirty clothes on the floor, leave your bed unmade… why would your folks recommend you to one of their friends?"

Brandon sighed again. "So I suck up to my parents."

"You suck up to everybody," Noah told him. "You never know where that next job is coming from. Every person in this restaurant, everyone on the street, everyone in the grocery store or at the movies—they're all links in a chain to your next paycheck. Does that make sense?"

After a moment Brandon nodded. "Yeah, it actually does when you think about it that way. I don't know why I'm being an ass to the folks," he added.

"Are you going to those sessions I recommended?" There were casual group-therapy sessions for newly released offenders. He hoped Brandon would take advantage of them.

"Not yet," Brandon admitted.

"Go to one," Noah pressed him. "Look, there are all these pieces that have been laid out to help you. Pick them up and put them together to make yourself a new life. You owe it to yourself to try."

"All right."

"Action steps?" Noah prodded him. "I'll see you in a week. What are we going to talk about?"

Brandon held up a finger. "I'm going to keep applying for every job I see." He held up another. "Be nice to the folks." Another finger. "Go to a stupid meeting."

"What about exercise? You running?"

"You're telling me to run?" For the first time Brandon cracked a smile. "I think that violates the terms of my parole, Noah."

"Yeah, yeah, smart-ass. You know what I mean. Blow off some steam in a healthy way. You said you used to run back in high school. Get back to it. Set goals. Get healthy. Deal with the anger that builds up. You hear me?"

"Yeah, all right."

"I like to jog," Christie said, passing by again.

"Oh yeah?" Brandon sat back in his seat. "You never joined the track team in school."

"Didn't have time. Too busy working. With Dad not around..." She trailed off, but she didn't need to explain. Noah knew Christie and her sister, Monica, had helped pay the bills when their dad took off. That was the thing about small towns, Noah thought. Everyone really did know everything. Or at least thought they did.

"I think we'll take the bill, Christie," he said, trying to derail what was happening. Knowing already he was too late. He'd have to have a private word with Christie and give her some advice. Brandon could turn a corner and spend the rest of his life on the straight and narrow path. Or he could take up where he'd left off and destroy her life along with his own if those two started dating.

"All right, I'm out of here," Brandon said when they'd settled the bill. "Next week?"

"That's right. Good luck," Noah told him and watched him leave, not missing the smile Christie sent Brandon's way when he passed her.

Hell. More trouble.

Christie veered off to greet a new set of customers, and Noah lifted his coffee cup to drain it. When he set it down again, Liam was taking a seat across from him.

"What's up?" Liam asked.

"Just met with Brandon Sykes. What's up with you?"

Liam took a menu from Christie when she came

back but didn't open it. "Coffee. Black. And a Danish. Something with strawberries in it."

"Got it. Be back in a minute," she told him and took the menu again.

"Killing time." He chuckled. "Getting away from Uncle Jed, to tell the truth."

"Yeah, he's a handful."

"What are we going to do about him?"

"What can we do?" Noah countered. He adjusted the fork to make his line straighter.

"If he stays, he's going to try to run the place. He might not be able to ride anymore, but he can sure talk."

"Let's take it one day at a time for now," Noah suggested. The truth was, he didn't have any idea what to do either. Liam was right; Jed would soon grow bored on the ranch without the company he'd enjoyed in town. He didn't know how to fix that.

"Hey, there's Carl. Shouldn't he be on his honeymoon?"

"I don't think they went yet, actually," Noah said. "Something about needing more time to plan a big trip. He and Camila spent a few weeks down in Mexico last month."

"Yeah, heard about that. Who's he with?"

Noah didn't recognize the man sitting across from Carl, but he could take a guess. "That's got to be the architect who's working on the school. Look, he's got plans. Let's go check it out."

"What about my Danish?"

Noah wasn't worried about the Danish. Christie

would track them down. He wanted to see what Carl was up to—and how hard it would be for his family to top it.

When he reached Carl's booth, he didn't wait for an invitation. He dropped into the seat beside the stranger. "Morning, Carl. How's married life treating you?"

"It's great so far. We've got big plans for the ranch."

"Got a name for it yet?"

"We're keeping the one it has. Laurel Heights. Suits us fine."

"What'cha got here?" Liam put in, sitting next to Carl when Carl slid over on his seat and tapping the large pieces of paper spread over the table.

"Plans for the Chance Creek High upgrade."

"Heard it's going to be pretty high-tech," Noah said.

"It is. We've been working with the teachers to figure out how best to support them during the upgrade and transition. I'm going to bring in a half-dozen experts later in the summer for intensive training programs for them, too. Next fall those kids are in a for a big surprise."

"Sounds great." It bothered Noah he couldn't simply feel happy for the town that it was happening. But there was the Ridley property to think about. "Feels like Chance Creek itself is getting an upgrade." He made a show of looking around. "Wonder what else is in store for this town?"

"There's a lot to do," the architect put in. "Name's Henry Woodruff. From Billings." He shook hands with Noah and Liam. "Little towns like this all over the

United States are getting rough around the edges."

"Maybe one thing will lead to another," Carl said. "But I like the old buildings in town. I hope people don't mess with those classic facades too much."

"Some of them are great. Others... could use an update," Henry said. "And some need downright repairs. The old grocery store for one. And that post office..." He shrugged sadly. "Beautiful building in its day. But the mortar between its stones is crumbling."

Henry was right, Noah thought. The grocery store was kind of a mess. It was crammed into an old building that once had been a general store and retained the atmosphere of an old-timey trading post. But it had been added to haphazardly, and its rugged exterior had slipped from charming to shoddy. It could use a face-lift.

Maybe that should be their project.

"Can't fix everything at once," Carl was saying when he tuned into the conversation again.

"No, that's right." Noah stiffened when he saw Olivia and Lance Cooper walk in. He knew they must be here to meet with Carl and the architect, and knew, too, he needed to get Liam out of here before his brother started something with Lance. "Hey, we'd better go see what Jed's getting up to," he told Liam and stood up. "Thanks for showing us your plans, Carl." He grabbed Liam's arm and pulled his brother along with him.

"What's the rush? I haven't gotten my Danish!" Liam complained but narrowed his eyes when he caught sight of the Coopers.

"Keep moving," Noah told him evenly. He signaled to Christie as they went. "Can we get that pastry to go?" he asked her. "Meet you on the street," he said to Liam. Liam took the hint and went outside. Noah breathed a sigh of relief when he was gone, although he regretted missing the chance to speak with Olivia. When they passed, he met her gaze and nodded slightly. She nodded back, a tiny movement but one that sent his heart beating harder.

Noah found himself smiling as he paid the bill. Flirting with Olivia wasn't smart, but it sure was fun.

AT LEAST SOMETHING was going right, Olivia thought when the meeting with Carl and Henry was over. She might not have gotten a chance to chat with Noah, who had been leaving as she had arrived, but she had to hand it to Carl—he'd come through on his promise to help her family try to win the Founder's Prize. Not for the first time, she wished the Ridley property had simply come up for sale and her family had the money to buy it fair and square. The Founder's Prize wasn't going to be awarded until October. It was early June. Far too much time for something to go wrong.

Outside Linda's Diner, she said goodbye to the others and walked toward the grocery store to do her shopping. She stopped when someone called her name.

"Olivia!" Caroline Selwich hurried to catch up with her. "Hey, what's the rush?"

"No rush, just running errands. Good to see you."

"You, too. How's your aunt? I heard there was quite a fuss at the Prairie Garden."

"You've got that right." Olivia filled her in as they walked together. Caroline knew all about Virginia. She was one of the first friends Olivia had made when she returned to Chance Creek. Caroline had grown up in Billings and moved here to take a position in the dentist's office in town. She was friendly, kind and open-minded, and her presence in Chance Creek had done much to make life here bearable for Olivia. She wished they got to spend more time together, but Caroline's boyfriend, Devon, demanded all her attention outside work hours. He was a loner. The kind of guy who liked a woman around and didn't want to share her attention with friends. Olivia had never been to Caroline's house and had only met Devon once or twice in town. She privately wondered what Caroline saw in the man, but it took all kinds, as her mother said.

"Are you free next Sunday for lunch?" Caroline asked when they reached the grocery store.

"Absolutely!" Olivia had learned to jump on any invitation Caroline made. She never knew when they'd get a chance to hang out, with Devon keeping her on such a short leash. "The usual place?"

"DelMonacos at noon," Caroline said happily. "See you there."

"See you."

Steel appeared at her side almost as soon as Caroline left.

"What are you doing here?" Olivia asked him.

"Snacks for the road," he said, holding up a bag of chips. "Meeting go good?"

"It went fine. You should have been there."

"I'm heading out of town."

Steel was always heading out of town these days, and he never answered her questions when she asked where he was going. "I talked to Virginia this morning," he went on. He followed her as she filled a basket with the supplies she needed. He was tall, with short, iron-dark hair. She knew other people found him intimidating, and he'd been a pain in the ass as a kid, but now he seemed to have elected himself her personal protector.

She wasn't sure how she felt about that.

"Oh yeah? What about?" she asked lightly.

"She wants us to throw a party."

"A party?" Olivia stopped short. "What kind of a party?"

"A big event. Her words, not mine. To shore up support for the school upgrade. Not everyone at the high school was on board with the renovations. Some people still aren't. They think we're rushing things. They might have a point."

Olivia blinked at him. "Wait, you don't think the school needs the upgrade?"

He shook his head. "It needs the upgrade: the issue is with the time frame. If we pushed it to next summer, everyone would have a lot more time to prepare for it. To be honest, the only logical reason to rush it like this—"

"Is to have it finished before the Founder's Prize

gets awarded," Olivia finished for him.

"Right. Luckily Martin Fulsom bought the company that's doing the renovation. That man loves to be in front of a camera. We're going to throw him a party and give him all the attention he can handle."

"How would that help?"

"When Fulsom gets in front of a camera, the nation watches," Steel said. "It won't take much prodding to get him to spout off about how great this project is going to be—and how fast he's going to get it done."

"And then everyone will be on board with the time frame." Olivia nodded slowly. "Because the whole country will be watching to see how it turns out."

"Exactly. So you'll take care of the party?"

"Me?" Heck, she wouldn't know where to start. *Party* wasn't even the right word for what Virginia had in mind. Gala was more like it. None of the Coopers had any experience with galas.

Least of all her.

"Better get Carl to do that."

"Carl's busy."

"What about Lance?"

"He'll help, but he's not a detail man. This... event... is going to take a lot of detail work."

"What about you?"

"Me? Come on."

She understood what he meant. Most of Chance Creek gave Steel a wide berth.

"So it's me or no one, huh?" Was she supposed to feel gratified?

They paused at Steel's truck. "That's right, and I need you to take this seriously. Don't flake out on me, okay?

"I'm not a flake—"

She just trusted the wrong people sometimes.

"I'll take it seriously," she told Steel. "I still think we're in over our heads."

"Then we'd better swim fast."

Chapter Two

"GROCERY STORE? YOU want us to refurbish the grocery store?" Jed said later that night when Maya and Stella had served up a meatloaf dinner.

"The outside's seen better days," Noah said. "We can spiff it up."

"The grocery store," Jed repeated.

The more he said it, the less of a good idea it sounded. "The post office, then?" Noah suggested.

"What's wrong with the post office?"

"I... don't know," Noah admitted. "What do you think we should fix up?" He'd been preoccupied with the state of the Flying W so long, he honestly hadn't thought too much about the rest of the town.

"We don't need to fix up anything. I've got a better idea," Liam said.

Noah turned to him. "Oh yeah? What?"

"A smear campaign." He picked up the newspaper Jed had been reading that morning and opened it. "Letters to the editor." He pointed at the page. "People complain in there all the time about all kinds of things."

"So?" Noah said.

"So we'll get them to complain about the school

43

upgrade. There'll be letters to the editor about it every day—until everyone thinks it's a bad idea."

"Who's going to write letters like that? Us? We'll look like fools." Noah was getting sick of the whole Founder's Prize thing. He had enough on his plate to worry about without this. He realized he never did talk to Christie. Probably better stop in at Linda's Diner again soon to see her.

"Not us. Other people. People who don't like the Coopers."

"A lot of people like the Coopers," Noah pointed out.

"But not everyone. You'll see."

"It'll backfire. When it's over, and everyone's mad, they're going to remember we're the ones who stirred things up. That won't win us any prizes." Noah turned the idea over in his mind. There had to be a better way—and to his surprise, one dawned on him. "On the other hand, people like to be nostalgic for the good old days."

"So?" Liam played with his water glass, clearly unhappy Noah had shot down his idea.

"So turn your plan around. Don't have people complain about what's coming—have them sing the praises of what we already have. Get people to write in about all their best memories about the school as it is. Plant the first few letters to really play up how changing anything about the school—even modernizing it—will ruin it. Use nostalgia as a weapon. Other people will join in. Everyone likes talking about themselves. Get them to talk about specific incidents that wouldn't have happened if everything was high-tech."

"I like it. It's devious," Jed said.

"Hell, Noah, you're an evil genius." Liam grinned.

Noah frowned. Liam was right; he'd gotten carried away. "We're not trying to stop the project," he hurried to say.

"But—" Liam started.

Noah cut him off. "We want to cause enough pushback that they miss the deadline, that's all. The money is there. The plans are there. Once we win what's rightfully ours, we'll let it go through next summer. In fact, we'll even help it along next year if that's what it takes, because that's what's best for the town."

Jed and Liam made noncommittal noises, but Noah was resolute.

They were Turners, and that still meant something.

"HONEY, YOU NEED to cut your losses. I don't know what made you go back to Chance Creek in the first place," Olivia's mother, Enid, said the following afternoon. Olivia's fingers tightened on her cell phone as she stood by her bedroom window and looked out over the pastures spreading behind her house. She should be out there working with her brothers, but she'd been unsettled all day and needed to touch base with someone outside of Chance Creek. "The Coopers burned their bridges there a long time ago, and new ones aren't worth building. Come to New Mexico. You'd love it here."

It wasn't the first time her mother had extended the invitation, but Olivia knew she'd never accept. Chance Creek was in her bones. When everything had gone wrong for her family, Enid had divorced Dale so fast her parents' marriage seemed over before they reached Idaho. Looking back, Olivia realized her mother must have offered Dale a stunning deal, and her father must have cooperated. Enid hadn't asked for a share of the ranch, and he hadn't contested the divorce. He'd felt so guilty about taking them all down.

Olivia felt guilty, too.

Almost as soon as Enid had taken them to her sister's ranch in Idaho, she'd left again to go looking for work. That's what she'd told them, anyway. Later they found out she'd left town with a man. A high roller who'd wined and dined Enid, told her he loved her, squired her around the country for a few months and then admitted he already had a wife. Enid had found a job in New Mexico, where an old friend had settled down, but by the time she'd gotten her act together, Olivia and her siblings had put down tentative roots in Idaho, and Aunt Joan, disgusted by Enid's behavior, had allowed them to stay. Olivia's family had fractured again.

As years went by, Olivia saw little of her father, visiting him in jail only once or twice. Dale didn't like her to see him like that, and he wasn't much of a letter-writer, either. He never mentioned Thorn Hill, so neither did she, figuring the bank had probably repossessed the ranch and sold it off to pay the mortgage. When Dale died, she and her siblings learned they would inherit the ranch, after all. Some anonymous partner of his had been renting it out to a tenant to keep it running all those years. Olivia could only wonder why her father had never explained that.

Now she was back in Chance Creek, and she meant to stay. Besides, she still found it hard to forgive Enid for leaving her and her siblings behind when she'd made her break for freedom. Olivia turned her back on the view outside her window as Enid went on.

"I know I let you down in the past, but that was a long time ago. I'm a different person now. I think everyone is entitled to one screwup, don't you think?"

"I'm settled here. For now, at least." Olivia didn't want to argue over the past. Turning to the window again, she watched a crow fly across the pasture, circle around and head in the other direction.

"Well, any time you change your mind, you know where I am. I miss you. All of you. How's Tory?"

Olivia wasn't fooled by her mother's nonchalance. She'd always been uncomfortable with her role as messenger between Tory and their mother. "Good, as far as I know. Busy." Tory had been a massage therapist in Seattle for years now and seemed to have no intention of coming back. She called about once a month, and they chatted over their news, but Olivia felt like her sister was slipping away.

"Everyone's always busy," Enid said. "Or something else."

"What does that mean?"

"I think all of you kids are stuck in the past. Punishing yourselves—and me—for what went wrong instead of getting over it and moving on. Take you, for example. Nothing that happened back then is your fault. You know that, right?"

No. She didn't know that. She was the one who'd brought the sheriff to their door.

If she was being honest with herself, she was the reason Enid left, too. As angry as Olivia was that her mother had abandoned her, she supposed she couldn't blame Enid for not wanting to stick around when her husband went to jail.

And Dale only went to jail because of what she'd allowed Maya Turner to see in her family's barn. Her real mistake had been to imagine that a Turner could ever be a true friend to a Cooper.

"I'm not stuck in the past," she said. "I like it here." For some reason she thought of Noah Turner.

"You want to be a rancher?"

The conversation was becoming far too uncomfortable. Olivia wasn't sure what she wanted to do with her life. "If there was another career I wanted to pursue, I would," she told her mother. "Hey, it's getting late. I've got to go."

Her mother sighed but didn't push the matter. "Before you do, one thing. I'm sending you a book."

"A book?"

Enid chuckled. "It's the darndest thing. You know I had a storage container."

"Yeah?"

"I finally went through all that old stuff. No sense

paying to keep things I don't need, right? Anyway, I was going through a bunch of old books and found one from the library. The Chance Creek library. I figure I'd better return it."

"After all this time?" Olivia laughed. "I doubt they want it back."

"I know… I was going to take it to a thrift store, but there's something unsettling about not bringing a library book back where it belongs. It's a loose thread from my past. If I send it to you, will you deal with it?"

"Why not send it right to the library?" Olivia crossed to her mirror and checked her reflection, wondering what Noah saw when he looked at her. His kisses kept running through her mind. That's why she'd called her mother to begin with—to distract herself.

"I want to know it got there. I need closure."

"What if they fine you a million dollars?"

"Don't even tease me about that. It's been keeping me up at night." Her mother laughed again, but Olivia heard the strain there. This was about more than a library book, she thought suddenly. This was about making sure the past stayed in the past. Pain shot through Olivia. For her mother, Chance Creek was the past, not the present. Was she making a mistake trying to create her present here?

"Come see me soon, okay?" her mother said.

"Sure, Mom." Olivia hung up, suddenly restless.

She needed to figure out what she really wanted to do with her life. Like her mom said: stop living in the past and start building her own future.

Right after she figured out how to put on a gala for an eccentric billionaire and his entourage of socialites and investors.

Olivia sighed and left her bedroom. If she wanted to pull this off, she needed help, but from whom?

She considered all the likely people in town. Mia Matheson was a wedding planner. She probably could branch out, but it was nearly summer, and Olivia had a feeling she'd be booked back-to-back right now. There was Autumn Cruz. While Olivia knew Ethan Cruz to speak to, she was less familiar with his wife, who ran a lovely bed-and-breakfast on their ranch, which would probably be hopping right now, too.

For some reason her thoughts kept trailing back to the Halls. Ella Hall, to be precise. She didn't do events—she ran an equine therapy program. But she'd once been a Hollywood actress, and she must have gone to dozens of galas. She'd know exactly what it took to impress a bunch of media moguls. Since she wasn't in the hospitality business, she wouldn't be wrapped up with other events.

Olivia glanced at the time on her phone. Despite what she'd said to her mother, it wasn't that late, and suddenly she had the urge to get away from the ranch. Forgoing a phone call, Olivia drove to Crescent Hall, impressed as always by the Halls' imposing three-story home. With its tower and wraparound porch, it epitomized late-nineteenth-century Gothic architecture. The large spread always looked tidy and affluent. In comparison, Thorn Hill was downright seedy. Her brothers ran the ranch with a minimum of outside help, and she pitched in, far more interested in those kinds of chores than household ones. No one made mowing the front lawn a priority or fussed with potted plants and sweeping the porch.

Maybe it was time she stepped up and took on those chores, Olivia thought. Just because her mother hadn't been much of a homemaker didn't mean she couldn't become one. She wanted to be proud of Thorn Hill, right?

So why did the idea of buckling down and taking care of it make her squirm?

Olivia thought that through as she got out of her truck. Was it because her family had made their mistakes so openly, and everyone knew about them? Was she afraid to even try to succeed at anything after so much failure? It was as if she was superstitious about fixing the place up. Like fate would strike them down if they tried to improve their lot.

Her heart was in her mouth by the time she knocked on the Halls' front door. After all, she didn't know Ella more than to say hello to in the store. She remembered the Hall boys from when they were kids, but they were a few years older than her. If Ella declined to help her, this visit would be very awkward.

Regan Hall answered the door with a wide smile that eased Olivia's tension a little. She'd pinned her auburn hair on top of her head and held a broom in one hand.

"Oh, thank God," she cried. "Now I can't possibly mop. You've saved me!" She opened the door wider and ushered Olivia in. "I hate mopping," she confided.

"I hate it, too." Olivia felt better already. She followed Regan to the kitchen at the back of the house.

"What's new?" Regan asked her. She pulled out two tall glasses. "Lemonade?"

"Sounds great," Olivia said. "Where are all the kids?"

"Out with the guys or napping. We women get a couple of hours of quiet a day so we can get things done."

Olivia knew there were a lot of kids underfoot at the Hall house. With four couples in the main building and bunkhouse, all of them with multiple children, you could almost call it a horde.

"Is Ella around? I have a question for her," Olivia told her.

"Sure, let me find her. She's probably outside." Regan handed Olivia a glass and went out the back door, returning a few minutes later with Ella.

"Good timing, I was just coming in." Ella was a tall, stately woman, whose beautiful features and charming manners made it clear why she'd had so much success acting in movies. Olivia couldn't believe she'd given it all up to move to Chance Creek, but Ella seemed to adore working with horses—and both children and adults who'd been through traumatic experiences.

"I know this is a little strange." Olivia's awkwardness reappeared. She'd better simply blurt it out, she decided. "I need to put on a big party. Kind of a gala. A lot of important guests will be there—including Martin

Fulsom."

"*The* Martin Fulsom?" Regan raised an eyebrow.

Olivia nodded. "The billionaire," she confirmed. "I... need help." Would Ella understand?

"From me?" Ella cocked her head. "I did some entertaining back in LA, but... mostly I hired it out, you know?"

"And that's fine, but I need to know what it is I'm supposed to hire out," Olivia said in a rush. "Where do I have it? What do I need? Tables? Food? Flowers? Music? I don't even know where to begin. I know it's a lot to ask, but... I thought maybe you could give me some pointers?"

"Well... sure," Ella said. "I'll try. I think Regan should join us, though. She's better at entertaining than I am."

"Did someone say entertaining? I want to help, too." Storm Hall came in. She was Zane's wife, another California girl with blonde hair that hung to her waist. "I love throwing parties, but I'm not very good at it, either," she added, shooting Olivia a conspiratorial grin. "I'm due at the shop, but count me in for anything." She kept going. Olivia knew running Willows, a woman's clothing store in town, had to take up most of her time, but she appreciated the offer. As Storm headed for the front door, Heather—Colt Hall's wife—walked in.

"Did I miss something?" she asked, setting grocery bags on the kitchen counter. She was a practical, pretty woman who owned the hardware store in town.

"We're helping Olivia throw a gala for a bunch of

important, out-of-town guests," Ella told her. "It has to be really snazzy."

"I'm not sure what I can do to help, but just ask." Heather moved to put away the groceries she'd lugged in.

A booming cheer from outside startled Olivia, and she moved to see out the window over the kitchen sink. "What's going on?"

"Oh, those are just the weekend warriors," Regan said. "From the training camp. They must be on their way to the obstacle course. They use it a lot."

"How's that business going?" Olivia asked, trying to see the men, but no one was in sight.

"The obstacle course is in the woods," Heather explained. "You can't see them from here, but believe me they're there, and they come thundering through like a herd of elephants every now and then. The kids love it."

"I bet they do." Olivia laughed.

"They've got ten to twenty campers there at any given time," Ella said. "And there's about eight ex-SEALs, soldiers and marines running the thing."

"I didn't realize it was such a going concern," Olivia told her. "You never see anyone in town."

"None of the guests get to go to town." Regan laughed. "It's a full-on extreme experience. We're not supposed to go anywhere near them."

"Huh."

"But let's talk about the gala." Ella grabbed a pad of paper and pen from a nearby drawer. "Come and sit. Let's brainstorm."

"Maybe Autumn Cruz would rent out the guest ranch for a day," Heather said. "It's a fairly large venue."

"There's the town hall," Regan said.

"But it's not nearly as impressive," Ella pointed out.

Olivia heaved a sigh of relief as the other women began to brainstorm ideas.

Maybe she could pull this off after all.

NOAH HAD EATEN only a couple of hours ago, but it had been a light affair—a couple of sandwiches he'd grabbed when he'd arrived home before heading out again to tackle evening chores with Liam. Normally, either Maya or Stella cooked a more substantial meal, but they were off to dinner and a movie tonight with friends, so he, Liam and Jed had been left to fend for themselves. Jed had made it known he meant to go into town to dine at DelMonaco's. A friend was picking him up, and Noah figured they'd meet up with some of their card-playing buddies.

Liam had peeled off a half hour ago toward town, as well, to start to gather letter-writers for the nostalgia campaign against the updates to Chance Creek High, so when Noah let himself in the back door of the house, it was unusually quiet inside.

When was the last time he'd been alone like this? Noah couldn't say. He wasn't sure he liked it, either. The quiet made it all too easy to think about his family's problems. Jed wasn't going to be happy for long isolated on a ranch when mobility was difficult for him. Maya and Stella had been sad to see their cousins go. Now they needed to help more with the outdoor chores, which left them overwhelmed on the household front. He needed to talk to Liam—and Jed—about doing their share here in the house, but as he looked around, he realized it was going to take a concerted effort on all their parts to get their home back in shape.

And that was just cleaning. The truth was, the Flying W had seen better days. It needed painting, a new kitchen floor. New… everything.

But they didn't have money for that.

He wished his cousins were still here. Those extra hands would have helped a lot right now. He couldn't work the ranch, work his job and come up with some way to prevent the Coopers from taking the Ridley property all at the same time. As much as he hated to think they'd mess with Pittance Creek, Jed was right; the Coopers were capable of stealing—

Noah stilled, one hand reaching to open the refrigerator to look for leftovers.

What was that?

He'd heard a noise, a soft scrape, like the front door opening.

Someone was here.

Was Olivia stealing the damn clock again?

Noah chose swiftness over stealth, raced through the kitchen, burst into the living room and caught her red-handed. "Put it down!"

"Damn it!" Olivia set it back on the mantel with a thump. "Why are you always here?"

"Why are *you* always here?" he shot back. "Someone might think you were after more than that clock."

Olivia gaped at him, and to his surprise she flushed.

Heck, maybe she *was* after more than the clock.

Interesting.

Noah forced himself to stay where he was. He needed to stop being attracted to Olivia. Out of all the women in Chance Creek, she was the most off-limits. But if he was honest with himself he found her—

Pretty much the only woman he was interested in.

"I was just on my way home," she said. "I've had a really good day, so I thought—"

"You thought you'd waltz in here and steal my clock." Looking her up and down, Noah knew exactly why she pushed all the buttons of his libido. She was a country girl through and through. Boots, fitted jeans that hugged her curves and made him hungry to touch her. A blouse with a couple of buttons left open. Silky hair he'd like to wrap his hands in. She was lively and quick to smile and a little crazy to boot. The perfect antidote to his cautious, controlled personality. It didn't take a genius to see he was looking for something to spice up his humdrum life.

Even if he knew there'd be consequences.

"Exactly." She actually moved toward the clock, as if to pick it up again.

"For heaven's sake, Olivia." Jed would be back soon. Or Liam. Or his sisters, and if they walked in here and saw Olivia in their living room, there'd be hell to pay.

She reached for it.

Noah snapped. He came at her like a linebacker, ducked down to flip her over his shoulder and whisked her right out of the room—and out of the house. If she stayed any longer, he couldn't answer for what he might do. Not in anger because she was stealing his clock, but out of the lust that consumed him whenever she was around. If he kept making moves on her, things would get complicated fast.

"Noah!" Olivia's unladylike shriek pierced the quiet summer evening, and despite all of it, Noah laughed as he set her down on the front stoop. He hated to let go of her, so he kept his hands resting on her hips.

"If you're going try to steal my clock, you're going to pay the consequences," he told her sternly.

"Oh yeah? What consequences?"

She was daring him to kiss her, he realized. Tilting up her face with that cocky grin of hers.

Ah, hell, Noah thought. He was only a man. He leaned down, cupped her chin and met her mouth with his own, kissing her deeply, sliding his other arm around her waist to pull her close.

Her soft body in the circle of his arms felt too good. His pulse raced as she matched his hunger with her own. Her arms linked around his neck, and she went up on tiptoe, arching into him.

What were they doing? Playing with fire. Dancing with the devil. But Noah let the moment linger on. Maybe he wouldn't get this chance again. He wanted to savor it.

When he finally broke away, he was breathing hard, and so was she. He snatched another kiss because he couldn't help himself.

"What are we supposed to do?" he asked. He didn't need to explain what he meant.

"Nothing." Olivia ran a hand over her hair to smooth it back into place. "I mean it, Noah; we can't act on this."

"We're enemies," he agreed.

"Exactly."

Noah's heart sank at the certainty in her voice. "I want to do this, though. I want you," he confessed.

Olivia bit her lip, stared off into the distance as if she was thinking it over, and finally shook her head. "We can't have a relationship," she reiterated, "but that's not what you want anyway. So I propose..." She trailed off.

"You propose what?" They were taking a chance standing so close to each other on the front steps like this. Where had Olivia parked her truck? Noah scanned the lot, empty except his own vehicle. She needed to leave.

"I propose we have sex."

Noah looked down sharply. Swallowed hard. "Sex?"

"We'll get it out of our systems. We're like forbidden fruit for each other, right? Forbidden fruit drives you wild until you eat it. Then it's just... fruit."

Noah couldn't believe what she was saying. Did she really think they could fuck each other out of their systems?

He didn't like the sound of that at all. He didn't think the feelings that sparked between them were just... fruit.

Still, she was offering something he'd thought about a lot. He wanted to make love to Olivia.

Noah thought fast, until a smile tugged one corner of his mouth. If she wanted sex, they'd have sex, and he'd take a chance that once would be enough for her. But he'd do his damnedest to make sure it wasn't. No matter what she thought, he did want a relationship.

Even if he knew they couldn't have a future.

Reason warred with the animal desires raging inside him. Desire won.

Why was he surprised?

"Okay," he finally managed to say, working hard to form the syllables in a suddenly dry throat. "Yeah, forbidden fruit. Getting it out of our system. That sounds about right."

"When can we meet? And where?" Olivia was all business, like she did this all the time, but Noah knew she didn't. Knew that underneath her bold personality she was softer than you might think. She was a library geek at heart, after all, even if she never went around the library these days.

"Where?" Noah chuckled. Given the way their families were feuding over the Founder's Prize, he'd just thought of the perfect place for their tryst. "The Ridley property."

Olivia laughed. "Hell, yeah. It's a good place for secrets." Noah wasn't sure what she meant by that, but she went on before he could ask. "I'll text you." She began to back down the steps.

"When?"

Olivia shrugged. "When I can get away."

He nodded. He could live with that. "Not too long, though," he said.

"No." She shook her head. "Not too long."

"OLIVIA? DID YOU hear a word I just said?" Lance thumped his glass on the table several days later.

Olivia straightened. Her brother was right; she'd been daydreaming... about Noah. The man she wasn't supposed to care for. The man she was going to sleep with. The last time she'd seen him she'd talked a bold game, offering flat-out to make love to him to rid him from her system—

And he'd agreed.

What was she doing?

It was like slipping into a forgotten mineshaft, the floor collapsing under her feet, sliding in a wash of dirt and rubble to land who knew where.

This was a disaster plain and simple. She couldn't kid herself that she wasn't half-crazy for him. The desire she felt for Noah was like something alive within her, gnawing at her until she couldn't concentrate on anything else.

"Well?" Lance demanded.

"Well, what?" She picked at her scrambled eggs, not hungry. Consumed by thoughts of what making love to Noah might be like. Would he be tender or rough?

Would he take his time… or take her fast?

"The creek's down. It's too early in the year for that. We've got a lot of summer ahead of us."

Olivia snapped out of her reverie. "How far down?"

"Six inches at least, and it'll keep going down; I've been watching it. There's no rain in the forecast."

Worry replaced the warm, heady feeling her daydreams had produced. The water from Pittance Creek was vital to their ranching operation. Vital to Noah's ranch, too. Thorn Hill and the Flying W. Two sides of the same coin. Two banks along a creek. A creek that was running low on water.

"We have to keep an eye on it," Lance said. "Morning," he added when Steel walked in, poured himself a cup of coffee and joined them at the table.

"You talking about the water?"

Olivia nodded.

"It's not looking good," Steel said grimly. Olivia's two brothers were both dark, brooding men, but Steel's melancholy always seemed to run deeper. Olivia worried about the demons that haunted him. "There's something else," Steel went on. "Money. We're running low." He stared into the depths of his coffee cup. Lance exchanged a look with Olivia.

Olivia took this in. Low on water and low on money. Not a good combination for a ranch already skating on thin ice.

"I'll look for work," Lance said.

"No." Both brothers looked up at Olivia's emphatic statement. "If you go out to work, we'd end up needing to hire more hands. I'll get a job."

"Doing what?" Lance asked. A fair question. Olivia didn't have much experience off the ranch. Not for the first time, it seemed to her like she'd been drifting through life these past years. Letting life happen to her rather than making any decisions.

"I don't know," she said truthfully. "I guess we'll find out."

Chapter Three

WATER SLOSHED IN the bucket Noah carried when he stumbled on the uneven floorboards of the stable. He exhaled in relief when he saw none of it had spilled. Right now water was on his mind, and spilling it seemed like a bad omen.

He tuned out the musty smells of hay and animals as he went about tending the horses, thinking back to the night he'd kissed Olivia. Forbidden fruit, indeed. His heart quickened, and he couldn't tell if it was excitement or anxiety. On the one hand he couldn't believe Olivia would really go through with it. On the other hand...what if she did—and actually got him out of her system that way? Better not to be with her at all, rather than get a taste of the forbidden and then be banished from the garden forever. He'd lose his mind.

If he didn't lose his mind over the state of the Flying W first. He sighed, glancing around at the interior of the stable. The crooked beams caught his eye like they always did, and he ached to force them to line up somehow. Which was impossible, of course. The beams were crooked because the weight of the roof had shifted over the years, which had probably happened because snow always accumulated in one corner where the shingles were all torn up. Crooked beams were the least of his worries.

He couldn't afford repairs like that right now, not if a drought was coming. His family would need to dedicate all their efforts to the cattle in the months to come if it got dry. That didn't stop him from being frustrated, though. His fingers itched to get right to fixing the stable. It was a project that could be completed, and then he'd have something lasting to show for it. Didn't matter how much water you gave your cattle today; they'd still be thirsty tomorrow.

He wished his cousin Eli was here to consult with. He could call him later, but it wasn't quite the same. When he'd been here, Eli had always talked Noah down whenever the responsibilities of running the ranch had piled up too high. His quiet wisdom helped.

But there was nothing to be done about it. Eli was back in Colorado now.

When Noah left the stable, empty bucket swinging, he met Jed and Liam coming in from tending the cattle. Jed's limp was pronounced today. Noah suspected he was overdoing things.

"Looks like a damn good thing I came back, eh?" Jed tossed his head toward the stable Noah had just come from. "You let the place go all to hell without me around."

Noah gritted his teeth. He, Liam and their sisters had been doing everything they could, but Jed wouldn't acknowledge that. "How's the herd?" he asked, hoping to change the subject.

"Where'd it all go?" Jed asked. "Back in my day the herd stretched from here to the creek."

Noah doubted that. He caught Liam rolling his eyes and wondered if Jed had been like this all morning.

"Since Dad passed we've had to downsize the operation a little. Not enough people working here to keep up with a herd that size, so we sold some off."

"This one claimed the same thing." Jed hooked a thumb at Liam. "Sounds like an excuse for laziness to me. Next you'll buy some of Carl's robots to run the operation."

"That isn't fair," Noah said against his better judgment. "Given how many people work here now, there's actually more cattle per person than ever. And that was before the rain stopped."

Jed made a dismissive sound. "Better get used to it, at any rate." He indicated the parched grass with a sweep of his hand. "If the Coopers win the Ridley place, things are going to look like this all the time, drought or no drought."

"We don't know they would—"

"Don't worry about the Coopers," Liam said. "I'll take care of them."

Noah didn't like the sound of that, and he didn't like the way Liam was trying to prove himself to Jed. Sometime soon he'd need to sit his little brother down and explain that surly old relatives criticized because they had nothing better to do and not for any personal reasons.

They met up with Maya when they reached the main house. She looked tired, but she straightened when she saw them and forced a smile.

"Everything okay?" Noah asked.

"It's fine." She didn't sound fine, though. "I couldn't sleep last night. Thought we were simply going through a dry spell, but everyone in town yesterday was talking about a drought. How bad do you think it will be?"

"Hard to say at this point." Noah didn't even want to think about it.

"At this rate I'm not going to have much produce to sell. I was hoping to turn a profit and help out a bit around here."

Noah considered the matter. He'd hoped for that, too. "What about selling more baked goods?" he suggested.

Maya frowned. "I'm running a farm stand, not a bakery."

"It could be both."

"I guess so."

Noah hated seeing her so discouraged, but none of them had experienced true adversity before. They'd all have to make sacrifices to keep a roof over their heads. "We need your stand to be profitable. We need more cash. We can barely afford to pay our field hands."

"We could cut back on the hands if you quit your job."

Noah shook his hand. "I just told you we need the cash."

"Of course. You get to hold on to your passion project, but you want me to give up my garden." Maya folded her arms over her chest.

Noah laughed. "First of all, I didn't say to give up your garden; I said to bake some pies and cakes, too. Second of all, you think I like being a parole officer?"

"Hell, yeah! You love telling people off when they break the rules. It must be a dream come true."

"Do not." Was that really how people saw him? "Look, keep your garden for now, but if our well gets low, we'll have to set priorities."

"It won't get that bad, will it?" Maya asked.

"A drought like this can make a family lose their ranch," Noah said. Jed was nodding, and Noah realized his uncle would know a thing or two about hard times.

"We'd better be more vigilant. Especially when it comes to the Coopers," Liam put in.

Noah's stomach sank. "What do you mean?"

"Remember when Olivia tried to steal the clock that one time?"

Noah winced. Yeah, just the once.

"Good citizens are supposed to report crimes like breaking and entering and attempted theft. It won't matter what they do to fix the school if we expose them as the criminals they are. Next time Olivia tries to steal it, we'll catch her and turn her in."

"You'll tell Cab?" Noah asked. He didn't like the idea of Olivia being hauled into the sheriff's office.

Grinning, Liam picked a newspaper off the table and shook it at Noah.

"We'll tell everyone."

"IF I HAD any experience, do you think I'd be looking for a job like this?" Olivia rustled her stack of résumés in frustration.

Allison, a cashier at the local hardware store, frowned. "If it were up to me, I'd give you a chance, but Heather was specific about the requirements. I can call her if you want. Maybe she'll make an exception."

"No, don't do that." Olivia swiped the résumé out of Allison's hands. Heather had already volunteered to help her organize a gala. If she asked for any more favors, she'd feel like a beggar. She hoped no one could see her cheeks burning as she left. When she pushed through the front door, however, she blinked against the glare and the dust. Damn drought.

Olivia walked aimlessly through the streets of downtown Chance Creek. She'd checked off the grocery store and the main restaurants, which all asked for references, which she didn't have. Secretarial jobs were a no-go; she'd barely used a computer in her life and didn't know any of the software packages. She was beginning to regret taking on this responsibility, even knowing it was the best thing for Thorn Hill and her family.

It wasn't that she hadn't worked before. She had— for a restaurant that had gone under several years ago. When she'd tried to track down the owner for a reference, she couldn't find her.

The post office came into view, and she sighed. Worth a shot.

"First you have to take a government exam. Then comes the background check," the woman behind the counter said when Olivia asked about employment opportunities.

"Exam?" That would take too long. She needed money now. "Never mind."

"Hold on, Olivia," the clerk said as she turned to leave. "We've got a package for you."

At least her visit hadn't been a total waste of time. The clerk returned with a neatly wrapped parcel with a New Mexico return address. Of course: the book her mother wanted her to return. The package bore a sticker for express shipping. Her mother was serious about tying up this loose end.

Deciding she couldn't take any more job hunting today, Olivia made the library her next stop. On the way she unwrapped the package and surveyed the battered old book within. *The Unbearable Lightness of Being.* Sounded like the sort of thing her mother would read. Olivia preferred whodunnits, when she had time to read at all.

It hadn't always been that way, though. Her steps slowed as she approached her truck. Even as a child she'd read far above her age, getting lost in complex and weighty books. It wasn't until real life got too complex and weighty that she'd started looking for lighter fare between the pages.

She'd created a new version of herself after her father had gone to jail—a cardboard cutout of the girl people expected her to be. She'd dumbed herself down. Made herself small.

Which was... kind of awful, now that she thought about it. Was that why life held little spark these days? Because she wasn't being the person she could be?

With one hand on the truck's door handle, Olivia shook her head. This was her life, and she had to accept it. Which meant stopping this pity party and getting to the library.

Deciding a walk would clear her head, she left the truck where it sat and kept going. It was only when she stepped through the front door of the old library that she woke up from her daydreams and looked around. It had once been a huge old house but had contained the library for so long she had no idea who'd lived here. It was dim and quiet, a dusty sanctuary. She hadn't been here in ages and had forgotten how comfortable a place it was. As a kid, she used to come all the time, escaping the chaos of home and school. She could pick out a book, curl up in some shadowed nook and read for hours, hidden from the world.

Why had she given that up? There were libraries in Idaho, for heaven's sake.

Although...

A memory rose in her mind. She'd visited the town library near her aunt's place once, a cold, modern building with security like an airport. Its starkness had unnerved her, and she'd never gone back. She'd let her disappointment steal another source of joy away from her.

Had she been punishing herself all this time?

Olivia shook the uncomfortable thought from her

mind and focused again on her surroundings.

Good old Chance Creek didn't have any security system, and Olivia went straight past the checkout counter; she'd deal with her mother's book in a minute. First she wanted to get reacquainted with the place.

She walked the aisles between the stacks, running her hand along the spines of the books and losing herself in the memories. She'd volunteered here for a few years, too. She'd loved the work. She paused when her fingers caught on a spine that jutted out from its row. She frowned and nudged it back on the shelf so it was in line with the others. Then she noted another book that had been pushed too far back. She tugged it forward. There were books out of line all over the place. Olivia began to tidy them.

"You'll be here all day if you try to do *all* of them."

Olivia jumped and spun to face the cheerful old lady who had appeared in the aisle beside her. She almost didn't recognize the woman at first, but as the words she'd spoken echoed in Olivia's mind, she recognized the silly old in-joke. "Marta? I didn't know you still worked here!"

Marta embraced her. "Every day. Time was you'd be here every day, too. Was a bit of a shock when you moved away, learning how to get on without you. Never realized how much help you were until it all fell back on my shoulders."

"Oh, stop." Olivia found her cheeks warming for the second time that day, blushing at Marta's kind words. "I was a kid. If anything, I must have gotten in the way."

"A more helpful child I've never had the pleasure to meet," Marta said solemnly. "Could hardly get my own to help me with the dishes."

Olivia laughed. "That's a new one. Most people who remember us Coopers from back then don't have anything nice to say."

Marta pursed her lips. "With good reason, some of them. But you are not your parents, Olivia. I knew even then you'd be the one to turn over a new leaf for your clan. Remember how you used to like helping me? Lord knows I could use some help now."

Olivia lit up. *Finally.* "You're hiring?"

"Volunteer help," Marta clarified. "We're really strapped for funds right now, and things are falling apart. I know times are hard and a library doesn't seem so important to folks, but a town needs a library."

Olivia hated to see the strain on her old friend's face, but she had her own problems. "I'd love to help," she told Marta truthfully, "but my family's having a pretty rough go of things, too. I need a real job so I can help our bottom line, or we'll all go under. I'm sorry."

Marta nodded. "Don't worry, dear. I understand. Best of luck in finding a job."

"Speaking of that, I'd like to photocopy some résumés while I'm here." She still had a good stack left, but at this rate she'd need to hand one out to every business in town before she got anywhere.

"Of course. Right this way."

Olivia handed over a résumé, and Marta fed it into

the machine. The librarian tinkered with the copier for a minute, frowning. "Hmm. Might need to restart it. Give me a moment." She pressed a button, and the lights on the screen died. She pressed it again and plunged the library into darkness.

"Darn it," Marta said. "Blew a circuit again. Give me a minute."

"Everything all right up front there?" a man's voice called from the back.

"Everything's fine, Allen," Marta called back. "Sit tight; we'll have lights back on in a minute." She hurried away, and Olivia waited patiently. It seemed the patrons were used to it. Olivia could hear several people chatting.

The lights flickered back on. "There we go," Marta said, returning. A minute later she handed Olivia her new résumés, still warm from printing.

"Thanks," Olivia said, glancing at her watch. "It was really nice to see you again, but I've got to run. Need to get my aunt to her doctor's appointment." She sighed, already longing for the days when the nurses at the Prairie Garden took care of all that. "I'll be back soon, though, I promise—oh, and here." She handed Marta the book her mother had sent her.

"What's this?" Marta held it up, then opened it to the page where an old-fashioned system listed the due date by which the book was supposed to be returned. "Well, this is a little overdue, isn't it?"

"Thirteen years," Olivia said ruefully. "My mom had it in a storage locker for a long time. She found it a couple of weeks back and sent it to me to return."

"You tell her thank you. I'll get this little beauty right back on the shelf where it belongs."

"You still want it after all this time?" Olivia asked.

"This was a wonderful book back then, and it's a wonderful book now. I still have a place for it."

DRIVING ALONG THE parched dirt road toward town, Noah ached to lay on the gas pedal and cut his commute time in half, but the last thing he needed was for Jed to see him being irresponsible. Normally he would have taken it slow, basking in the warmth of the sun and letting the endless blue sky and rolling fields lull him into an almost meditative state.

He doubted Jed had ever even heard of a meditative state. His uncle must be seeing something completely different when he looked out the truck's windows, because to hear Jed tell it, everything in the world was wrong, and most of it was Noah's fault. Part of him wanted to stop the truck and tell Jed he could walk to his doctor's appointment, but another part of him wondered if that was exactly what Jed wanted. His uncle had made it more than clear he'd rather not go to the doctor's at all.

"You stopped those Coopers from fixing the school yet?" Jed asked, breaking Noah out of his dark musings.

Noah shook his head. How many times did they have to go over this? "Liam's still working on the newspaper thing. Don't know what else you expect us to do. You do understand the school board has officially signed on to the Coopers' plan, right?"

"Guess it's too much to expect for you to take family matters seriously. What with you spending all your days away from the ranch."

Noah frowned. "I have a job, Jed."

"Which I would have expected you to quit by now. What's the matter with you, boy? Can't you see the ranch is falling apart?"

Noah wanted to bang his head against the steering wheel. "We need money to fix it," he forced himself to point out calmly. The old man was nervous, that was all. Noah wanted nothing more than to restore his home to its old glory. It wasn't his fault things hadn't gone right in a long time.

"That's what it's all about with you kids, isn't it? Money's the answer to everything. That's what brought the Coopers down in the first place, you know that? Money-grubbing little scoundrels. Couldn't be content with what they had, always wanted just a little more. Wouldn't be half-surprised if that's why they want our clock so bad—just to pawn it off to an antique shop."

Noah wasn't sure that was true. Thorn Hill had started out as a fairly comparable spread to the Flying W, but the Coopers always seemed to be unlucky. Olivia's father had been pretty shifty, though. "What do you propose we do about the ranch, then?"

"Don't need a cent to repair a building, just gotta be willing to work. Cut down the trees yourself, cut the lumber and build whatever you need to build."

"After you've bought the equipment to do that, and

after you've let the wood cure a few years, and..."

"Back in my day, when people respected the Turner name, any family in Chance Creek would have been honored to lend us a sawmill and a hammer—and a hand to wield it, at that. Excepting those damn Coopers, of course."

Noah fell silent as they finally pulled into town. For the first time, he thought Jed had hit on a kernel of truth. Despite what Jed might think, people still respected the Turners, and Noah had no doubt they could lean on their community for help in their time of need. What had kept him from even considering that option?

Honor? Integrity?

Pride?

Whatever. It was an idea to keep for the future—if things got worse.

Jed's attitude didn't improve during the appointment, but at least for the moment his ire was directed toward the nurses and doctor rather than Noah.

"I want a second opinion," he snapped when the doctor told him they needed to start looking into surgery for his hip.

"You're entitled to seek one out, naturally," the doctor said, not rising to Jed's bait. "But your hip joint is damaged. There's not a pill for that. If we don't replace it, it's only going to get worse with time."

"We don't need a second opinion," Noah cut in quickly. "I think my uncle's just a little shocked—"

"Don't talk about me like I'm some kind of child, boy. And what do you mean 'we'? Since when are you my spokesman? Figures you'd be all for them putting machine parts in me—trying to turn me into one of those robots you're so in love with, huh?"

The doctor raised his eyebrows.

"Don't ask," Noah mumbled.

The doctor bit back a smile. "I can't make you go in for surgery, Jed, but I do strongly recommend it. You don't have to schedule it right now, either—we can wait for the shock to wear off. It's quite normal to experience anxiety about a procedure like this. If it helps, I can refer you to a counselor who can help you through the process. In fact, seeing as you're a rancher at heart, I wonder if equine therapy might work well for you. There's a woman in town—"

Jed shook his head emphatically. "I don't need no counselor, and I don't need no equine whatever-it-is."

"It's okay to need help, Jed," Noah told him. "And it's okay to be afraid."

"Afraid?" Jed fumed. "To hell with that! What I am is brave enough to tell you I know what's best for my own body, not like the rest of you cowards too scared to ever question authority."

Noah took Jed's arm to stop it from flailing. "Can we schedule another appointment to talk again?" he asked the doctor.

"Sure thing. Any time you're ready."

The moment they stepped out into the waiting area, Noah wished they'd stayed in the examining room. "You again!" Jed roared, catching sight of Virginia. "Did you follow me here so you could gloat over my afflictions?" He started toward her so quickly Noah wondered if the doctor had somehow fixed Jed's hip when he wasn't looking. "You'll be sorry to hear I'm fit as a fiddle."

"A fiddle that hasn't been tuned in years." Virginia swung her umbrella to keep him at bay. "I haven't heard a racket like that since baby Steel tried to build a drum set out of the cookware."

Despite himself, Noah chuckled. That vision just didn't mesh with the secretive, intimidating Steel he knew.

"And you!" Jed wheeled on Olivia. "Don't you have a clock to steal? Or is it too much to hope you came here to apologize?"

Olivia looked at him, slack-jawed. "I, uh, we're really just here for an appoint—"

"You leave her out of this!" Virginia advanced on Jed and launched another attack with her umbrella.

Jed caught it in a strong, calloused hand. "You think you can tell me what to do? Ha!" He yanked the umbrella from Virginia's grasp, gripped it in both hands—

And snapped it in half.

"YOU...YOU..." VIRGINIA SEARCHED for words, and when they didn't come, she bashed Jed with her pocketbook, staggered backward, caught her balance, lunged forward and bashed him again. Olivia thought she saw tears in her aunt's eyes, though she couldn't say if they were from hurt or anger. She supposed she shouldn't be surprised. Virginia loved that old umbrella.

This wasn't the place for a brawl, though. Virginia needed surgery on her ankle, and she couldn't get it if she was kicked out of the doctor's office the same way she'd been from the assisted living facility.

As the fight grew louder, she saw a doctor emerge from the back room to see what the ruckus was. He said something to the receptionist, who picked up the phone and dialed.

That couldn't be good.

"Virginia, please—" she started, but Virginia swung her purse at her before she could continue. Olivia stepped back and looked to Noah. "Help," she mouthed.

Noah jumped into the middle of the fray and fended off swipes from both Jed and Virginia. "Jed just received some bad news," he told Virginia, as if that would settle her down.

"Did they explain to him there's no cure for his personality?"

"What are you here for? An infusion of common sense?" Jed retaliated.

Noah grabbed Jed by the arm and forcibly removed him from Virginia's vicinity. "We'll be happy to reimburse you for the umbrella or buy you a new one," he called back over his shoulder.

Virginia humphed. "Trust a Turner to think everything's so easily replaceable. That parasol belonged to my grandmother. You want to make it up to me, you can start by returning something else irreplaceable: my clock."

Jed dropped the broken halves of the umbrella to the floor. "Why, I ought to—"

"Respect the peace and your fellow citizens? Good," Cab Johnson, the local sheriff, said. "That's exactly what I hoped you'd say."

Noah was the first to break the awkward silence that followed his interruption. The sheriff must have been nearby to get here so fast. "Sorry, Cab. This is all a misunderstanding—"

Jed cut him off. "What did I tell you? All you're good for is sucking up to authority."

Noah turned on him. "There's a difference between sucking up and being a responsible—"

"All right, that's enough out of everyone." Cab turned his back on Olivia and Virginia, and focused on Noah and Jed. "You know, I might have expected this from the Coopers, but I thought you lot were supposed to be above all this."

Ouch. Olivia's first instinct was to give the sheriff a piece of her mind, but that would just prove his point. With great difficulty she bit her tongue and held back. She really needed to rehabilitate her family's image, which meant she needed to get the school upgrade done. Better talk to the Hall women soon about the gala.

She focused on Cab again.

"You don't have to like each other," he was saying. "Don't even have to pretend to get along. Just stay out of each other's way, and I think we'll be fine."

"Good," Jed muttered. "Not even Shakespeare

could act like he liked that old biddy."

Virginia rolled her eyes. "Shakespeare wrote the plays; he didn't act in them, you bitter old coot."

"Are you or are you not going to keep the peace?" Cab demanded, looking at first one and then the other of them. "Well?"

"We were just leaving." Noah took Jed's arm.

"As soon as he's gone, I'll be fine." Virginia nodded toward Jed.

"Then my work here is done." Cab left with a tip of his hat to no one in particular. Olivia thought Noah would follow, but he lingered.

"I bet Virginia isn't afraid of surgery," he said dryly to Jed.

Jed flushed with anger. "What the hell is that supposed to mean, you little ingrate? Ain't got no problem with surgery."

"I'm glad to hear that. Would you like to schedule an appointment now?" a doctor said, approaching from one of the nearby offices. He must have listened to the whole fight, Olivia realized.

Jed froze, then nodded stiffly.

"You'll be called in a just a few minutes," the doctor told Olivia and Virginia. He turned back to Noah. "This shouldn't take long. I've got some reading material to send home with you. You should read through it together, as soon as possible," he added to Noah.

Virginia went to gather up the broken pieces of her umbrella, sat down hard in one of the chairs lined up against one wall and smoothed her skirt, looking worn out despite the show she'd just put on. Olivia took the pieces from her hands. "After this we'll find someone who can fix your umbrella."

"Humph." Virginia turned away, and Olivia's stomach sank. Her aunt wasn't just tired; she was sad. That umbrella had really meant a lot to her.

Noah and Jed reappeared a few moments later. Jed kept walking, never once glancing their way.

But Noah did. He winked at Olivia, and a private smile curved his lips.

She had no doubt what he was thinking about, and her heart skipped a beat. He still meant to go through with their date, if they ever had a chance.

Good.

Chapter Four

"**I** CAN'T FIND a job," Brandon said when he met up with Noah at Linda's Diner the following day. "It's impossible."

"Nothing's impossible," Noah assured him. "You have to work at it, but you'll get there if it's what you really want."

"Easy for you to say. The whole system's rigged to help people like you succeed, whereas it's all stacked against me."

That caught Noah off guard. "People like me?"

"Born rich, from a respected family. Probably never had the chance to slip up even if you wanted to."

Noah frowned, but not because Brandon thought he had it easy. It was to be expected for a parolee to lash out, blaming an unfair system rather than taking responsibility for his actions. What bothered Noah was that the accusation brought him back to the day before, when Jed had busted him for sucking up to Cab. He didn't care what Jed said; Jed criticized everything he did anyway. What bothered him was that he'd said it in front of Olivia. Was that how she saw him? As a spineless goody-goody looking for a pat on the head?

He sure hoped not.

"I'm not rich," he told Brandon evenly. "And even if I was, that wouldn't mean I didn't have my own challenges."

Brandon shrugged. "Maybe. And maybe if I could go back I'd do things better. But seems to me you get one chance, and if you screw it up there's no hope of fixing it."

"You're right." Noah was satisfied when Brandon straightened in surprise. "It is harder to rebuild once you've broken the law. It's harder to do most things, I'd imagine, including getting a job. The lesson here is that actions have consequences. It's probably difficult to see right now, but in a way that's a good thing."

Brandon let out a bitter laugh. "Oh yeah? How do you figure?"

"Dealing with the pain of those consequences now will help you make better decisions in the future. Not only better for society, but better for yourself. It's understandable that in certain situations you might be tempted to cut corners. This gives you a reason not to. In fact, in sticking to stricter rules than most people have to deal with, and overcoming more difficult obstacles, you're going to build a lot of discipline, perseverance and integrity. Those values will serve you well, not just through this process but the rest of your life. You might feel impossibly behind right now, but if you take this chance to develop a strong character, you'll be ahead of the average person in the long run."

Brandon made a noncommittal noise. Noah obviously wasn't getting through to him. And he really needed to get through to him. His parolee was disenfranchised, running out of hope and more concerned with the present moment than his future.

In other words, he was dangerously close to reoffending. Noah couldn't bear to see Brandon throw it all away now, and he'd do whatever he could to keep that from happening.

"Okay," he went on, "maybe you're not in the mood to think about the future right now. I get it. So let's talk about your current—"

"You boys doing all right?"

Noah nearly groaned when Christie appeared, her gaze fixed on Brandon. Why on earth had he brought Brandon back here? Caught up in his longing for Olivia, the escalating feud between Jed and Virginia, and Jed's constant, irritating presence around the Flying W, he'd forgotten all about the flirtatious waitress.

"We're good," he said firmly.

"Actually—" Brandon caught Christie's hand when she started to turn away. "I could use a glass of water."

Funny how he hadn't mentioned being thirsty when their original waiter took their orders, Noah thought.

Brandon held on to Christie's hand far too long until Noah cleared his throat. By the time he let go, Christie's color was high.

"I'll be right back," she said breathlessly.

"What I was saying," Noah continued when she was gone, "is that you don't have to wait for your situation to get better. There are things you can do right now that can improve your quality of life."

"Like what?" Brandon's eyes traced Christie's path through the restaurant.

"Building your community would be a great first step. Like we talked about before, the more people you know and who trust you, the more opportunities will naturally come your way. But it goes way beyond that. Once you get used to feeling ostracized by society, it's easy to forget what it feels like to have a strong support system. You might not even realize how much you miss—"

"Here you go, honey." Christie was back. She leaned across Brandon to place his water on the table, the position leading to a lot more body contact than seemed necessary. She caught Noah glowering at her and winked at him. "Okay then, I'll get out of your hair, let you get back to your serious business."

"Wait," Brandon said before Christie even began to move away. He touched the brim of the glass. "I was actually hoping to get water with ice in it."

"My bad." She leaned in again to retrieve the glass. "Be back before you know it."

Noah ran a hand through his hair and watched Brandon in silence. The parolee didn't seem to notice at first, his gaze focused on the waitress as she walked away, but when he glanced back, he caught Noah looking and shifted uncomfortably. "So, uh, you were saying about a support system?"

Noah said nothing. This time when Christie came back, she took one look at Noah's face, set the ice water on the table without fanfare and scurried back to the kitchen.

"Are you two dating?" Noah asked when the kitchen door swung shut behind her.

Brandon eyed him. "What's it to you?"

"I'm your parole officer. It's my job."

"To meddle in my love life? I don't think that's any of your business."

"It's my business if I think you're building a destructive relationship."

Brandon set his hands on the table and leaned toward Noah. "Weren't you just telling me I should build my community? You don't know what it's like to be in prison. It's been a long time since I've been with a woman."

"That doesn't mean—"

"You keep telling me I need to connect with people." Brandon cut him off. "But the first time I try to, you give me hell. What makes you think she's going to be a bad influence on me, anyway? She seems nice."

Noah cleared his throat. "She does, actually. Seems like a good woman."

Brandon's eyes widened as he finally understood. "Wait—you're saying I'll be a bad influence on *her*? Fuck you, man—you're supposed to be on my side." He stood up, bumping the table in his haste to get away. His water sloshed in its glass.

"Hold on, there." Noah got up, too, but he had to collect his jacket and wallet. By the time he managed it, Brandon was already at the door. "You're twisting my words. Hey!" He rushed to catch Brandon and bumped into two people coming in.

"Noah! Perfect." Liam waved something in his hand at Noah. "Check out—"

Noah forced his way around him and Jed, but by the time he poked his head out the door he couldn't see which way Brandon had gone. Besides, he couldn't just leave without paying.

He crossed paths with Christie on his way back in. "Brandon had to go," he told her curtly and led his brother and uncle back to his table. Christie took their orders, and Liam laid a stack of papers before him. Noah struggled to get his irritation under control.

"Look at these," Liam said. "First batch of nostalgia letters for the school. Some of them are gold."

"Others are from people who clearly never graduated," Jed muttered.

Liam waved him off. "Seriously, give them a read."

Noah picked up one at random and skimmed it. It could use a little cleanup, for sure. There was a lot of rambling in the beginning about the author's childhood that had nothing to do with the school, but there was heart to it, too, a simple, honest account that made Noah wish he'd been around for a time when he hadn't even been alive. When it got to the point and talked about good times at Chance Creek High, it was touching.

"These... these could actually work." He started on a second letter.

"What, you didn't think I'd pull it off?" Liam demanded, but beneath his sour expression, Noah could tell he was proud.

"You're right. I should never have doubted you." Noah didn't want to alienate his brother, but he was still torn about delaying the renovation and tech upgrade project at the high school. "Let's keep it positive, though. Some of these letters are a little… rough."

"As well they should be," Jed said. "I say we focus on those, let everyone know how the Coopers are trying to ruin our town."

"A majority of the teachers had to vote for the renovation to go through," Noah reminded him. "If we publish letters that call them stupid—or malicious—for supporting the renovation, all we'll do is make them close ranks against us and double down." He picked up and waved the first letter he'd read. Knowing Jed never was much for tact, he appealed directly to Liam. "You were right, man, letters like this are gold. This guy talks about how incredible his teachers were, then goes on to argue that all this technology will keep the next generation of students from building those close personal relationships with them. The Board will be a lot more inclined to listen to letters that start out by praising the school." He clapped Liam on the shoulder. "Look for more like this one. Great work, man."

Liam squared his shoulders and nodded, but Jed's expression remained stormy. "Still nothing but talk in the end. We ought to do more."

"I think Liam's doing plenty," Noah said. He had to keep them both on the straight and narrow path.

"I disagree," Jed said. "I think we should take action."

"Maybe you should collect testimonials, too," Noah suggested. "Like you always say, the Turners were more respected back in your day." Liam opened his mouth to protest, and Noah shot him a significant look, praying he'd understand. "There's got to be plenty of folks around who remember those times and still have a lot of respect for you. I bet you could get better testimonials out of them than Liam or I could hope for."

Jed chewed on that for a moment. "I suppose I do have a lot of pull in this town. Might as well put it to use."

Christie came to bring them their orders and talk turned to the ranch and the work that needed to be done there. Noah let out a sigh of relief when they left him alone at his table to run some errands around town. He sat back and nursed his coffee. When had it become his role in life to blow smoke up everyone's asses?

"Why the long face?"

A lean man with a dark goatee and a matching dark Stetson sat across from Noah, putting an end to his moment of peace and quiet.

"Mahoney," Noah greeted the young deputy. "How you been?" He'd worked with Patrick Mahoney awhile now. Noah could count on him to have his back, and he appreciated that.

"I asked first." Mahoney reclined in his seat.

Noah rested his head in his hands. "Wish I could say things were good, but they aren't." He wouldn't mention his family's troubles. "It's my parolee. Keeps flirting with the waitress over there." He nodded at Christie. "Pretty clear she's in it for the thrills of dating a bad boy, but I'm worried she'll get in over her head. Don't want her to end up on the wrong path. 'Course when I brought that up, Brandon snapped and stormed out."

Mahoney shrugged. "Can't say I blame the guy." He leaned forward and studied Noah intently. "You ain't never fallen for the wrong gal?"

Noah started to deny it, then paused. On the surface Mahoney played the part of the devil-may-care, doesn't-play-by-the-rules deputy, but Noah knew it was an act. Underneath, he was studious, disciplined and a genuinely good guy.

"I guess I have," he admitted.

Mahoney's eyebrows shot up. "Oh yeah? Who?"

Noah took a deep breath. "You'd better keep this under your hat."

"SORRY IF WE'RE getting ahead of ourselves," Ella said when Olivia finally got another chance to stop by Crescent Hall. "It's your party, after all. We should have waited for more input from you before putting down so many ideas."

"Are you kidding?" Olivia leafed through the binder Ella had put in front of her. "I'm the one who should apologize—you didn't have to do all this. This must have taken ages."

Regan waved a hand. "With all these little ones

around, there's a lot of time for chatting and brain-storming while we keep an eye on the kids. It was nice to have a project to talk about."

Olivia chuckled when she reached a page headlined *Regency Theme*, with several question marks after it. "Aunt Virginia should love this one; it'd be like reliving her youth."

The other women laughed, except Storm, who leaned in seriously. "We first put the idea down as a joke." She ran her hand down the early entries in the list of notes, written in a variety of hands and colors. It included entries such as "quadrille dance battle" and "How to Marry an Earl trivia game." Farther down, however, the entries grew serious, including a detailed Regency menu and cost estimates for what it would take to fit each guest with appropriate clothing. "The more we talked about it, the more we fell in love with the idea," Storm explained.

"The girls over at Westfield run a Regency bed-and-breakfast," Heather added. "I'm sure they'd be honored to help us put it on."

"And get this," Ella began.

"Miss Hollywood Starlet, always working the net-working angle," Regan teased.

Ella held up her diamond-clad ring finger. "That's Mrs. Hollywood Starlet to you," she said archly, then turned to Olivia. "What I was trying to say is, this party is mostly for Martin Fulsom's benefit, right?"

"More or less."

"He's the one behind that crazy reality show at

Westfield. If we can pitch it to him as promotion for both his Chance Creek projects, tied together by the Regency theme, I'm sure he'll be all over it."

Well hell, that was something.

"Not to mention the teachers," Regan said. "They're a bunch of big old nerds at heart, so they'll eat it right up."

"Plus, Regan's biased," Heather added with a grin.

Regan nodded. "Jane Austen's writing played a role in bringing me here and changing the course of my life, so she holds a special place in my heart. And besides, teachers really do love to play dress-up."

They all waited for Olivia's reaction. When she didn't reply right away, Storm bit her lip. "Whoops. We didn't mean to give you such a hard sell, I swear. It's only one idea—and it's your party, after all."

In response, Olivia picked up a pen and drew a thick dark line through the question marks in the title, transforming them all into a single exclamation point. "I'm in!"

Driving home again, she spotted Carl heading into Fila's Familia, a popular local restaurant that his wife owned with Fila Matheson. An idea popped into her head, and she pulled over, parked and hurried after him.

"Hi, Carl. Mind if I join you?" She caught up just as he was sliding into a booth. She saw Camila disappearing back into the kitchen. The newlyweds must have already greeted each other. Olivia thought it was sweet Carl came here for dinner.

"Oh hey, Olivia. Go ahead." He gestured to the

bench seat across the table, but the yummy smells that swirled through the air of the Afghan-Mexican fusion restaurant were making Olivia hungry.

"Be back in a sec." She went to the counter to order.

Juana Valentin, Camila's cousin who had recently moved to town from Mexico, greeted her at the register and recommended their latest addition to the menu: *gorditas de flor de calabaza*. Olivia didn't know what that was, and she'd been skeptical when Juana and Camila started adding "authentic" Mexican dishes to Fila's menu, but she'd quickly learned Juana knew what she was doing. When Olivia returned to Carl's booth, she carried a plate laden with pastry shells stuffed with squash flowers.

"Surprisingly good, right?" Carl said when she'd polished off her first *gordita*. "I've never eaten a flower before."

Olivia nodded, then remembered why she was there. "I've got a proposition for you."

One of the corners of Carl's mouth quirked up. "I'm not stealing any clocks—even if they do fetch a good price on the black market."

Olivia rolled her eyes. Carl had been her unwitting getaway driver one of the times she'd tried to take her family's grandmother clock back from the Turners. "This isn't about the clock. You're doing really good work with the school," she went on as Carl's gaze fell on the folder in front of him, which was stuffed with paperwork no doubt connected to the project. "But it isn't the only place in town that could use some help. I was wondering if you might be able to help me raise money for the library."

"You don't think the school's enough to win the prize?"

"This isn't about the prize. I've known the librarian since I was a kid. She's having trouble keeping the lights on. I know you're busy, but it was so easy for you to get sponsorship for the school. If you could just reach out to some of your contacts—"

Carl finally looked up. "Easy?" He put his pen down. "You know I'm trying to be a rancher now—not a businessman? I'm busy."

"You said the same thing before you started on the school."

"That was a special case—" He broke off. "Look, 'busy' doesn't begin to cover what I am these days. Not only am I starting a ranch right when Chance Creek is heading into a drought, but I'm also trying to run it like Camila's family's ranch back home in Mexico. I'm trying to figure out how to grow the ingredients she can't get here, which means designing a whole new system of greenhouses."

"Never mind. I'll figure out another way."

"Try me in a few months, when I've managed to check a few things off my to-do list."

Olivia nodded and made small talk for the rest of the meal. If Carl couldn't help her, she didn't know who could, but she couldn't blame the man for being over-whelmed right now. Embarrassed she'd even asked, she hurried to finish and said goodbye. On her way out, she almost bumped into Caroline, who was walking in.

"Hey," she said, glad to see her friend. "Are you here to eat dinner? I'll sit with you if you are." She could use a good chat.

"Just getting takeout," Caroline said apologetically. "I've got to hurry. We're still on for Sunday, though, right?"

"You bet." Olivia was disappointed, but no doubt Devon was waiting for Caroline at home. He was always impatient when she wasn't there with him. "How's work?" Olivia asked to prolong the conversation.

"Busy. I—hang on, let me get this." Caroline drew her phone out of her purse, frowned and answered it. "Hi. Yes, I'm at the restaurant. Devon, I just got here. Yes. Yes, I know. I'll be home as soon as I can, okay? What?" Her shoulders slumped. "Sure. I'll stop and get them." She hung up, her lips pinched in a thin line. Olivia didn't like the pain in her friend's eyes, and she almost reached out to touch Caroline's arm. Devon was so damn overbearing sometimes.

Before she could, Caroline straightened. "Lottery tickets, can you believe that? Like we've got the money to spare. Devon calls it our retirement plan, but it's stupid, if you ask me. And somehow he's never the one to buy them; it comes out of my earnings." She swallowed and looked around swiftly, as if someone might have overheard her.

Olivia smiled sympathetically, but inside her thoughts were churning. Things didn't seem to be going well in her friend's relationship. She wished she knew how to help. "I'll walk you to the gas station." She was pretty sure that's where Caroline would buy them.

"Great. Let me pick up my food first."

Several minutes later they reached the head of the line at the station, and Caroline picked out several lottery cards of different kinds.

"Sorry I was so cranky before," she said when she'd paid for them. "It's just… when they announce the winners, Devon will get so disappointed, he'll be a bear to be around for half the day. I wish he'd stop buying them."

"You're the one buying them," Olivia pointed out. "You could stop. At least it wouldn't be your money down the drain."

"We live together. It's pretty much *our* money," Caroline said.

"You aren't married."

"We're cohabitating. That's like a common-law marriage. That's what Devon says."

Olivia bit back an unkind remark. Devon didn't deserve Caroline. Never had. "What do *you* say?" she asked.

"I think marriage takes a ring and a ceremony." Caroline bit her lip, then quickly lifted the bag of food from Fila's. "I need to go. Don't want dinner getting cold."

"Of course. See you Sunday?" The last thing Olivia wanted was to push things and end up ruining their friendship.

"Yeah. Sunday," Caroline echoed, but she didn't look back.

Olivia watched her go. She wished she knew how to convince Caroline to leave Devon and strike out on her own. The man seemed determined to suck the life out of her friend. Checking the time, Olivia decided to run back to the library. Maybe she could find a book on the subject. She ended up spending an hour in the psychology section reading about controlling men and accommodating women. She still wasn't sure how best to help Caroline, but she was doubly determined to do so now that she'd read how common it was for guys like Devon to escalate to becoming abusive.

Her dark thoughts made her restless, and she found herself driving over the speed limit several times on her way home. Catching herself again, and slowing down, she decided she needed a distraction.

And she knew just the ticket.

Olivia parked far up the lane to the Flying W and sprinted the rest of the way, slowing when she came in view of the house.

No one seemed to be around, although several trucks were parked out front. She had no doubt Noah and his family were finishing up chores for the day. When she tested it, the front door was, once again, unlocked. The Turners never learned. She crept inside, into the living room and across to the fireplace. She had just placed her hands on the clock when a pair of strong arms wrapped around her waist.

"You're not taking that." Noah's voice tickled her

ear.

She wriggled a bit, realized she wasn't getting away and sighed. "You could hand it over to make up for the umbrella."

"Not going to happen." Noah tightened his grip, and suddenly Olivia was far too aware of the powerful arms beneath her breasts and the hard frame pressed against her back.

A moment later she became aware of something else, too.

"Feels like you're in the mood for something," she said acidly.

"I'm serious, Olivia. You're lucky Liam's not here. He's ready to call the sheriff on you—and make sure your photo's in the paper, too."

That got her attention; the last thing she wanted was to end up in jail—or in the paper. "I guess it's a good thing you were the one who caught me," she said softly.

"Yeah." His arms tightened around her, and he kissed the top of her head. "Really, though. You need to get out of here."

Much to her chagrin, he let her go and led the way to the front door. Outside, she paused at the top of the steps. "Virginia hasn't bought a new one, you know."

"New what?"

"Umbrella. After that spat at the doctor's, I tried to find someone to fix it, but I couldn't, and she won't buy a new one. Big waste of my time, really." She gave him a wicked grin. "Which means not only do you owe me a clock, but also you owe me time. A lot of it."

"What did you have in mind?"

"How about we settle up tonight, at the Ridley place?" She could still use a distraction. Besides, with Devon's example fresh in her mind, she would remember that men weren't worthy of trust—or love. She'd get Noah out of her system for good and move on with her life.

He smiled, and Olivia's insides tangled into a tight knot. Moving on wouldn't be that easy. "I guess it's only right to make amends," Noah said, "but you're not getting that clock."

"Then I'll need to charge you more time."

"A man has to pay his debts." Noah looked around, then leaned forward and snatched a quick kiss. "Now get out of here," he said with a smile.

Olivia found herself grinning, too, despite all ups and downs of the day. But as she walked down the driveway to where she'd parked her truck, her smiled died on her lips when a sheriff's cruiser drove by.

She recognized Deputy Patrick Mahoney and realized he must be going to see Noah. Had Noah called him when he spotted her trying to steal the clock? Had the rest of it been a way to delay her until they got here?

Heart in her mouth, she waited for the sheriff's cruiser to slow down and signal her to stop, but it passed right on by.

So he wasn't after *her*. Was Noah the one in trouble?

Olivia laughed bitterly as she picked up her pace.

Noah Turner in trouble?

That'd be the day.

"AREN'T YOU GOING to offer me some tea or lemonade?" Mahoney drawled. He stood in the doorway, scanning the front hall with a trained eye. "Where are your manners, Turner?"

Truth be told, Noah had forgotten them. The deputy didn't seem to be here on any official business, but his showing up right after Olivia left had shaken Noah. Had Mahoney seen her?

"I bet you offered Olivia tea," the deputy added slyly.

Yep, he'd seen her.

Noah sighed and led Mahoney to the kitchen, then fetched them both glasses of lemonade. "What brings you all the way out here?"

The man laid a file on the table and flipped it open. His expression grew serious. "I pulled some records on your Juliet, man. You need to hear this."

"Records?" Noah's eyes narrowed. "I never asked you to do that."

"It's a thankless job being your friend, Turner. Come take a look. You're going to want to see these."

Noah knew he shouldn't, but Olivia and her family were so secretive, and he ached to understand her better. He handed a lemonade to Mahoney and took the files he held.

"You ever wonder why the Coopers skipped town in the first place years back?" Mahoney asked.

"I know why. Dale went to jail. Enid was pissed and divorced him. She took the kids to live with her sister in Idaho." His stomach tightened in anticipation of what

Mahoney would say. Was the deputy about to tell him Olivia had been complicit in the crime—when she was eleven years old?

Mahoney tapped one of the papers, moving it a little. Noah moved it back so its edges lined up with the rest of the stack. "They were under investigation for poaching," the deputy began.

Noah frowned. "Poaching? That carries a fine, not jail time."

"Yeah. Thing is, the sheriff—Cab Johnson's father—caught Dale in his hunting cabin, and he found a lot more than bear traps there, if you catch my drift."

"No, I don't," Noah said. "If you're here to warn me about something, tell it to me straight."

"Fair enough. Dale and his associates were storing weapons there—real weapons. Lots of them. Assault rifles, things like that. Dale was convicted along with several other men of smuggling arms over the border into Canada."

Noah frowned. He had to admit that sounded pretty bad. Assault rifles were banned in Canada. "What's that got to do with Olivia?"

"The sheriff knew something was up, had his suspicions what he'd find if he could track Dale down, but he didn't know the location of his hunting cabin. So he asked Olivia a few questions one day…"

"And she cooperated." That was a trick to play on a little girl, getting her to rat out her dad. "She cooperated," he repeated. "Which means she wasn't a part of whatever Dale was doing."

"It also means she grew up in a family that doesn't think twice about running on the wrong side of the law. Think about that, Noah; you're a parole officer."

"You have any evidence she's ever committed a crime?"

"Can't say that I do. Not sure that matters, though."

Noah frowned. He knew what Mahoney was trying to say, but this new information only made him feel for Olivia.

"Look, I'm pretty sure Steel's been involved with smuggling, too. Possibly other crimes. He's a pretty shady guy. Takes after Dale."

"But you don't have any proof."

"No."

"What about Lance?"

"I didn't see anything on him, other than a suspicion he cheats at cards." Mahoney grinned suddenly. "I've heard more than a few complaints about that over the years, but to my way of thinking Lance might just be good at the game."

"Thanks for the tip."

Mahoney grew serious again. "Olivia's trouble for a guy like you, Noah. Come on, anyone can see the attraction. You're a straight-laced guy with a lot of responsibility hanging on your shoulders. Olivia's this wild child you want to save."

"She's not a wild child." The memory of her reading in the stacks of the town library crossed his mind again. Far from it.

"She's not the girl for you. Step away while you still

can."

"I appreciate your concern."

Mahoney sat back. "But you're not going to listen to me."

Noah shrugged. "I don't know what I'm going to do."

"Liar. You do, too. You're going to sleep with her. And then you're going to regret it. Well, don't say I didn't try to stop you." Mahoney drained his glass and stood up. "See you around, Turner."

"See you around." He let Mahoney show himself out, then realized the man had left his folder behind. On purpose, Noah was sure. Noah stacked the papers inside it and pushed it away. Maybe Mahoney was right; maybe he shouldn't get tangled up with a woman like Olivia.

But he wanted to.

Several hours later, when darkness had fallen, Noah let himself out of his house quietly so as not to attract the attention of Liam or his sisters, who'd all come home in the meantime. He couldn't tell them where he was going, and he didn't want to lie, either. He preferred to slip away unnoticed.

He breathed easier when he turned his truck out of the lane onto the country highway that led to Thorn Hill. Not that he was going to pick up Olivia there; they'd agreed via text she'd walk out to the main road and wait in a nearby turnoff. He supposed they could have met at the Ridley place, but that would be two vehicles for someone to spot. Best to keep things simple. Besides, if he couldn't take her on a real date, he'd make up for it by playing the gentleman in other ways.

Unfortunately, just as he reached the turnoff where Olivia waited with her arms crossed, he spotted another vehicle's lights approaching in the oncoming lane. What if the other driver saw them? He pressed on the accelerator and passed her by, hoping Olivia would understand.

As soon as the other truck was out of sight, Noah pulled a quick U-turn and circled back to her. Olivia looked pissed.

"Didn't you see me?" she asked through the open window. She yanked the door open and climbed into the passenger seat before Noah could hop out and do the honors. "What was that about?"

"Being careful, that's all. We can't afford to be seen together."

Olivia looked away. "Sure."

Noah's jaw tightened. She had to understand where he was coming from, but he wasn't sure how to fill in the ensuing silence. He was grateful when they reached the Ridley property.

"What is it with you and turnoffs today?" she asked when he drove on past the lane leading into it.

He nodded at a copse of trees ahead, silhouetted against the starry sky. "There's another lane that leads to a field behind those trees. I'll park there where no one will see us. Don't want to be interrupted, do we?"

"Whatever."

Uh-oh. He wasn't scoring points with his cautiousness. "You don't want Steel or Lance to know you're with me, do you?"

"No," she said shortly, but she kept her head turned away.

Once parked, Noah came around to open her door and took her hand before she could pull away from him. When she let him hold it, he figured all wasn't lost.

They picked their way down an overgrown path to the abandoned farmhouse, a nondescript old building whose windows were boarded up.

Noah wished he could refurbish it, or tear it down and build a new one. He hated to see something useful like this fall apart. His own house needed work, though. No need to take on a new project, even if his family did manage to win the Founder's Prize.

"Are we there yet?" Olivia joked as they broke through some bushes and found themselves near the house's front porch. He was gratified to see she'd regained her sense of humor.

"Do you want to be inside or outside?"

"I don't think we can get inside."

"What kind of talk is that for a burglar?" Noah could have kicked himself the moment his words left his lips. Olivia moved away abruptly, and he followed helplessly, wondering if there was any way to salvage this date. "Let's try in the back," he said and led the way around the house. They found a flagstone patio and a back door Noah was able to force open with his shoulder.

"Ugh. It smells in here." Olivia shivered and wrinkled her nose.

"Yes, it does." Noah looked around. The building seemed structurally sound but that was all anyone could say about it. "Outside?"

"Definitely." She returned out the door they'd come in and waited while Noah opened the picnic basket he'd packed earlier and pulled out a blanket. She helped him spread it on the flagstones, and they unpacked the rest of the contents. Noah lit a wide candle and placed it to one side where it wouldn't catch anything on fire.

Now he could make out her expression, which was drawn and wary.

"This is better," he said with false cheerfulness and set about pouring her a glass of wine.

"I guess so." Olivia took a sip and visibly relaxed.

Noah relaxed a little, too. It was a beautiful night. The air was warm. Insects sang in the long grasses nearby, and stars were winking into existence in the night above them. If he could stop sticking his foot in his mouth, everything would be fine.

He handed her a foil-wrapped sandwich, and for a few minutes they were too busy eating to talk. Noah searched for something to say. "Wish our families weren't always at each other's throats."

"You know what they say: if wishes were horses, beggars would ride."

"Maybe we could do something about it." That seemed far-fetched, even to him. Olivia didn't bother to answer. "I'm glad you're here, anyway. Back in Chance Creek, I mean," he went on, wanting to bridge the distance between them. "Your family was gone a long time."

Olivia stilled. Sent him a cryptic look. "I know, believe me."

Too late, Noah realized he'd walked into another minefield. "I just meant—"

"It's my fault, you know," Olivia said suddenly. "That's been on my mind a lot. Dad went to jail because of me, and he never got out again." She set her sandwich down on her paper plate. Her words were light but Noah felt the pain behind them.

He was surprised she'd admitted that, and he softly asked, "What happened?" He needed to hear it from Olivia, even if he'd read it in Mahoney's file earlier in the day.

"I was dumb. Just a stupid kid. Thought I was doing the right thing reporting a crime and instead helped Cab's dad bust my father."

"What do you mean?" That didn't quite jibe with what he knew.

"I used to play here all the time—with Ma—" She cut off suddenly. "With one of my friends. I had a treehouse back that way." She pointed off into the distance. "Hung out in it whenever I could. Explored all over the place."

Noah could imagine it, but he wondered what she'd been about to say before she'd bit back her words. Who had she come here to play with? And why didn't she want him to know?

"One day we found a field of marijuana growing on

the property. I mean, I can't believe someone managed to hide a crop that large for so long without us knowing, but it wasn't where we usually hung out. I was walking first, and as soon as I spotted it, I knew exactly what it was. I'd seen pictures in books in the library. I got my friend out of there before she could figure it out. She didn't realize what she'd seen, thank God. I didn't know what to do. I figured if someone else found it, they'd blame us. We live right next to that property, and people always said things about my dad. It wasn't his crop," she added. "He never sold drugs."

Noah nodded.

"I brought it up to my mom casually. 'What would you do if you saw something against the law?' She was busy doing housework and gave me a brush-off answer: tell the authorities. Now I look back and realize that was a load of baloney. Mom didn't like what Dad did, but she never reported him. Anyway, the next day when Mom dropped me off at the library I walked over to the sheriff's office and told the sheriff all about it."

Hell, Noah thought. And all the while the sheriff had his eye on her father.

"He asked me a bunch of questions. Wanted to know where everyone in my family was so that when he went on the Ridley property, if there was trouble with the growers, none of my folks would be close enough to get hurt. Seemed a reasonable question. I was only eleven," she added defensively. "I told him where everyone was—including where my dad's hunting cabin was. I had no idea he knew my father was...." She trailed off and looked down.

"Poaching?" Noah supplied, testing the waters. Would she tell him Dale was running weapons over the border?

She shot him a look he couldn't interpret. "Did Maya tell you that?"

"Maya? What would Maya know about it?"

Olivia studied him a moment longer and shrugged. "You're right. He was poaching."

He was doing far more than that, Noah thought, but somehow he couldn't bring himself to tell Olivia what he'd heard. "Sometimes we don't really know the people we love." Noah wished he could make things different for Olivia. She'd lost Dale much too soon, and he had no doubt she'd loved him as much as he'd loved his own father.

"If I wasn't such a loudmouth, maybe my dad would still be alive today."

SHE NEEDED TO shut up. Olivia didn't know why she was telling Noah all of this. He was a Turner, for God's sake; it wasn't like he would understand.

"Olivia—you're not to blame."

Olivia shut her eyes. Of course she was. "You're flirting with the daughter of a criminal," she said bitterly. "And I'm the one who gave him up. Doesn't that bother you? Or is my checkered past part of the allure?"

"Come on."

"Well? Is it?" She wasn't sure why she was pushing

him, except that if he was going to ditch her, she wanted him to do it now, before he could break her heart.

Which was ridiculous, she thought. She already cared for him, far too much. Even now, she was willing him to touch her hand. To kiss her. She wanted him to hold her. To make everything else go away.

He didn't reach out to her, though. She could tell he was searching for the right thing to say. Why didn't he ask her the obvious question: Had she ever committed a crime?

"Look," Noah said finally. "I'm not with you for some kind of weird thrill. Not like that, anyway," he added with a quick grin before growing serious again. "I can't pretend I don't have questions about your family, though."

"Like what?"

"Your brothers… Rumor has it Lance cheats at cards."

She relaxed a little. Was that all? "I wouldn't play against him. He took a ton of my allowance away when I was a kid."

"Heard Steel's had some trouble, too."

Olivia stiffened. "Steel… is his own man. I can't clear up anything for you there." It was the truth. Her oldest brother had so many secrets she'd stopped trying to fathom them. Sometimes she thought he was following in their father's footsteps; sometimes she wasn't sure.

"What about Tory? She hightailed it to Seattle, right? Never came back?"

Olivia bit her lip. Tory was a sore subject. "My sister is as honest as a sunset," she told Noah. "So is my mom, which is why she left my dad."

"And left you, too," Noah pointed out.

Ouch.

"And left me, too," Olivia repeated. "Just like everyone does sooner or later."

Noah winced. "Look—"

"No, don't say it. I know you're not interested in some long-term deal with me, and I know I came out here on my own volition, but I've changed my mind." She stood up. "I want to go home."

Noah stood, too. "Olivia—"

"I mean it, Noah."

"Look, I'm sorry. I didn't think—"

"That's the problem. Neither of us thought this through. This isn't going to work between us. So let's not even try. Take me home." She tossed the dregs of her wine from her glass and bent down to start packing away the picnic.

Chapter Five

HE'D BLOWN IT. Big time.

Grilled Olivia like she was one of his parolees. Forced her to drag her family secrets into the candlelight.

He was an ass.

An ass who was about to lose his one chance with the woman he wanted. Noah couldn't stand to let the night end like this. If he did, he'd regret it. He wasn't willing to lose her because of what other people had done in the past. To hell with that.

Noah thought fast. If he wanted to salvage this situation, he needed to do something radical. Something that would prove to Olivia he was far more serious about being with her than she'd known.

"I've got an idea."

"What?" Olivia reached to fold up the blanket.

"We'll go to the Dancing Boot. Have a drink or two. Dance a little. Have a real date."

Olivia stood up slowly, the blanket still in her hands. "Are you crazy?"

"Not in the least. I don't care what anyone else thinks. I was trying to save us from being hassled by our families, but what the hell? Let them hassle us. We can take it."

"You'll ruin your reputation." She moved away and finished folding the blanket.

Noah pursued her. "Who gives a damn?"

"I thought we were going to have sex and forget each other."

"I don't think I can forget you." He leaned in and kissed her. "In fact, every time I'm near you, I want you more." He grinned. "Besides, you just said you weren't going to have sex with me. At least at the Dancing Boot I can cop a feel or two."

Olivia rolled her eyes, but a smile was tugging at her lips. "You're incorrigible."

"I'm something," he agreed. "What do you say?"

Olivia tilted her chin up to look at him, and he bent to catch her in a kiss. Tangling his hand in her hair, he moved her closer and showed her how much he wanted her. They were both breathless when he pulled back.

"Come dance with me," he urged her, squashing the little voice in his head that said this was a big mistake. Olivia's proximity had released something reckless in him, and he was going to see it through.

"I'm going to regret this, but like you said, what the hell."

Noah grabbed the basket, took her hand and set a fast pace for his truck before she could change her mind. They were quiet on the drive into town, but Olivia sat close to him, and Noah kept a hand on her knee, tracing patterns over her denim-covered thigh with his fingers until she squirmed. She was right; what they were doing was insane. But it felt damn good.

"Haven't been by this place in too long," she said when he parked at the Dancing Boot.

Noah nodded. "Know what you mean. Work can take over your whole life if you let it." He hadn't had much time for fun lately, either.

Inside, he led her to a quiet spot on the edge of the dance floor. Once they'd claimed their table and placed an order, Noah led Olivia to the dance floor. The music was slow tonight, and he took her in his arms and swayed along with the other couples.

This was what he wanted: Olivia in his arms.

She smelled good. Felt good, too, with her breasts pressed against his chest in a very distracting way. He liked the curve of her waist under his hands. Olivia relaxed against him, and Noah sighed. Heaven.

He didn't want a fling with this woman. He wanted it all. A relationship that progressed step-by-step. One that strengthened the ties that bound them—not one that cut them for good.

What had he been thinking, agreeing to a one-night stand?

He'd been thinking of the Turner–Cooper feud of course.

Noah moved with Olivia, shifting his hands just for the excuse to feel her body. Why should he let ancient history dictate his future with this wonderful woman?

He needed to stop thinking of her as a Cooper. He needed to start thinking of her as simply Olivia. Ever since he'd seen her make sure each puppy in front of the hardware store got the same amount of love, he'd known she was the one for him. She'd suffered a lot, but what counted was the size of her heart. He wanted a wife who loved like that. Who was warm and affectionate. Who cared about the puppies of the world—and the people around her. Olivia cared—a lot.

"This feels good," he told her, murmuring into her ear.

"You're kind of old to be going through a rebellious phase, aren't you? Although I guess it makes sense."

He chuckled. "In what way?"

"You probably never stepped out of line before."

"Sure I did. Once," he added and felt her laugh. "Seventh grade. Can't quite remember what was going on that year. Hormones, maybe. Anyway, I played it pretty cool at the start of the year, not paying attention in class, slacking off on homework. I even skipped class once or twice."

"You crazy man, you," Olivia teased him.

"Only until report card time. Then the remorse hit me, hard. I tried to clean up my act, but by that point it was too late to improve my grades. Usually when they handed them out, I'd open mine right away, then run home to show my parents. That time I shoved the unopened envelope in my backpack and took my time getting home. I sat at the dining room table for an hour with the envelope in front of me, just staring at it. When my dad caught me at it, he sat across from me. Didn't say a word, just picked up the envelope and looked it over. Felt like another hour before he put it down again and looked me in the eye. 'Son,' he said, 'no matter how long you stare at that thing, it won't make what's in it any better. But you'll get another one in a couple of months, and it's up to you whether it's better or worse.' Then he got up and left."

Noah smiled at the memory. He missed his father.

"At first I thought he was telling me not to worry about it. That I didn't have to open the envelope and confront the truth, as long as I worked harder and got better grades next time. But that wasn't it at all. I realized later what he meant was if I wanted to improve my grades, I had to open the envelope and see where I stood. Only then I'd know what I needed to do to fix them."

They were quiet for a little while, and Noah could almost hear the gears turning in Olivia's head. "Maybe you're right," he went on. "Maybe I'm ready to rebel again. I want the world to know about us. We'll see where we stand when they do and go from there."

"I still think you're crazy." But she nestled in his arms.

Noah breathed a sigh of relief.

Everything was going to be all right after all.

OLIVIA LIKED THE way she could feel Noah's chest stir when he spoke, liked the solidity of his body against hers. The dance music swelled like waves crashing over her, but Noah kept her anchored. She wasn't half as sure as he was that this was a good idea. She was a realist. Still, she appreciated Noah for taking this chance.

"Steel taught me a lesson once. Kind of a different one, though."

"Oh yeah? What?"

"I had nightmares when I was little, and I slept with a night-light. It helped at first, but it didn't light up the whole room, so I started looking for monsters in the corners that were still dark. I made Mom get me another one, but then the closet was still dark. It was Steel who put his foot down.

"He came into my room one night and took the lights out. I fought and argued with him at first, but he sat with me for an hour or so, playing I Spy with me. It was such a challenge, trying to pick out the objects in the darkness, I forgot to be scared. Steel gave me the lights back before he left, saying I could plug them back in if I wanted, but he warned against it. 'When there's light,' he told me, 'you'll always fear what's in the darkness. But if you let your eyes adjust to the darkness, you can see what's really there.'"

"He sounds like a good brother," Noah said.

Olivia laughed softly. Sure. A real sweetheart. Probably best not to tell Noah how the rest of that story went.

The evening after Steel had unplugged her night-lights, she'd gone to bed with a newfound confidence. She could see in the dark, and she could see there was nothing there.

Except suddenly she wasn't sure that was the case.

Something rustled, a soft scrape that could have come from anywhere in the room. She'd pulled the blankets to her chin and told herself it was nothing—until she'd heard the breathing. Heavy, slow, rhythmic. After a minute she'd been able to pinpoint its source.

There was something under her bed.

Mustering all her courage, she'd pushed aside the blankets, getting ready to make a run for the light switch. She leaped out of the bed—

And tripped when fingers closed around her ankle.

Her shriek should have woken the whole house, but a second later, a hand covered her mouth, and a familiar voice hissed, "Shh!"

Steel kept his hand there until she'd gotten under control—too terrified to cry.

"You missed the whole point," he told her in a rough whisper. "I didn't teach you about seeing in the dark just to convince you there wasn't anything there. I did it to teach you to keep your eyes open—because you never know when something will be. Fear is what keeps us alive. Remember that."

Olivia pressed her face into Noah's chest, wanting to forget that memory. Wanting to forget her parents' fights, her father's refusal to walk the straight and narrow path, the splintering of her family when it all came to a head. She wondered now what Steel had known to make him feel the need to do that to her. He'd always been her father's confidante, and Dale had run with a crowd that was nowhere near respectable.

If she was honest, she'd never asked her brother

because she didn't want to know what her father was involved in. But she'd taken the lesson. She'd started sleeping with a baseball bat beside the bed. Kept her eyes open whenever she was alone. And tried to remember that at the end of the day, she could only count on herself.

If she was smart, she'd remember that now.

Then Noah cupped her chin and kissed her—

And Olivia forgot everything else.

MAHONEY WAS A lunatic if he thought Olivia was capable of any dangerous crime.

As Noah broke off the kiss and gazed down into her eyes, he knew he was in too deep to turn back now. The more time he spent with her and the closer they got, the more he realized what a strong, brave and beautiful woman she was. He leaned in for another kiss, and she welcomed him hungrily.

How on earth had some incident with a clock over a century ago come to be more important than what he and Olivia had between them right now? It was more than that single incident, though. Something happened every generation, some trivial slight that set the families off again and kept the war alive. This time it was the Founder's Prize, he realized. Why couldn't city council have come up with a way to award people for working together, instead of pitting families against one another to determine who was the best? That didn't seem very civic-minded, now that he thought about it.

Noah pulled back and searched Olivia's face. What

if they could bring their two families together? The drought and the hard times all around could work in their favor. His family couldn't disown him no matter what he did. He doubted the Coopers had much leeway when it came to Olivia, either. Their families needed them, which meant they had leverage.

He was about to say so when she went up on tiptoe to recapture his mouth. Noah forgot all about the future.

All he knew was he wanted Olivia.

Right now.

OLIVIA COULDN'T HELP herself. She stole kiss after kiss while her hands explored the broad expanse of Noah's back.

Why had they waited so long to do this? Because they were afraid of the consequences? Whatever else her family might be, Coopers were survivors. No matter how hard things got, a Cooper could bounce back and land on her feet. There would always be pain in life, and no amount of worrying could prevent it. She needed to just go for what she wanted, like she was doing now. Take the good in life where she could get it and deal with the bad when it came.

There was a lot of good to take just then. Olivia wanted Noah so badly she felt dizzy. She'd missed this heady, wonderful feeling.

"We should go somewhere," she said between kisses. "Run away together, and forget everyone else."

"I wish we could, believe me."

She knew what he meant; they weren't the types to leave their families high and dry. Her sigh was almost a groan. "Let's slip away for the night, then."

"That I can do." He took her hand, as eager as she was, and Olivia's pulse thrummed as he led her through the crowd. Why had they ever left the Ridley property in the first place? It was private, and right now she wanted to be alone with—

Noah stopped in his tracks, and Olivia bumped into him. "Hell," he muttered.

Looking around Noah's shoulder, she spotted Liam and immediately understood his reaction. She might have talked a good game about going public and confronting their families, but now that exposure was a real possibility she quickly realized she wasn't ready for it at all.

She ducked back behind Noah. "Run," she hissed.

"Too late. He's already seen us."

Liam crossed the room to confront Noah. She couldn't hear what they said over the din of the music, but Liam got up in Noah's face, and Noah shoved him back.

The crowd was churning at the edge of her vision, and she turned to see two more men forcing their way through. Was that—?

Lance and Steel.

How did everyone know to find them here? Olivia glanced around, took in all the cell phones focused on them. Had someone filmed her and Noah? Put it on social media and alerted everyone?

As she hesitated, unsure what to do, Noah pointed, Liam swung around and both men, who'd been about to come to blows, presented a united front against her brothers. Steel stepped right up to Noah, Lance right behind him. She didn't catch his words, but when Liam shoved him, Lance pushed him back.

"Stop!" Olivia winced when Lance threw the first punch. Damn it, now everyone would say the Coopers had started it, even though it was the Turners' fault. Typical.

Lance caught Liam in the shoulder, and Liam clocked him on the side of the head. Then Steel was on Liam, punching him in the gut. Liam doubled over, and Steel went in for the kill, but Noah tackled him to the ground. Then the circle closed around them as each side's supporters started throwing punches of their own.

Olivia fought a rising panic. Someone was going to get hurt—this was real fighting, not a boozy, drunken brawl. The worst part was she couldn't root for either side. She didn't want Noah hurt, but she didn't want anything to happen to her brothers, either.

She pulled out her phone. Who could she call, though? Cab?

She didn't want the sheriff involved.

A notification on her screen caught her eye. It was photo taken near the time she and Noah first arrived. It showed them dancing together. They'd both been tagged in it, and the caption read, "Has hell frozen over?" She nearly didn't recognize herself in the picture. She looked so peaceful and in love.

Who had shared it? Why couldn't everyone just leave them alone?

The fighting surged her way. Nearby Noah grappled with a stranger.

"Noah!"

He didn't even hear her, and she gasped as the crowd surged against her again. In the chaos nobody noticed her struggling to get free. Olivia pushed back, trying to create some room to breathe—

To escape.

A stray elbow caught her in the face—

And darkness reached up to swallow her.

Chapter Six

WHAT THE HELL was he doing?

Noah blinked the sweat out of his eyes, noticed his hands were bloody and took in the crowd brawling around him.

He was a parole officer, for God's sake. Not a fighter. How had this gotten so far out of control? Someone must have called the sheriff by now. He'd lose his job. Lose the money his family needed.

For what? For—

Noah swore. Olivia. Where was Olivia?

He took a deep breath and stepped back into the fray. Found Liam and wrapped his arms around his brother's waist, ducking as Liam swung at him with a haymaker. Noah dragged him out of the crowd, and Liam stopped thrashing when he saw who'd grabbed him.

"Where's Olivia?" Noah demanded.

"Why should I care?" Liam lunged back toward the melee, but Noah grabbed him again.

"We've got to find her. We've got to get out of here."

"We've got to teach these Coopers a lesson they

won't forget."

Noah had to restrain him again. This time he dragged his brother toward the door. "We're better than this. We don't brawl—that's Cooper territory. Think about my job."

Liam closed his eyes. "Shit. Your job." When he opened them again, he grabbed Noah. "Let's get out of here."

"Not until I find Olivia."

"You go back in there, and you'll make it worse. I saw that photo and knew Lance and Steel would come and beat the shit out of you. That's why I came."

"Photo?"

Liam filled him in as he hustled Noah outside. Noah heard sirens in the distance. "Whatever's going on with you and Olivia, everyone knows about it. What the hell were you thinking?"

"I wanted—" It all seemed stupid now. Thinking he could bridge the gap between the Turners and Coopers. Thinking he and Olivia stood a chance. That was—

Naive as hell.

"There's my truck," Liam said. "You got yours?"

"Yeah."

"You okay to drive?"

"Yeah." He hated the thought of leaving Olivia behind, though.

"She's got her brothers," Liam told him. "They wouldn't let her leave with you anyhow."

"It isn't right—" He had to go back.

Sirens blared much closer this time, and red and

blue lights flashed over them as Cab Johnson pulled in.

"Damn it. Now you've done it, Noah."

Cab climbed out of his patrol car and faced them. "What's going on here?"

Liam crossed his arms. "If anyone has some explaining to do, it's the Coopers."

Noah stepped forward and cut him off. "I should be the one to explain. I took Olivia out dancing. Someone took a photo of us. Liam came to help me. Lance and Steel came, too—looking to sort me out."

"And you all thought you'd fix this with your fists?"

"The Coopers started it," Liam protested.

"And I bet you tried real hard to stop it."

Liam looked away. "There wasn't any stopping it, Sheriff."

Cab grunted. "Don't think you're going to get off easy. You've crossed a line here. Come on."

"Inside?" Liam asked when the sheriff turned toward the club. "But—"

"Get your ass over here now."

Noah and Liam exchanged a look but followed the sheriff. What else could they do? Inside, the fight had ended, but chaos remained. Someone had turned the lights on, giving Noah a clear view of the destruction: overturned chairs and tables, blood and broken glass on the floor. People reeling from their injuries. But more than anything, Noah was shocked by the faces he saw. These weren't strangers.

They were neighbors. Acquaintances.

Friends.

How many of them had gotten hurt in the heat of the moment? In the dim light, it had been too easy to swing first and ask questions later.

His heart skipped a beat when he spotted Olivia. She was leaning against Steel's shoulder, a tissue clamped to her nose, which was oozing blood. Had she been in the fight?

Could he have hurt her?

His stomach flipped.

No. No way. Not even accidentally. His radar was clear where she was concerned.

"Come here." Cab led him and Liam to where the Coopers stood bunched together. He waited until Noah and Liam had caught up, then turned to the rest of the crowd. "Everyone, listen up, because I'm only going to say this once. If you've got an injury, or property that was damaged, you call these idiots. The Coopers and the Turners. They're the ones who started it; they're the ones responsible for fixing it."

"But—" A look from Cab stopped Liam cold.

"He's the one who started it," Lance said, pointing at Noah. "He's the one who took advantage of my little sister."

Olivia snorted, then gave a little cry of pain and clamped the tissue more firmly to her nose. "No one takes advantage of me. Everything would have been fine if you'd just left me alone."

"Both of you quiet down," Steel snapped.

All around Noah, people talked in hushed tones.

"I'm going to make something clear right now." Cab

ignored the interruptions. "You two families are done causing trouble in this town. Next time I'm called out, someone's spending time behind bars. Got it? Now get out of here. And expect a bill for all this damage. You all can split it."

Noah tried to catch Olivia's eye as he followed Liam out the door, Cab walking between them and the Coopers to keep them separate.

Olivia avoided his gaze, and he realized with a sinking heart whatever had started between them was now over.

It was his own stupid fault for bringing her to the Boot. Thinking they could smooth over a hundred years of family rivalry with a dance.

If he tried to pursue her anymore, he'd probably wind up in jail.

Noah drove back to the Flying W in silence, hoping to get home and go to bed without further incident, but his sisters were awake and had obviously heard what happened.

"Oh, my God, you're hurt!" Maya rushed to him when he entered the house. She touched a bruise on his face. Noah shrugged her off. Stella hung back but looked just as concerned.

Liam grinned wolfishly. "You should see the other guys."

Maya swatted him in the shoulder. "It isn't funny." She turned to Noah. "And this isn't okay. You need to stay away from Olivia."

Noah sighed. "Guess you saw the picture." He sat

down in one of the easy chairs.

Maya nodded, and Stella spoke up. "All of my friends made sure we did. What were you thinking, dancing with her? You'll end up setting this town on fire over it."

"Besides, she's an awful influence," Maya agreed. "Look at you. You never fight."

"Maybe he should try it more often," Liam said, clapping Noah on the back. "He's good at it. Should have seen the way he beat down those Cooper bastards."

"Fuck off." Noah shoved his brother away just as Jed came into the room.

"What's all this racket?"

"Noah's got the hots for Olivia Cooper." Maya sat down on the couch. Stella joined her.

Jed scowled. "Wish I could say I didn't believe it. But I wouldn't put it past you. Always were a shifty one."

Liam narrowed his eyes at Noah. "Jed's right. Can't help but wonder how much you're actually working that parole officer job and how much time you've been sneaking off to see Olivia."

"I haven't—"

"Look at you!" Jed interrupted him. "Those Coopers really beat you down, didn't they? Thought I raised you to fight better than that."

"You didn't raise us," Noah snapped. He wasn't going to sit here and take all this. Jed was part of the problem. "Dad did, and he didn't teach us to fight. He raised us to help people, not hurt them. The Coopers haven't done squat to us."

"They were the ones who started that brawl," Liam argued. He was still standing up, pacing back and forth.

"We chose to fight back. There wouldn't have been a brawl if we'd just left." Noah wasn't sure that was true, but he wasn't going to give Liam an inch right now.

"Olivia tried to steal our clock!" Maya put in.

"Because she thinks it's hers. Hell, the only reason the Coopers care about the clock is because of the way we rub their noses in it, and honestly, I think the only reason we care about the clock is so we can lord it over the Coopers. When was the last time anyone set the damn thing? It's been stopped for as long as I can remember. If it wasn't for the feud, that clock would probably be rotting in the attic by now."

"What about the school?" Jed demanded. "We're the ones who built it, and now they're trying to take all the glory away from us."

"No matter how they upgrade it, they can't change the fact we built it in the first place," Noah pointed out. "We set the bedrock, and the Coopers are adding to it. Maybe they can't build something from the ground up like we did, but we couldn't either right now. If our families worked together, who knew what we could accomplish."

He caught Stella nodding thoughtfully, but the rest of his family exploded.

"Are you crazy?" Liam asked.

"Did Olivia brainwash you?" Maya exclaimed.

"She's leading you around by the apron strings already," Jed said darkly.

"Look, I'm not saying we have to work with the Coopers. It's like Cab said, we don't even have to like the Coopers. All we have to do is stay out of their way. We can't tear apart this town for our own stupid vendetta."

No one looked convinced.

"What about you? Did you learn your lesson?" Jed challenged him. "You going to leave that Cooper girl alone from now on?"

"That's none of your business." And just like that he lost the room again.

Liam crossed over to confront him. "It is our business. Olivia can bring us all down by going through you."

"He's right," Jed said solemnly. For once he didn't sound angry or spiteful, and Noah was surprised by the faraway look in his eyes. "Maybe you think you can change her, boy, but you can't. Coopers are trouble. Always have been, always will be."

"Know what?" Noah stood. "That's baloney. The Coopers never had a bad reputation in this town until the Turners gave them one."

"You know Virginia will kill you if she finds out you were with Noah," Lance hissed at Olivia as they slipped in the front door of the main house at Thorn Hill.

Olivia only shrugged, continuing to press a Ziploc

bag of ice she'd gotten from the bartender to her nose. Lance had been like this the whole way back from town. She'd hoped his fury might fade during the long drive, but if anything he'd only worked himself up even more. Steel, as usual, had kept quiet, but Olivia thought he was pissed, too.

When they reached home, Olivia hopped out, hoping to escape to her room, but inside Lance confronted her again.

"Why are all the Cooper women like this? Betraying the family when it suits you, cutting and running at the first opportunity. I guess you and Tory can't help being messed up with the example Mom set for you."

"Lance!"

"It's true."

Olivia got in his face. "Don't you dare talk about Mom that way. She did her best."

"Her best wasn't very good, was it? Your best ain't all that hot, either. You're the reason she left in the first place, after all."

Olivia shoved him, dropping the bag of ice on the floor.

He shoved her back.

Steel got between them. "That's enough. Go to bed, both of you."

"Gladly." Olivia scooped up the bag of ice and headed for the stairs.

"We aren't done talking about this," Lance yelled after her.

"Yes, we are," she called back over her shoulder.

As she lay in bed that night, though, she found it impossible to get comfortable, her thoughts buzzing like flies in her brain. It wasn't fair. She hadn't started this conflict. Neither had Noah. They weren't to blame for what their ancestors had done, so why did they have to pay the price?

The trouble was, she was dependent on her family—and this ranch—for everything, which made it impossible to get away from the feud—or to influence how it went. Oliva sat up, scooted closer to the headboard and plumped her pillows behind her. She'd always wanted to base her life around her home and family. But she'd never realized before how that tied her hands. Lance and Steel were the ones who really ran the ranch. She only helped on the periphery. That gave her little standing when it came to making decisions. Was that why she was attracted to Noah? Was she going through her own rebellious phase?

She knew one thing for sure: she wanted to feel proud of herself when she looked in the mirror.

How long had it been since that was the case?

Olivia thought back—and back—and back. Probably not since she was a little girl, unaware of her father's brushes with the law and her mother's discontentment with her lot. Before everyone else's actions had crushed the pride out of her. Before her own actions had ruined everything.

Olivia stopped the familiar train of thought and rewound. It hadn't occurred to her before that while she'd inadvertently led the sheriff to her father's hunting cabin years ago, she'd already been suffering the consequences of other people's actions. She'd gone to report the field of marijuana plants because she'd been afraid her own family would be blamed—because her father tended to do things that were against the law.

That was his fault; not hers.

She thought back over her early years. There'd been so many unspoken rules in her house about what you could share with outsiders and what you couldn't. So many secrets and lies. So many arguments. The feeling—

The feeling it was the Coopers against the world.

That feeling had run her life, Olivia realized.

It was still running her life.

Pretty soon it would stop her from being with Noah. Was she willing to sacrifice her happiness to uphold her family's beliefs?

What was the alternative?

Independence, Olivia realized. The ability to really feel she could make good decisions for herself and carry them through, no matter what the rest of her family thought.

Suddenly she understood her mother and Tory in a way she never had before. It wasn't that they'd left in order to hurt her; they'd left in order to break free of the prison of being a Cooper.

Could she blame them?

Should she leave, too?

She drew her knees to her chest and wrapped her arms around them, wondering what it would be like to be free of all of this. She would be able to make decisions without worrying what everyone else thought. Work, school, life—all of it could be sorted out in a jiffy. She'd have so much more energy for the things she wanted to do.

Leaving Thorn Hill—and Chance Creek—felt like a betrayal, though. Not just of her family, but of herself. This was where she pictured herself when she thought about the life she wanted to live.

Did she have to leave to be free of the past?

It would certainly make things easier, she mused, but that didn't mean it was impossible to stay and still make changes.

Mostly, she needed to change her mind.

Olivia got up and paced the room. She had to stop drifting along. She needed to make a few simple decisions and then stick to her guns about them. If she wanted independence, she needed a job, which meant she needed something on her résumé to prove she deserved to be hired.

Why not start by volunteering at the library? She could work there every chance she got, rack up some hours and earn a reference from Marta, who'd be happy to help her get back on her feet. At the same time, she'd figure out what she really wanted to be and what steps she'd need to make to accomplish that.

She'd make a real plan. Become her own woman. On her way, she'd learn to make enough money to help make Thorn Hill a going concern again. That would take the pressure off Lance, and maybe he'd settle down. Meanwhile, she'd do what she could to fix up their home. Take a page from the Halls' book and keep the place tidier. Plant some flowers out front, maybe.

She'd spent far too much time feeling like a victim and waiting for someone else to fix her problems. That stopped right now. She was ready to solve them herself.

Olivia woke the next morning filled with determination. Her nose was still a little tender, but not too bad, and the bruising around it was barely noticeable. She took her coffee outside and, when she was done, left her cup on the back porch while she went for a walk to clear her mind. She stopped by the banks of Pittance Creek, lost in thought until a noise penetrated her concentration.

No, not a noise—

A lack of one.

Usually the water in Pittance Creek burbled and chuckled over its rocky bed.

Now all she heard was the quiet ripple of water.

The creek—

Olivia stared in shock. She'd never seen the water running this low.

"It's pretty bad." Lance came up beside her. "We're not getting near enough water in the channel."

Which meant they'd need to bring in water for the cattle, who usually drank from a channel that forked off from Pittance Creek. Which would put more load on their well. "That's not good."

"Not good at all." Lance surveyed the creek. "Bet the Turners are diverting plenty."

Both families had dug side channels decades ago to divert water for their needs, the Coopers to water their stock, the Turners to irrigate their fields. Fences prevented the animals at Thorn Hill from walking right down to the main branch of the creek and fouling it. That ensured that Pittance Creek remained a healthy waterway, supported fish stock and didn't erode. Cattle could do a number on a creek bed.

The Turners' irrigation channel started upstream from the Coopers' channel.

"You think they're taking more than their share?"

"Come and see."

Fifteen minutes later, they stood across from the opening to the Turners' channel. Lance was right; plenty of water fed into it, but Olivia didn't think that was because of some nefarious action Noah's family had taken. The way the creek ran and the positioning of the opening of their channel looked exactly the same as it always did. It was a quirk of the creek bed here that kept the smaller waterway full, while the water level in their own channel was dwindling.

"We've got to fix this," Lance said.

"What do you mean?"

"We can shift that rock and dig a little there." He pointed, and Olivia's stomach sank.

"Divert their flow? How is that going to help us?"

"Less for them means more for us."

"It's not their fault our channel isn't deep enough; that's what we need to fix."

"What we need to fix is the Turners always getting

in our way."

"How are they getting in our way?" she demanded.

"Come on, I don't need to explain this to you. You're a Cooper." He stalked off back toward the barn. Olivia followed him.

"We need to dig our own channel deeper," she said again. "Let's get the tractor."

"Tractor's busted. Everything's busted around here. Every time we start to dig ourselves out of trouble, the goddamn walls cave in again! We can't catch a fucking break!"

Lance's outburst slowed her steps to a halt, and she watched her brother keep striding away. She hadn't realized Lance's anger was so tied to the health of the ranch. She gazed around her and took in the brownish cast to the land, the desiccated pastures and the dust devils whipping in the light breeze.

There was a lot of summer ahead of them, and while she'd been buried in her private worries, Lance had borne the brunt of the concerns about the ranch.

She hurried to catch up with him again. "What would Steel say to do?"

Lance shrugged and increased the pace. "Ask him— if you can find him. He's never around when I need him these days." He kept walking, and Olivia kept following, but with every step she felt she was moving farther away from the future she wanted.

This summer could break her family.

Was she really going to turn her back on them just when things got really tough?

HE HADN'T HEARD a peep from Olivia. Hadn't dared to text or call her yet. Noah was going crazy trying to figure out what to do next. There wasn't much he could do for the next couple of hours, he thought as he followed Maya into the Chance Creek Reformed Church. He probably wouldn't see her here.

He'd come because he and his family needed to shore up their image, which he was afraid his behavior—and Liam's—had damaged fighting at the Dancing Boot. It hadn't been difficult to convince Stella and Maya to come along, but Liam had refused to fall in line with the idea. He said he had nothing to be ashamed of and was far too busy to take time out to listen to a sermon. Noah thought he was making a mistake, but he let it go; he couldn't force his brother to come along. Jed acquiesced as if going to church was a weekly event for him, although it had been some time since that was the case. As they entered the building, he led the way.

Noah took his place in a pew near the front beside Jed and his sisters, and tried to remember when his attendance at church had been more regular. He supposed that was years ago. Recently he was lucky to make it once a month. He'd become sloppy about it, the way he'd become sloppy about a lot of things, and that made him more like his uncle than he cared to admit. It embarrassed Noah to realize he'd begun to think he deserved people's respect simply because he was a Turner, not because he was doing anything worthy of it.

It was time to change his ways, starting with more regular attendance here on Sundays and more participation in the rest of civic life in Chance Creek.

That decision made, Noah sighed as he took in the plain white walls and high ceiling of the church. He'd always liked its peaceful simplicity. A man could think here. Clear his head. Find a better path. Looking around, he noted the Coopers were conspicuous by their absence. But the small church was full, and people were definitely noticing his family.

He faced front again. He had to admit he'd hoped for a glimpse of Olivia. He couldn't believe they'd come so close to being together—and how their evening had ended instead.

But that was life, wasn't it? You fought for what you wanted, but you didn't always get it.

When Reverend Joe Halpern ascended to the lectern, Noah was still thinking about Olivia, wondering what it would be like to stand up before the preacher to marry her.

Was that even possible in a world where Turners and Coopers hated each other?

He didn't know. Besides, it was way too soon to think about marriage.

Noah couldn't lie to himself, though; he was thinking about it. He'd always been a man who wanted to share his life with a partner—a woman who'd help him bring the Flying W back to its glory. If you took away the Turner–Cooper feud, Olivia fit the bill. She worked hard. Loved Chance Creek. And even if they hadn't talked about it, he was sure she had ambition. She certainly had grit and intelligence. All qualities that made her compatible with him.

Reverend Halpern braced his hands on either side of the lectern and swept his gaze across the congregation.

"Forgiveness," he boomed suddenly. Noah straightened his spine, and he noticed everyone else sat up, too. Halpern usually wasn't so direct.

"That's what we're going to talk about today. When was the last time you forgave someone? Truly forgave them, not just gave lip service to the idea?"

Noah shot a look Jed's way. His uncle's baleful expression told him forgiveness was the last thing on his mind. Beside him, Maya sighed, not in a sympathetic way, but in a fashion that told him she wasn't interested in forgiveness either. Only Stella was nodding.

"You are responsible for your actions. No matter what anyone else does, no matter what feelings you experience in response to it, you are the one in control of your body—and your thoughts." Halpern waited to see if everyone was listening. "If you think angry thoughts, you have decided to think angry thoughts. If you think about revenge, it's because you've decided to be vengeful. There is always another alternative."

Noah glanced at Jed again. His uncle had leaned forward and was glaring across the aisle—

At Virginia, Noah realized with a shock. He hadn't seen her enter the building. She was alone—

And she was glaring right back at Jed.

"Remember that pride goeth before a fall," Halpern continued.

"Listen to the reverend, Turner," Virginia hissed

across the aisle at Jed.

"Mind your own business, you old bat," Jed shot back.

"Jed." Noah reached out a restraining arm, but Jed brushed him off.

"Mind *my* business?" Virginia stood up. "I am minding my business. And my thoughts. And my thoughts tell me you're a thief and a scoundrel, and you owe me a clock!"

Jed surged to his feet, too. Halpern gripped the edges of his lectern and glared at them. "Jed, Virginia, pipe down!"

Maya covered her face with her hands. Stella had slid down in her seat, as if that could hide her. Noah had had enough. If Jed wanted to make an ass out of himself, that was his business. "I'm leaving," he told his sisters.

"Me, too," Maya said.

Stella followed them quickly out of the pew.

"Get back here. Cowards," Jed yelled after them.

"Everyone settle down," Halpern said. "Let's all try to—"

Noah didn't hear the rest. He was already halfway out the front door.

"Aren't we waiting for Jed?" Stella called after him as she and Maya struggled to keep up in their high heels.

"Hell, no. He can get himself home. I'm sick of all of this." Noah kept going down the steps and across the parking lot. "Halpern's right; we've got to stop holding a grudge. Why can't we forgive the Coopers for what they've done in the past? Start over with them?"

"Because they don't deserve our forgiveness," Jed called from the top of the stairs. He hobbled after them, crossed the parking lot as quickly as he could, caught up and yanked the passenger side door open. "Get out of my way," he told Stella, and she did, coming around to Noah's side. Noah pulled his door open, too, and both his sisters slid into the rear seat.

"Don't you walk away from me, Jed," Virginia hollered from the top of the church steps. "I'm not through with you."

"Let's get out of here!" Jed banged on the dashboard.

"Hold on," Stella said. "I'm not even in."

"You know what?" Noah rounded on Jed. "You should be back there in church. You need to hear that sermon more than anyone else."

"I don't need to do anything. I said, drive!"

"And I said wait," Stella snapped from the back seat. She was still tucking her dress around her and putting on her seat belt.

"How are we supposed to hold up our heads with you going off half-cocked all the time?" Noah demanded.

"Jed Turner, you get out of that truck and face me like a man!" Virginia smacked her hands on the glass of Jed's window, making all of them jump.

Jed slapped the window back at her. Virginia swore at him.

"We're losing influence in this town. Can't you see

that? You made it worse today," Noah told his uncle.

"Did not." Jed balled his fist and banged on the window harder, but Virginia kept it up, slapping at the glass with both hands.

"Did, too."

"Jed Turner, you are a coward and a reprobate. Get out here, so I can give you the beating you deserve," Virginia yelled.

"None of this would be happening if it weren't for the Coopers," Maya said.

Noah half turned in his seat to confront her. "I think it's pretty lucky that we have the Coopers. Otherwise we wouldn't always have someone to blame for our own shortcomings."

Maya reared back. "That's not fair."

"Like hell it isn't. Look in the mirror sometime. You won't see a paragon of virtue."

"Noah," Stella cautioned, but he was on a roll.

"It's been a long time since this family has done anything to be proud of, and we're all at fault, every one of us."

"Goddamn it, Virginia, get out of here," Jed shouted through the window.

"All right, I'm ready," Stella announced. "Noah, you'd better get us out of here before Virginia breaks that window and strangles Jed."

"She'd be doing us a favor," Noah muttered, but he put the truck in gear and started to drive.

WHEN THE PHONE rang, Olivia thought about ignoring

it, but when Marta's name appeared on the screen she accepted the call.

"Hey, Marta!" She tried for a chipper tone. "How are things? Enjoying your weekend? I was thinking about coming to see you."

"I think there's somewhere else you need to be right now," Marta said tightly. "I'm in the church parking lot. Virginia chased down Jed a few minutes ago, but the Turners took off before she was through with him, and now she's taking it out on everyone else, hollering at bystanders. You'd better come get her before she has a heart attack."

"On my way," Olivia said tiredly. She'd been spending a lot of time cleaning up Virginia's messes lately. She grabbed her purse and headed outside to her truck. When she reached the parking lot, the Turners were nowhere to be seen, but several members of the congregation huddled on the doorstep, watching Reverend Halpern remonstrate with Virginia. Olivia checked the time, realized the service should only be half-over and was grateful the rest of the congregation had stayed inside.

"I'll give Virginia a ride home," she announced when she'd parked and reached her aunt and the reverend.

"I don't need a ride home," Virginia snapped.

"Yes, you do." Olivia took her aunt's arm.

"You've had a lot of excitement," Reverend Halpern told her. "You'd better go with your niece."

Virginia humphed, but she allowed Olivia to lead

her to her truck. "That man. Preaching all the time," she fumed as she climbed inside.

"Virginia, he *is* a minister—"

"That's no excuse. A man of God should know when to shut his trap." Virginia waited for Olivia to get in on the other side. "As for you—"

"Here we go."

"Where were you when I needed backup in there? You're never where you're supposed to be. Always in the wrong place talking to the wrong people, telling them the wrong things. I guess I should know what to expect by now." Virginia tsked. "But to date a Turner? That's low, even for you."

"Give me a break!"

"Give you a break? What about me? Is it too much to ask for you not to humiliate me? I don't expect you to pick a winner, just anyone but a Turner. That's the least you could do after failing to stop Camila from stealing Carl."

"Excuse me?" Olivia, about to insert the key into the ignition, stared at her aunt. "What does that have to with anything?"

"Carl was our trump card. Camila's as good as a Turner. I wouldn't be surprised if she convinces him to shut down the school altogether. If you had half a brain, it would have been you standing up at the altar with him. Would have solved most of our problems right there."

"You have lost your mind, Virginia." Olivia had never once felt anything for Carl Whitfield, who was at least fifteen years her senior, and she was pretty sure he'd never given her a second thought, either.

"But it's like I said, I never expected you to manage to marry Carl. Just keep him from marrying a girl who could ruin us. That's all. The list goes on. You haven't given me one update on the gala you were supposed to have put together by now. Weren't you supposed to be getting a job? And, of course, back when you were a child you ruined things for all of us—"

Olivia turned the engine on and floored the accelerator. Virginia squawked as they lurched forward and clutched the edges of her seat. "What are you doing?"

"You said I ruin everything. Why not ruin our ride home?"

"Slow down!"

Olivia did, but she'd made her point, and Virginia was quiet the rest of the way.

By the time she dropped off Virginia and drove back to town to meet Caroline for lunch, she was more than ready for a break from her family. Caroline was at DelMonaco's before her, and Olivia gratefully slid into a seat across from her.

"You won't believe what happened. I can't believe it myself," Caroline said without preamble. She was beaming, and Olivia leaned closer, pleased to see her friend so happy for once.

"What is it?" She was grateful to forget her own troubles for a while.

"Remember the lottery tickets I bought the other day? I won! Olivia, I won fifty thousand dollars!" She lowered her voice when she named the number. "Fifty thousand! I'm going to put most of it toward my mortgage, but I'm going to splurge just a little bit and use some to fix up my kitchen. You know how bad it is."

Actually, Olivia didn't. She'd never been inside Caroline's house, but she'd driven past the humble older cottage in town. Caroline was so proud she owned it rather than renting. From what Olivia understood, she'd bought it several years after graduating from college, long before Devon came on the scene.

"Fifty thousand dollars!" The number was unimaginable to Olivia. "I'm so happy for you. You deserve something wonderful like that." If Caroline was careful, she could spiff up her kitchen and still take a bunch off what she owed on her mortgage. Her small house couldn't have cost too much.

"Thank you. I can't wait to tell Devon. He'll be home late tonight."

"He doesn't know?" Olivia bit her lip, trying to hold back the words she wanted to say but losing the battle. "Maybe you should keep it a secret for now."

Caroline's face fell. "Why would I do that?"

"I don't know." Olivia lost the courage to push the point. Caroline was so touchy where Devon was concerned. "What if he wants something different from what you want?"

"We have to pay off the house, and he knows I want to upgrade my kitchen. After all, I bought the tickets."

"That's right." She hoped Devon saw things the same way.

Chapter Seven

"NOAH? IT'S BRANDON. Man, you've got to help me. I can't get a job anywhere, and I need cash."

"Slow down." Noah put down the pitchfork he was using to muck out the stall of his favorite horse, Warning, and switched the phone to his other ear. "What happened?"

"The same thing that's been happening. I see an ad. I apply. I don't even hear back for an interview."

"We talked about showing up in person—"

"When I do that, the person in charge of hiring is mysteriously away. And when I come back, they're still away—"

Noah heard the desperation in Brandon's voice, and he knew something had to change, fast. He didn't have any answers, though. People were too worried about the drought to take a chance on a man who'd been in jail. He wondered if he could hire Brandon himself, but they were already stretched tight at the Flying W. Besides, that wouldn't give Brandon the experience of solving the problem himself. "Why do you need money so badly?"

"The cost of living—"

Noah listened to his gut. "You live with your parents. So what is this really about?"

"Christie," Brandon admitted. "She deserves more. I want to take her out to eat. To a movie. Dancing. I want to buy her things."

"What kind of things?"

"She needs a new stove. Hers is busted—"

"She has a job," Noah pointed out. "Let her buy her own stove."

"She said—" Brandon cut off.

Now they were getting to the crux of it, Noah figured. "What did she say?"

"She said she wants to be with a good provider. And before you flip your lid, that's what I want to be. That's what a man should be. What's wrong with that?"

"There's nothing wrong with that," Noah admitted. A woman like Christie had to think about the future. What if she had children? A man without a job wouldn't be much help. "Look," Noah went on. "You need to hang in there. I need you to trust me. This is the crucial part of the equation right here. If you slog through this and find a job—any job—you're going to be okay. If you reoffend, you can kiss Christie and your future goodbye. Got it?" There was no use pulling punches.

Brandon heaved a sigh. "Yeah, I got it. But this sucks."

"Check Silver Falls. Check everywhere you can. Go after every job. Persistence is going to pay off. I swear."

"Yeah, yeah." Brandon hung up.

Noah had barely pocketed his phone when Liam rushed into the stable, waving a fistful of papers at him. "Look at all of these letters about how much everyone loves Chance Creek High like it is right now. We're going to bury those Coopers."

"Shouldn't you let people send them in themselves? They're not going to look good coming from you," Noah pointed out.

"Way ahead of you," Liam said. "Everyone is submitting their own letter, a few each day. The paper can ignore some of them, but they can't ignore all of them. I'm going to post these around town." He waved the papers again. "I'll do that tonight, when it's dark."

"Don't get caught," Noah warned him.

"Stop worrying," Liam told him and left the stable.

Noah snorted. If anything, he was more worried than ever.

OLIVIA WAS CURLED up on the sofa with an old dog-eared paperback when Lance and Steel trailed through the living room, dressed in black and carrying flashlights.

"I don't even want to know," she told them.

"You're going to know," Lance said. "You're coming to help."

"Oh no, I'm not."

Steel tossed one of the flashlights at her. Olivia caught it automatically, and he grinned. "Come on. We need you."

Olivia marked her page and put her book down.

"The Turners have the right to irrigate their fields." Lance cut her off.

"We have the right to water our stock."

"You're right, we do. So let's work on dredging our channel tomorrow when it's light out."

"The Turners didn't wait for light when they made theirs deeper." Lance was already moving toward the door.

That got her attention. Olivia got up and followed her brothers through the kitchen and out the back door. "You think they diverted water into their irrigation channel?" she asked Steel. She didn't trust Lance to tell the truth.

"Doesn't matter if they did or didn't. Lance says we need more."

"Then let's work with the Turners to make sure it's fair—"

"Coopers don't work with Turners," Lance started.

"I'm out of town tomorrow. We'll take care of it right now," Steel said. Olivia knew he wouldn't change his mind, and the two of them outnumbered her. So much for being independent, she thought dispiritedly as they walked. She should go back to the house. Refuse to cooperate. What would they do then?

"What is your beef with Liam Turner?" Olivia demanded of Lance as they headed to the barn.

"My beef is with all the Turners."

"Baloney. You have it out for Liam. Always have."

"Not always."

Lance wouldn't elaborate no matter how she pestered him as they picked up tools and headed for the creek, and finally Steel shushed her. "We're getting close."

"I still don't want to do this."

"You're doing this," Lance growled at her. "Pipe down."

Olivia gave up. She'd never crossed her brothers before, and she couldn't seem to now, not when Steel was on Lance's side. What if he knew something she didn't? Furious at herself for failing to stand up to them, her heart in her mouth at the thought of Noah catching them in the act, she held the light for her brothers as they waded into the sluggish water of the creek and altered its flow toward their own side channel.

"Make sure you leave them enough. They'll be less likely to come after us," she hissed.

"They don't deserve—" Lance began.

"Quiet, both of you. We'll leave them some water."

"Steel—"

"I said quiet."

Lance shut up, but the way he hacked at the creek bed with his shovel told Olivia his anger simmered beneath the surface.

Someday that anger was going to blow them all to kingdom come, she thought.

"There. That will do it for now," Steel said.

"For now," Lance echoed and splashed toward the shore. He passed Olivia without another word and strode back the way they'd come. Olivia waited for Steel.

"We've started something that isn't going to end well," she told him when he was out on dry land.

"We don't have a choice," Steel said.

"We always have a choice."

She thought he wouldn't answer, but Steel stopped and stared into the darkness beyond the reach of her flashlight. "You're right. We do have a choice. I hope someday you'll understand mine." He was gone before she could question him, leaving Olivia to stumble across the fields on her own.

After a few paces she turned off the flashlight, let her eyes adjust and continued by the light of the stars. She'd disagreed with Lance plenty of times in the past, but this was the first time she thought Steel was in the wrong. It left her feeling untethered. She'd counted on her brother, especially after their father landed in jail and their mother left. Now she was on her own.

Which was exactly what she'd said she wanted, Olivia reminded herself. She needed to make her own decisions. Take a stand. This was the last time she'd help sabotage the Turners.

She hoped like hell someday Steel and the rest of the family would understand her choices, too.

NOAH KNEW SOMETHING was up when Liam and Jed met him on the doorstep of the house the following afternoon. He'd been up well before dawn to drive into Bozeman for an all-day meeting, part of keeping up his credentials for being a parole officer. By the time he got home again, it was nearly dinner. He was hungry and worried because he still hadn't talked to Olivia. He wished he could meet with her in person, rather than texting or calling, but he couldn't simply arrive on her doorstep.

"What's going on?"

"Nothing. Just coming to say hi." Liam stepped aside so Noah could pass. He and Jed followed him inside.

"You're freaking me out. What's going on?" Noah made his way toward the kitchen. Something smelled good. Stella was at the stove when he walked in.

"Jed and Liam tell you about their crazy idea?" she asked.

"Not yet. What is it?" When he spotted the pot roast she was lifting out, he nearly groaned with impatience. "Are there biscuits? Tell me there are biscuits."

"There are. Wash up first."

He moved to the sink. "What's the crazy idea?"

"It isn't crazy." Jed elbowed Noah out of the way and washed up, too.

"Well?" Noah asked when they were all seated. "Come on. Spill it."

Maya entered the kitchen and slid into her seat. "Have you heard—?"

"No. No one will tell me."

Stella served him a plate of pot roast and a biscuit. Noah knew he should wait for the others, but he was too hungry. He made short work of buttering the biscuit, dipped it into the gravy, blew on it and took a bite.

Heaven.

"Jed's opening a tubing business," Liam said. "We fixed the irrigation channel so it reconnects to Pittance Creek downstream and got more water flowing into it. It's perfect. We'll charge ten dollars a head and—"

Noah dropped his biscuit on his plate. "A tubing business? What are you talking about?"

"You know—people riding on inner tubes, like a lazy river ride at a water park. We'll rent out tubes, ferry people back when they're done for another ride—"

"In our irrigation channel?" Noah couldn't believe what he was hearing.

"You've gotta come see—"

"After dinner," Stella said firmly.

"But the creek's gone down—"

"We fixed that," Liam said. "The channel is full, and the water's the perfect speed. We made it so it loops back to the creek—"

"Ten bucks a head," Jed said with satisfaction. "That'll add up in hot weather like this."

"You fixed it?" All thought of food forgotten, Noah pushed back his chair. "How did you fix it?"

"The Coopers messed with the creek first," Liam said, but he wouldn't meet Noah's eye.

Hell.

"What have you done, Jed?"

"Liam worked the machinery," Jed said primly.

Noah just bet he did—under Jed's careful direction. Liam loved using the tractor's backhoe attachment. And Jed—well, Jed loved screwing things up between them and their neighbors.

"The Coopers messed with the creek first," Liam said again. "I went down there this morning, and there was barely a trickle coming into the irrigation channel. They changed the course of the creek last night, Noah. They're only getting what they deserve."

"If we're getting enough water to fill our channel full, how much did you leave the Coopers?" Noah demanded.

Liam ducked his head again.

Just as Noah had thought.

"If you left them nothing, then we're worse than them." He stood up.

"Eat your dinner," Stella told him.

"Not until I see what they've done."

"Noah, you're not going to fix it tonight. There's still water flowing in Pittance Creek. Eat," Stella ordered. "Besides, the tubing idea might be a good one."

"You can't be serious." Despite himself, Noah sat and scooped up more gravy with his biscuit. He was starving, and he needed to keep up his strength.

"Just for a little while, anyway. We need cash."

Stella kept the books. They must be getting awfully short if she was willing to do something like this.

"Do you seriously think people want to tube in our irrigation channel?" He couldn't think of anything more ridiculous.

"Some kids might. What else is there to do on a hot summer day in town?"

"They can go to Silver Falls or Runaway Lake," Noah pointed out.

"Not everyone has the time to go that far," she pointed out.

"Look, we've got the inner tubes, and we've already put out the word," Liam said. "We start tomorrow."

"You know the Coopers are going to retaliate."

"Let them," Jed said. "They'll be the killjoys ruining everyone's good time. Then people will remember who the true heroes of this town are."

Noah waited for everyone to laugh at that pronouncement.

When they didn't, he knew they were really in trouble.

"WHERE'S THE SHOTGUN?" Lance shouted when he burst in through the back door after dinner.

Olivia, hands deep in a sink of soapy dishes, shrieked, then fought to catch her breath. "Heck, Lance, don't do that. What do you need the shotgun for?" She wiped her hands quickly on a towel and rushed after him as he strode through the house toward the gun safe in the first-floor office.

"I'm going hunting. I'm going to get me some Turners."

"Lance, slow down! Where's Steel?"

"Where is he ever? I sure as hell don't know. He's not here helping me protect our property!" Lance kept going.

She remembered Steel said he'd be gone today. "What did the Turners do?" Olivia tried to keep up.

"They diverted the water. Now it's all running into their irrigation channel. Hardly any is reaching ours."

"So let me get this straight." Olivia put on a burst of speed, got past him and blocked his way, remembering the promise she'd made herself. "You diverted the water away from their irrigation channel, they diverted it away from ours and now you're pissed?"

"Get out of my way!"

"No!" Olivia shoved Lance back when he tried to advance.

"What the hell, Olivia?"

"Don't you see what you're doing? You're ruining everything for us! What are you going to do? Shoot Liam? Or Noah—or Jed? And then what? You're going to spend the rest of your damn life rotting in a jail like Dad did? How does that solve anything?"

"I'm just trying to—"

"You're just trying to make sure the rest of my life is as shitty as the first part was!" Olivia shoved him again. "If you wind up in jail—or dead—who's going to run this place? Who's going to put food on our table? Who's going to be left in my family, Lance? Huh? Tell me! Because Dad's gone, Mom's gone, Tory's gone and Steel's never around!"

She'd never shouted at Lance like this before, but now that she'd started, Olivia couldn't seem to stop. "I can't do this all by myself. So stop being so goddamn selfish, and start thinking for once!"

For a moment she thought Lance might push past and get the shotgun after all. Instead he turned on his heel and walked out and slammed the back door so hard the house shook. Olivia scrubbed at her face, wiping away the tears she found there.

She didn't know what Lance would do next.

Didn't know how to stop the feud from escalating even more. How was it going to end? With someone dead?

Her hands were shaking when she pulled her phone from her pocket, and it took her two tries to make the call to Noah.

"Pick up," Olivia muttered. "Pick up, pick up."

"Olivia?" Noah answered.

"We need to meet. To talk. Lance was coming to get his shotgun when he saw what you did to the creek. I stopped him, but I can't vouch for what he'll do. We need to stop this."

"I know. I told Liam there'd be more trouble."

She heard Noah breathing. Thinking.

"Where and when?" he finally said.

"Tonight. Camila's old cabin. It's empty, right?"

"You can't come here. Are you crazy? Liam's got a shotgun, too, you know."

"I've snuck onto your property hundreds of times." She let that sink in. "I'll be there. Ten o'clock."

"I'll be there, too."

Her phone beeped, and she looked at the screen. "I've got another call." It was Caroline.

"See you later." When he was gone, Olivia eagerly greeted her friend, hoping for a break from the day's worries, but Caroline's voice was too thick with tears for

THE COWBOY'S OUTLAW BRIDE

Olivia to understand her words.

"Slow down. Say that again. What happened?" Olivia clutched the phone, wondering how much misery one day could bring.

"He took it. My lottery ticket," Caroline sobbed. "He said he needs a new truck."

"Oh, Caroline." Olivia didn't know what to say. She wasn't surprised, but she'd hoped things wouldn't turn out like this. "You need to stand up for yourself. That money is yours."

"I... tried." She was crying so hard she could barely form the words.

"I'm coming over. We'll—"

"No!" Caroline cut right over her. "No, you can't come. I just need you to listen."

"But—"

"Olivia, you can't come over here."

Olivia took a deep breath. "Is he still there?"

"No. But I don't know when he'll be back, and he'll be furious if he knows I told you. He said—he said I'm always so selfish. I never think about him. It's not true—"

Olivia swallowed the fury that rose in her throat. "You're right it's not true. You think about him way too much. He's not good enough for you."

"You don't understand. He's had it hard." Caroline's sobs began to subside. "His parents treated him so bad."

And Olivia knew her friend was lost. They'd had conversations like this before, and once Caroline started defending Devon, she couldn't be budged. Olivia listened, hoping that her silent support was enough. Knowing it couldn't be.

When she'd heard enough, she tried one more time. "You deserve that kitchen upgrade and to pay off some of your mortgage. Don't you think?"

"Yes," Caroline said softly.

"Devon needs to give you back the lottery ticket."

"I know. He will," she said, though she sounded far from certain about that. "I'll wait for him to settle down and talk to him again."

"I hope he listens to you," Olivia told her.

But she doubted Devon would.

Chapter Eight

H E HAD TO be the stupidest man in the world for taking this chance, Noah told himself as he walked up the steps to Camila's old cabin. If Liam or Jed found Olivia on their land, there'd be hell to pay.

The door swung open, and Olivia pulled him inside. It was cool in the cabin and already had the musty smell of an unused home. Noah wanted to take Olivia into his arms and forget about everything that had happened in the past few days, but he couldn't do that. Not when their families were taking up weapons.

"We don't have water for our stock, Noah," Olivia told him. "The creek's so low now, it barely flows into the channel."

"Your family started this."

"Lance said your family diverted water first."

"Lance is lying. But you won't believe what Liam and Jed are up to." He filled her in on their plans, and for the first time, Olivia cracked a smile.

"Tubing? On the irrigation channel? That's—"

"Insane," Noah finished for her.

"And kind of... ingenious," Olivia said. "I mean, the water's only a few feet high, but how much do you need, really? Especially if it's kids we're talking about."

"He wants to charge ten dollars a head. Stella said we need—" Noah cut off abruptly. Hell, he hadn't meant to say that.

"You need the cash," Olivia said when he didn't. She nodded. "Don't we all."

"I'll make them change it back," Noah told her, although he wasn't sure how Liam would react to that. His brother was changing in ways he didn't like. He seemed brittle lately. Pushed to the edge.

"I'm not sure if I can keep Lance from starting something again." Olivia looked miserable, her arms crossed and her shoulders hunched as if she was cold, although the night was warm.

"I'm not sure if I can keep Liam on the straight and narrow, either. It might take me a day or two to convince him about the irrigation channel. Do you think you can keep Lance in line that long?"

"I can try, especially if I have your word that it will happen."

"You have my word." Noah paced the room. "I don't want it to be like this between our families." He turned to face her. "I want to be with you."

"I know."

"How about you? What do you want?" He had to know. Was there any hope for them?

"I want you, too."

Noah was suddenly aware of the cabin in a way he hadn't been before. It had four walls. A door that locked. Curtains that could be closed. Unable to keep away from her any longer, he stepped forward, caught her up and kissed her. He couldn't stop himself. He didn't care about the Ridley property, or the water, or his ranch, or anything else. Or rather, he did, but this was more important.

He wanted Olivia. Wanted to forget all the rest of his problems and simply be with her.

Now.

And Olivia wanted him. He felt it in the way she melted against him. The way she linked her arms around his neck and went up on tiptoe to meet his kiss willingly. Now that he'd started, he couldn't seem to stop, either. He tightened his embrace, pulled her body against his and groaned.

She felt so damn good.

"Olivia—"

"Yes," she said definitively before he could even finish his sentence. "Me and you. Together. Now. Screw everyone else."

She slipped her hands down between them, tugged the hemline of her shirt up and over her head, and stepped back a moment before crashing against him again and reaching for another kiss.

Hell, yeah. Screw them all.

Noah reached over his head, grabbed a fistful of his shirt and tugged it off as well, breaking off the kiss only momentarily before tossing it away, tugging Olivia close so he could undo her bra.

"You and me," he echoed. "Just you and me."

"Just you and me," she agreed.

As her bra fell to the floor, he palmed her breasts, and Olivia moaned.

Noah could barely think straight. He wanted more. Needed to touch her everywhere.

This was the only answer that mattered. What was between them—the longing, the lust, the… desire—was far more important than what the rest of the world was dishing out.

And she was kicking off her boots and undoing her jeans, and he was tugging them down, and she was fumbling with the button at his waist and tugging at his jeans—

And then they were in a heap on the floor, and Noah didn't care, because he needed—

Olivia slipped out of her panties in a maneuver that gave him glimpses of everything he wanted to see. He didn't know how he got naked. But it was quick, and suddenly he was free, flipping Olivia onto her back, settling between her legs, nudging her thighs apart and—

Oh, God.

This was what he wanted. What he needed.

Where he belonged.

Forever.

OLIVIA GASPED AS Noah pushed inside her with one strong stroke, sensation bursting through her like clear water running over dry earth after far too long. She clutched at his shoulders, slid her hands to his hips and tugged him back inside her when he pulled back.

Noah followed her lead, plunging into her again, and Olivia arched her back, sighing at the wonder of it. He filled her perfectly, tugging her further toward ecstasy with every stroke, and Olivia wished it would last forever.

She wanted more. Much more.

As Noah increased his pace, she met his rhythm with her own and lifted her hips to meet his thrusts. His fingers dug into her skin in answer to her own urgency. She lifted her head to kiss his neck, run her lips along his collarbone.

All she needed was Noah. He was here in her arms—inside her—and that was everything. She didn't care what happened next.

Noah worked in and out of her, building the pressure, coaxing her to a climax she already knew would dwarf any she'd had before.

Noah was right for her. He was meant to be here between her legs. Meant to love her—to make her—

Olivia cried out as pleasure exploded through her and arched her back, crying out again and again. When Noah joined her, his gruff sounds echoing her cries, she hung on to him, riding the storm of his pleasure, too.

When it was over, he collapsed on top of her, gathered her up and cradled her against his chest, turning them over to the side.

"You and me." He didn't say more, and he didn't need to; he'd already said everything.

They were perfect together.

They were all each other needed.

She was never going to let him go.

As Noah caught his breath and held Olivia in his arms, he knew he was lost. Here they were lying on the bare floor of an empty cabin, and it felt like heaven. How would it feel to be with Olivia in more comfortable circumstances? What would it be like to plan a whole life with her?

He wanted a whole life with Olivia. A life of waking up to her, of sharing his days with her. Learning all about her. Growing together.

He didn't want to sneak around.

What was the alternative, though? Leave Chance Creek? Start over? He couldn't walk out on his family the way his mother had.

Noah glanced at Olivia, who was staring at the ceiling, too. It was a mystery he couldn't hope to solve. Not without asking his mother some difficult questions.

Olivia must have sensed his scrutiny. She touched his face. "You're thinking."

He nodded. "About my mom."

"Anything in particular?"

Noah shifted, trying to get comfortable on the hard ground, and smoothed a lock of hair back behind Olivia's ear. He hadn't thought about his mother much recently. He didn't talk to her as much as he should. Their conversations were always so stilted, and he supposed it was his fault. He still blamed her for what she'd done and how his life had changed so suddenly when she'd left.

"I won't walk out on my family the way she did."

"I'd never ask you to."

"I know."

"Tell me about her." Olivia turned on her side to face him, and for a minute Noah got lost in wonder over the beauty of her body. She was comfortable in her skin in a way he appreciated. Her curves entranced him.

But she'd asked him a question.

"She left pretty soon after your family did. Went to Ohio, where she had some family. She works for an insurance company, has a boyfriend. They take vacations at a time share in Florida." He found it all hard to understand.

"It must have been difficult when she left."

Noah nodded. "She laid things on the line for us. Told us she'd never live on a ranch again. Told us she loved us, but that if we came with her, we'd have to leave all this behind. We all decided to stay."

"Oh, Noah. What a decision to have to make."

"At least she was truthful. In that way she did us a favor. I would die away from the ranch," he confessed. "This is my home." He knew Olivia understood.

"Strange how both our families fell apart at the same time."

She didn't know the half of it. Should he tell her how his father had taken care of Thorn Hill during William's absence? That the job had fallen to him when Dale died?

His father had wanted that kept a secret.

"When I marry, it's going to be forever," Olivia said

with determination, breaking into his thoughts.

Noah softened. "Me, too." He edged closer and found her mouth again.

"What are we going to do?" she asked a few moments later.

"I don't know," he told her honestly. "I'll take care of the water issue as soon as I can, but—" His phone buzzed. Noah fished around in his clothes until he found it.

Brandon again.

"Shit." He gave Olivia an apologetic look. "This might be important."

"Go ahead."

"What's up, Brandon?" Noah disentangled himself from Olivia and sat up.

"Still no job. Noah, something's got to give."

"There's no way you went to Silver Falls and knocked on every door."

"I'm doing the best I can—"

"Well, it isn't good enough, is it?" Noah snapped. "Suck it up, Brandon. I know it's hard, but you're the one who got yourself into this mess. You're the one who has to get yourself out of it."

Silence stretched out on the other end of the line. "Thanks for nothing," Brandon said and hung up.

Hell. Noah scrubbed a hand over his face. That had been a real mistake.

"What was that about?" Olivia asked.

"One of my parolees about to go off the deep end." Noah scrambled to his feet and reached for his jeans.

"I've got to go. I promise I'll fix the creek. Just give me time. First I need to keep a good man out of jail."

"What about us?" Olivia asked, already pulling on her clothes.

"I want to see you again. Soon." He shook his head. "I don't know how we do this," he confessed. "I don't want to hide—"

Olivia chuckled. "After the other night, I'm down for hiding—at least for now. See you here tomorrow night?"

"Yeah. Good." He snatched another kiss that was nearly the undoing of him, then pulled away. "Tomorrow. Same time."

He slipped out the door.

SEX WITH NOAH had been better than she'd ever imagined. Good enough she was already anticipating doing it again. Olivia wished they'd been able to spend the night together. What would it be like to curl up in bed with him? To wake up by his side. Did Noah snore?

Would she mind if he did?

As she dressed Olivia tried to pinpoint what it was about Noah that was so different. She'd dated other men, but she'd never felt the urge to think of something permanent with them. With Noah, it was as if they were reaching for each other, meeting in the middle rather than one or the other of them calling the shots and setting the tone of their relationship. It was more... mature.

Olivia laughed.

That was a sexy thought.

Maybe maturing had its perks, though. Noah was a man who'd showed he stuck around in adversity, both in the context of his life with his family and in the context of her relationship with him. He didn't cut and run at the first sign of trouble, like so many people did. Noah would be a rock for his wife and kids to depend on.

She could use a rock.

Could she be a good wife to a man like Noah?

Could he even think of her that way?

As she finished dressing and paused near the door to gather her thoughts before sneaking back to her own ranch, Olivia wondered if she was fooling herself. Maybe Noah liked her because she was wild. Saw her as a diversion from the rest of his life—a diversion he'd grow tired of someday.

Why would the happiness that had eluded her all her life arrive now, of all times?

She let herself out of the house and scanned the area. The lights were on in the main house, and shadows crossed back and forth in front of the windows. Olivia hugged her arms over her chest, finding it hard to believe she'd ever be invited in there. Noah liked her— but it would take a lot more than that to overcome the distance between their families.

The hike back across the pastures to where she could cross the creek to her side seemed far longer than it had on the way here. Alone under a field of stars, she wondered if she had taken yet another wrong turn with her life. Being with Noah had been wonderful, but instead of sating her desire for him, she'd simply fanned it.

She knew what she wanted: a ranching life by his side.

It seemed impossible they'd ever have that.

When she finally let herself into her own house, it was quiet. Her brothers must be already in bed, ready for another long day tomorrow. Virginia would have gone to sleep hours ago.

Or maybe not. Sometimes her aunt suffered from insomnia.

Olivia stepped into the living room and stopped, struck dumb by the sight that greeted her. Virginia snoring in a rocking chair near their brick fireplace.

And a very familiar clock sitting front and center on the mantelpiece.

She had crossed to stand before it when her phone buzzed. Pulling it out of her pocket, she answered it.

"Olivia?"

"Caroline? Caroline, where are you?" Olivia was already racing back toward the door. Caroline sounded awful, her words slurred and her voice thick with tears.

"Home. I... need you."

"I'll be right there."

Chapter Nine

B Y LUNCHTIME THE following day, Noah was ready
to give up hope he'd ever find Brandon. He wasn't
at his parents' place. Noah had checked last night and
come back again several times today. Brandon's parents
didn't have a clue where he'd gone either.

And they didn't seem in much of a hurry to search
for him.

Noah had texted Olivia twice. Once to say good
morning, and again to tell her he was still looking for
Brandon and hadn't even gotten to talk to Jed about the
water. He hadn't gotten an answer, and he wondered
where she was, but before he could try to track her
down, he needed to find Brandon, or the man might run
off the rails for good.

He was nearing the end of his patience when he ran
into Cab at the sheriff's station, where he'd hoped to
find Mahoney.

"Just the man I've been looking for," Cab said.

Noah wished he'd avoided the place, but it was too
late now. He followed Cab into his office and sat on
one of the hard wooden chairs the sheriff indicated. Cab
took a seat behind his desk.

"If this is about the other night…"

"Of course it's about the other night. I can't have my parole officers beating up people at the local bar," Cab said.

"I know." Noah hung his head. He did know. He wasn't one for starting fights. Usually.

"No one's pressed charges. Not even the owner. Everyone knows there's tension between your families. There always is. The question is, can you get your people under control?"

"Yes." Noah tried to sound far surer than he really was. Truth was, controlling Jed was like trying to control the wind. As for Liam, his brother was getting more trigger-happy by the minute. He wasn't sure why. He'd grown up like the rest of them hearing stories about Coopers being the enemies, but Liam seemed to have it out for Lance in particular.

"I've got this under control," he said again.

Cab shook his head but didn't press him, and when Noah didn't get up to go, he leaned back in his chair. "Something else on your mind?"

"Yeah," Noah finally answered. He filled in Cab on his progress—or lack thereof—with Brandon. "I'm afraid he's going to reoffend," he finished. "He's desperate for cash to impress Christie, and he can't find work. It's a dangerous combination."

"I'll let my deputies know, and we'll keep an eye out. Maybe he's holed up with Christie somewhere."

"I checked her house, too."

"Maybe he took her out of town."

"Could be." Noah sighed. The puzzle was wearing him down. He wanted answers. Now.

"Listen." Cab sat forward. "I know you don't want to hear this, but I'm going to say it anyway. You're doing your job, and at some point you'll have to sit back and let Brandon make his own mistakes."

"But—"

Cab held up a hand to stop him. "No buts. It's his life, not yours. His choices. Things don't always line up all nice and neat." He nodded to the edge of his desk, and Noah realized he'd been lining up everything on it. Cab's pencil holder, stapler, calculator…

"Sorry."

"No problem. But you need to hear what I'm saying. You can't control Brandon. You can't control Jed or Liam, either."

"You just asked me to," Noah pointed out.

"I asked if you could. You said yes. Which means you're delusional."

"Hell, what do you want me to do then?" Noah had the urge to get up and start pacing. Only Cab's calm gaze kept him in his seat.

"I want you to control your own actions. Even if Jed or Liam start something. Hell, even if the Coopers start something—you need to hold back. Be the calm one in the middle of the storm. Got that?"

"Yeah, I got it."

But he didn't know if he could follow through.

A half hour later, he parked his truck in front of his family's home and slowly made his way up the front steps. Inside all was quiet. He went upstairs to change into work clothes, but when he came back down, he heard a noise. Noah stopped. It was coming from the living room. As he stepped into the doorway, a blur of movement caught his eye, and he reached out instinctively—

And caught Olivia around the middle, hauling her back against him as she flailed around trying to get free.

"Olivia! What are you doing here in the middle of the day?" He glanced at the mantel. There was the clock. She hadn't gotten it.

But she'd been trying. Again. Less than twenty-four hours since they'd made love. And she looked... haunted.

"I brought it back. I've got to go—Caroline's in the car."

"Brought it back? From where?"

"From Thorn Hill. Virginia stole it. Noah, I have to go—"

"Virginia hasn't set foot on the Flying W in decades." He didn't know what Olivia was up to, but he didn't like the idea she'd come here and lie to his face. Bad enough she'd been trying to take the clock again. Didn't she know Liam would turn her in if he caught her? He couldn't bear the thought of Olivia in trouble like that. "Liam's out to get you. You know that, right? You want to end up in jail like your dad?"

Olivia's mouth dropped open. "You think I stole it—after we—are you kidding?"

"It doesn't matter," he said quickly. "Look, the

clock is where it belongs, so no harm, no foul, but you have to get out of here before—"

"I didn't take it!"

"Shh! I just said it doesn't matter—"

"Wow," Olivia said. "Just… wow. Fine. I'm out of here." She yanked her arm out of his grip.

"Olivia, wait—"

"Hell, no. I'm not sticking around for this. I tried. Remember that when you're wondering what happened to us. I tried. You're the one who refused to give us a chance. What is wrong with men? You're all insane!"

And she was gone.

"It really was an accident," Caroline said for the tenth time when Olivia parked in the Chance Creek Reformed Church lot. She didn't know where else to go. After collecting Caroline from her house last night, she'd brought her back to Thorn Hill, guided her past Virginia, who was awake and crowing about successfully stealing back her clock, and put her to bed in her room, where Caroline had sobbed her eyes out before finally falling asleep.

She'd spent the morning trying to convince Caroline to go to the sheriff, but Caroline refused. Her eye was swollen shut, and dark bruises marred her arms, but she wouldn't budge, and Olivia knew she couldn't force Caroline to press charges against Devon. When Virginia forced Lance to drive her to the Prairie Garden to visit friends—more like intimidate them, Olivia thought—Olivia knew the chance had come to return the clock.

She'd brought Caroline with her. With that errand accomplished, Olivia had driven to the church. Now Caroline sat buckled into the passenger seat of Olivia's truck, refusing to get out.

"Why are we stopping here?" she demanded.

"Because we're going to talk to Reverend Halpern. He'll know what to do."

"There's nothing to do," Caroline cried. "This is all my fault. I shouldn't have yelled at Devon. I was the one who started it."

Olivia wasn't sure she could stand much more of this. "He's the one who hit you! Caroline, what he did isn't right. You know that, don't you?"

"I wish I'd never won that money." Caroline huddled into the seat, and Olivia lost what composure she had remaining.

"He's going to kill you sooner or later!" Olivia snapped her mouth shut. Had she gone too far?

Caroline stared at her in shock.

"Men who hit women don't stop." She had to press forward now. "They keep on hitting. And they do worse."

"I—it wouldn't come to that."

"What if it did? Is that what you want? Do you want him to kill you?"

"No!" A tear streaked down Caroline's face. "But I don't know what to do."

"Leave him."

"And go where? He's living in my house." Her voice rose as she spoke, and Olivia understood. Caroline thought she was in too deep; she didn't think she could get out. Now they were making progress.

"It's your house. You can kick him out."

Caroline shook her head, her tears falling faster. "I put him... I put him on the title. And on my credit card. My bank account. On everything."

Olivia let out a ragged breath. She didn't know what to say to that. This was legal territory she didn't have answers for.

"He took all the money out of the bank," Caroline sobbed. "He took the lottery ticket. Everything. It's all gone. I can't leave; I have nothing." She was losing control, and Olivia ached for her friend.

"You still have to go. Now. Today, Caroline."

"I can't even pay for a plane ticket!"

"I'll take care of that."

"You don't have any money either."

"Do you trust me?" Olivia demanded, making up her mind what to do. She was done letting men call the shots.

Caroline nodded.

"Then no more questions. I know what to do."

"What took you so long?" Liam asked when Noah joined him at the Burger Shack an hour later.

"I was doing something." Noah wasn't going to elaborate. He'd spent the last thirty minutes pacing a trail around their living room, going over and over his conversation with Olivia, wondering how everything had gone so wrong. Cab was right, he told himself for the twentieth time. You couldn't change people. Olivia was who she was. She'd spent the night with him, then tried to steal his clock. It didn't matter if Virginia strong-armed her into doing it or if she thought she deserved it because once it had belonged to her family. She hadn't knocked on the door and asked for it; she'd walked into his house and tried to take it.

He was a parole officer. A man who believed in the law. Could he be with someone who flouted it so openly?

Liam led him to a table, and they both sat down.

"I got Coach Latham coming to talk to us. You remember him, right?" Liam asked.

Noah forced himself to focus. Coach Latham had run the Chance Creek football team like a military unit. Noah had appreciated his orderliness. The predictability of practice. You always knew where you stood with the man.

"He's going to write a letter?"

"I'm still trying to convince him. That's why you're here. He'll listen to you."

Maybe, Noah thought. He still didn't like this letter campaign, though. What would Olivia think if she knew what they were doing?

And you call me the thief, he could hear her say. She'd be right to condemn him. Working against them this way wasn't any more honorable than stealing a clock.

Noah stifled a groan. God, he'd been a self-righteous prick back at the Flying W. Who cared if Olivia was trying to steal the damn clock? Hell, it should belong to the Coopers. He had to find Olivia and apologize.

It was too late to leave now, though. Coach Latham was coming through the door.

"There's the man who took us to Regionals," he boomed when he spotted Noah. "Noah Turner. Best running back a coach could want."

"Hey, Coach Latham. How are you?" He wished he'd slipped away. He couldn't stand what this feud was doing to him—making him participate in undermining something so good for Chance Creek. It bothered him even more to be helping get other people involved. "You know, Coach—"

"Call me Daniel. You're not a kid anymore, are you?"

"No." Even though sometimes he wished he was. Life had been a hell of a lot easier back then.

"What's this about a letter? Writing's not my strong suit, you know. Give me a ball to throw, and I'm your man…"

"It's about the school." Liam gestured to the booth, and Coach Latham sat down, blocking Noah's way out. Liam went on to explain what they were doing and what they wanted from him. Noah, more uncomfortable by the minute, looked for a way to excuse himself but failed to come up with one.

"Well, boys, I guess I can jot down a memory or two," Latham said when Liam was done. "But I got to say, this upgrade sounds like a great deal."

Liam shot Noah a look that said he'd better jump in

and seal the deal. Noah opened his mouth, closed it again, tried desperately to think of what to do and was grateful when the door burst open again and Virginia Cooper strode in.

"Where is she?" the old woman shouted.

The hum of conversation in the restaurant faltered, then surged again as people craned their necks to see what was happening.

"Olivia? You here?"

Noah half stood, his present predicament forgotten. Had Virginia gone right over the edge? He wondered why Virginia thought Olivia would be in the Burger Shack, but taking in the old woman's appearance, he guessed this wasn't the first place she'd looked. Her tidy bun had slipped to one side. Her face was flushed, her hands shaking.

"Coach, let me out, would you?"

Latham stood up, and Noah brushed past him.

"Virginia? You okay?" A glance over her shoulder told him she was alone. How had she even gotten to town?

"No, I'm not okay. She stole it! That girl just up and stole it, and I bet you put her up to it, you Turner weasel! After all my work—"

"Stole what?" Noah pulled out his phone but wasn't sure who to call. Would Olivia even pick up if she saw his name? He couldn't call her brothers. Cab? Maybe—

"My clock!"

Noah faltered. "Clock?"

"You know exactly what I mean, you stupid...

Turner. My clock. The one your ancestors stole from my family. The one Jed wouldn't give back."

"You stole the clock?" Noah's heart sank. Hell, Olivia had been telling the truth?

And he'd accused her of being a thief. Driven her away.

"Of course I took it. Didn't you see my umbrella?"

"Umbrella?" He couldn't keep up.

"I left its broken shards on the mantel so you'd know justice had been served." She lifted her chin. "When I find Olivia, I'm going to—"

"Virginia, calm down. Liam, get her a glass of water or something." Noah urged her over to their booth, where Coach Latham helped her into a seat. He hadn't seen a broken umbrella, but Olivia had been carrying a purse—a normal-size one, not the tiny thing she'd carried at Camila and Carl's wedding. Maybe she'd shoved the pieces in there.

Virginia sat down, still sputtering. "Don't even bother to look for her when I'm done. You won't find a trace of that ungrateful—"

Noah wanted to kick himself. He'd jumped to conclusions, hadn't listened to a thing Olivia said.

He was such an idiot.

Would Olivia ever forgive him?

Liam came bearing a water glass and a look on his face that said Noah had to have lost his mind, but Noah didn't have time to explain.

"Where have you looked for Olivia so far?" he demanded of Virginia.

"Everywhere! The grocery store, the hardware store, the feed store, Linda's Diner, DelMonaco's, even that foreign place."

"Fila's?"

"That's the one." Virginia sniffed. "She's not at any of them."

Noah went over the list in his mind, then nodded. It was a long shot, but he knew one place Virginia hadn't looked. "Gotta go," he said, already on his feet again. "Liam, Coach, make sure she gets home."

"Are you out of your—?"

Noah didn't wait to hear Liam out. He had to find Olivia and make things right between them.

"LOOKING FOR THIS?" Lance held out the key to the gun safe but lifted it high when Olivia grabbed for it.

"That's exactly what I'm looking for." She slammed shut the drawer she'd been pawing through, the one that usually held the spare key. They'd long ago figured one of them would be in the kitchen if the house was ever broken into. Someone was always in the kitchen.

"Finally come around and realized those Turners need shooting?"

"Not the Turners." Olivia jumped up, but Lance held the key out of her reach. "Come on. I don't have time for this."

"Who?"

Olivia hesitated.

"You want these keys, you're going to have to tell me."

"Promise not to get involved. No matter what."

Lance made a face. "Fine. I promise."

"Devon Host."

Lance gave her the keys and followed her into the study to the gun safe. He watched her fumble the keys into the lock. "What's he done?"

"Beat the shit out of Caroline and stole her money."

"So you're going to kill him?"

Olivia got the door open and pulled out the shotgun. "I'm going to get her money back." She gave him a quick recap of the situation as she locked the safe again and grabbed a handful of ammunition.

"Why the hell aren't you getting Cab involved?"

Olivia turned on him. "You're telling me to the get the sheriff involved? That's rich."

"Look, you aren't me. You've got a future—"

"Lance, you've got a future, too. You're a rancher, for God's sake. With a ranch. How many people can say that these days? I get that it's hard. I get you need more help. I'm trying. But right now I need to get Caroline's money and get her out of here." She pushed past him and made for the front door.

"I think this is a mistake." Lance followed after her.

"It won't be the first one I've made." She faced him one last time. "Remember—you promised. Stay out of this."

NOAH'S HEART SANK when he scanned the library parking lot and didn't see Olivia's truck, but he persevered and went inside. Marta was nowhere in sight, but he recognized Caroline Selwich sitting nearby, bent over her phone. Wasn't she a friend of Olivia's?

She looked up as he approached, and his breath hitched when he saw the large bruise swelling one eye. Hell, how had that happened?

"Hi, Caroline," he said awkwardly. "I'm looking for Olivia. Have you seen her lately?"

She nodded. "She was here about an hour ago."

Noah knelt down beside her chair. "You look like you could use some help. Have you seen a doctor about that eye?"

"I'm okay."

"You don't look okay." Noah's phone shrilled, and he grabbed it from his pocket. It was a number he didn't recognize, but he sure knew the name.

Lance Cooper.

He accepted the call. "Noah here."

"Olivia's in trouble."

A chill traced down Noah's spine. He got to his feet. "Where is she?"

"Caroline Selwich's house. She's going after Devon, Caroline's boyfriend. Says he hit her."

Noah turned, paced away and lowered his voice. "I'm looking at Caroline right now. She's got a shiner like you wouldn't believe."

"Olivia says he took Caroline's money. I promised I wouldn't interfere."

"I'm on my way."

"Good." Lance hung up. Noah faced Caroline. "I'm going to go get her."

"I don't know where she is—"

"I do. Sit tight. I'll be back soon."

THIS WAS NO time for niceties, Olivia decided as she walked up to the front stoop of Caroline's little moss-green house. With its white shutters and picket fence, it was cute as a button. Caroline kept the front yard neatly trimmed, and rose bushes edged the fence. It made Olivia sick to think of Devon taking it over.

She grasped the knob of the front door firmly, turned it, but it didn't open.

Was Devon not even here?

There was a truck in the driveway but no lights on in the house that she could see. Caroline's place was with walking distance of downtown Chance Creek, though, and there were a dozen places Devon might have gone on foot. Olivia let herself through the gate into the fenced backyard. The back door was locked, too, but a screened window was open beside it.

Olivia cradled the shotgun, reached into her purse and pulled out her pocket knife. Her father had given it to her when she was six years old and taught her a little whittling, although she'd never been good at it. The knife itself came in handy all the time, though. It was sure handy now, she thought as she slit a hole in the screen big enough to step through.

Inside she found herself in a neat bedroom she guessed was a spare one. The door was open, and she listened for a moment before moving into the hall. Five minutes later she'd assured herself no one was home.

Olivia wasn't sure if that was a good thing or not. With Devon out of the way, she could look for the money, but if he'd taken it with him, she was hooped.

She kept the shotgun at the ready as she picked her way through the house again, opening drawers and looking through Devon and Caroline's possessions, but finding nothing out of the ordinary.

She pocketed as much of Caroline's jewelry as she could when she found a box of it in the master bedroom and stuffed in her purse a small photo album she found on her friend's bedside table. Where was the money, though? Olivia tried to think like Devon would.

He'd claimed it as his own, which meant he'd put it somewhere he identified as belonging to him, too. Olivia looked over Caroline's pretty bedroom. Not here.

She crossed to a window and spotted a shed in the backyard. She'd bet Devon had taken that over when he moved in. Back out in the hall, Olivia was headed for door when another room caught her eye. She carefully pushed the door open wider.

An office.

It looked like Devon had claimed this room. Papers were spread over the desk. A jacket had been tossed on a chair, and a pair of work boots Olivia was sure Caroline would never allow in the house lay on their sides on the carpet.

Olivia hurried to search the desk, leaning the shotgun against it and using both hands to paw through the drawers.

She didn't find the money, but when she gave up in

frustration and scanned the room a second time, she noticed the wooden box on the bookshelf near the window. It was handmade. Rough. Like a project a kid might complete in high school shop class. A kid who wasn't very good at woodworking.

Had Devon made this himself once upon a time? She bet he had. It was locked with a small padlock, but she wouldn't let that stop her. She looked around for a way to break it, and her gaze lit on a big stone studded with fossils. That would do.

She smashed the stone down on the lock and busted the box wide open.

Bingo.

Caroline's lottery ticket and a slim stack of hundred dollar bills.

Olivia shoved all of it in her pocket, closed the box again, picked up the shotgun and turned to go. This was the most dangerous part. If Devon arrived home now, he'd catch her red-handed. She slipped through the house and out the back door, closing it carefully behind her, and made her way to the gate, going up on tiptoe to make sure no one was on the other side before she opened it and went through.

Almost there.

As she came around the house, she stopped, taking in two vehicles in motion on Caroline's street.

A man in a silver pickup spotted her and quickly pulled away. Lance. He'd followed her.

Before she could fully take that in, a Ram pickup pulled in right behind her blue Chevy. The front window rolled down and a head poked out.

Olivia swore.

It was Noah.

"OLIVIA, ARE YOU all ri—"

Noah watched in shock as Olivia burst into a run, threw her shotgun through the open window into her truck, scrambled up after it and wriggled through the window herself, her boot-covered feet the last to disappear before a second later the truck's taillights came on, the engine roared to life and she drove away.

"Hey!" Noah yelled after her. He turned his own truck back on, put it in gear and floored the gas pedal. "What the hell, Olivia!" he called out the window, although he knew she couldn't hear him.

He looked back, wondering if Devon had been chasing her, but no one followed her out of Caroline's house, so what had she been doing with that shotgun? And why had she run away?

He had to let up on the gas almost as soon as he floored it. In the middle of town, traffic just didn't go that fast. Olivia didn't stop long enough for him to catch up to her, but she was obeying the traffic laws. When she turned into the library parking lot, he breathed a sigh of relief.

By the time he parked his truck, she was already racing inside the building—without her shotgun, he was glad to see. He followed her inside and caught up just as Caroline put her purse down on her chair and threw her arms around Olivia.

"Thank you," she said. "I was so worried. I didn't know what I was going to do."

"It's nothing," Olivia said.

"I was worried, too." Noah gave a hard look at another patron who was watching the proceedings. The man turned back to browsing the stacks. "Olivia, what were you doing back there?"

"Caroline needed something. I went to get it."

"Alone? Armed?"

"Everything's fine."

Noah couldn't believe her nonchalance. "Lance called me. He was afraid you'd get hurt. What did you need to get?"

"Lance called?" She huffed out a breath. "He followed me, too. After promising he wouldn't."

"He thought you were in danger."

"Well, I wasn't. Like I said, Devon wasn't there." She opened her purse. "I found some of your jewelry, too," she told Caroline. She handed her a tangle of necklaces, bracelets and more, and Caroline gasped. "And this." She pulled out a small photo album.

Caroline took it from her. "It's my parents' wedding album. Thank you!"

"I thought it had to be special," Olivia told her.

"What about Devon? You need to call Cab," Noah demanded, still trying to calm down. When Olivia had appeared around the corner of Caroline's house with a shotgun, his heart had nearly stopped.

"We will. Right now."

"We will?" Caroline didn't look at all sure about

that.

"We will," Olivia confirmed. "It'll take time to work things out and get him out of your financial affairs, but you have what's important, right?"

A smile tugged at the corners of Caroline's mouth. "Yeah, you're right."

Noah decided he'd never understand women. How could a pile of jewelry and a photo album be worth risking your life?

"Olivia—"

"Look, I know I took a chance, but it paid off, so just leave it, all right?"

It wasn't all right. He could have lost the woman he loved. "What would you have done if Devon had been there?"

Olivia grinned. "I would have done the world a favor and shot him."

THANK GOD FOR libraries, Olivia thought as she pushed a metal cart laden with books between the aisles. This felt like coming home in an even more visceral way than it had to open Thorn Hill's front door when she'd moved back three years ago. The smell of the books, the dust motes dancing in a beam of sunlight, the murmuring of a patron asking Marta for help.

Why hadn't she volunteered earlier?

Shelving books ordered her mind and gave her something to do while Cab interviewed Caroline at one of the tables in back. Soon they'd have to go to the station, and then probably to the hospital to get Caroline's eye checked out, but for now Olivia was in her favorite place—

With her favorite man trailing her.

Noah hadn't let her more than three feet away since he'd followed her here. She figured he was suspicious about what had really happened at Caroline's house, but as long as Caroline had her lottery ticket and cash tucked away in her purse, all was well. She could start again, whether or not she was unable to untangle Devon from her old assets. Olivia wasn't sure if Caroline would have to sell her house and split the proceeds with Devon since he was on the title. That would be a crying shame, but at least Caroline had only owned the place a few years and didn't have much equity in the property.

Equity. Caroline had to explain the term when she first mentioned it to Olivia a year or two back. Olivia didn't know much about buying and selling property. There were a lot of things she needed to learn. Olivia was determined to start. She was ready to grow up. Ready to make something of herself. Volunteering at the library was the first step. She and Marta had talked it over, and Marta agreed she could start right away— while she was waiting for Cab to talk to Caroline. Through all of it, Noah had stuck close.

"Why did you run from me?" Noah asked again. He'd already put the question to her twice.

"Like I said, I was afraid what would happen if Devon came home. You'd have stepped in. Maybe gotten hurt."

"You could have gotten hurt."

"I had a shotgun," she pointed out. "Besides, I got away before Devon came home. If I was thinking straight, I would have called a locksmith and gotten the locks changed on Caroline's house, though."

"How did you get inside? Did she give you her keys?"

"Something like that."

"Olivia—"

"Noah, this is between me and Caroline, okay? You need to back off."

"Did you *break* into her house?"

"She sent me to get her things." Olivia bit back her exasperation. "I was helping my friend."

"But sometimes—"

"Are we seriously going to do this again? I didn't take your clock—I was returning it!" In all the excitement she'd forgotten Noah thought she was a thief. She spotted something down the row—something out of place. Olivia pushed her cart toward it, grateful to leave Noah behind.

"I don't know where I put it. I can't find it anywhere!" A woman's voice pierced through the quiet of the library.

"I'm sure we'll find it if we look for it," Marta assured her.

"I swear I'd lose my head if it wasn't attached," the woman went on. "I'm so scattered these days." It was Fila Matheson, if Olivia wasn't mistaken.

"We all are, honey. Let's go look again."

Olivia reached the object she'd spotted—and had to

smile despite her irritation. The small pocketbook had been inserted into a row of books at one end of a shelf. She imagined Fila had been engrossed in a novel when she'd done that and forgotten it when she moved down the row. She herself had done something similar countless times in this library.

Ignoring Noah, who was still trailing behind her, she left her cart where it was, pulled the purse off the shelf and walked toward the front of the library just in time to see Fila and Marta disappearing into the nonfiction section.

"Fila? I found it!"

Fila reappeared. "Thank goodness. I thought I'd lost my mind." She rushed over and took the purse. "This thing needs to stay attached to me at all times. I'm constantly setting it down and losing it."

"Glad I could help."

"Good thing you spotted that," Noah said.

Olivia bit back a sharp retort. He'd just accused her of breaking and entering her best friend's house. He didn't get to pretend all was well with them. "You'd better check if your wallet and credit cards are still in there," she said to Fila.

Fila's eyebrows shot up. "Do you think someone got into it?" She opened it immediately and pulled out her wallet.

Olivia caught Noah's gaze and held it. "There's a Cooper present. Can't take too many chances when one of them is around."

Noah sighed.

Fila paused, wallet in hand. "What's that supposed to mean?"

"You haven't lived in Chance Creek long enough. You don't know I'm a hardened criminal."

Fila's gaze slid from her to Noah, and one corner of her mouth quirked up. "Glad you warned me. Here I thought you were just a nice woman who worked at the library."

"I never said you were a hardened criminal," Noah said.

"But you thought it," Olivia told him. "And that's enough."

Fila backed away. "Thanks again for finding it, Olivia, you're a life saver." She went to check out her books.

Noah waited until Fila had moved to the counter. "I probably deserved that."

"You did."

"I know," he admitted. "And I don't blame you for being pissed. You're right. I thought you were stealing the clock, and I didn't give you a chance to explain."

"You changed your mind?"

"Yeah, even before I ran into your aunt, and she set me straight." He shook his head. "She shouldn't have needed to, though. I don't know why I was being such an idiot." He took her hand. Rubbed his thumb along her palm. "I think I'm just not used to trusting anyone to get too close. Outside my own family, that is. And even then…"

"Yeah, I know." For a moment neither of them said anything. Then Olivia bit back a smile. "Virginia will be so pissed I brought it back."

"Why did you?"

Olivia blinked at him. "Because we don't need things any worse between our families than they already are."

Noah nodded. "I don't know what to do," he confessed. "Nothing's going right these days. My job doesn't earn enough. My ranch is facing a drought. My family's about to lose its chance to win the Ridley property, you keep taking chances you shouldn't and I can't see you without starting a riot."

Olivia chuckled. "Yeah, that last part is a drag."

"I want to see you again, you know." Noah moved closer. "You're all I think about."

Olivia caught Fila grinning as she scooped up her books and left the building. Marta busied herself behind the desk.

Olivia touched Noah's arm. "I think about you a lot, too."

"I think we need to—"

When a bit of plaster dropped down from a discolored patch in the ceiling nearby, they both jumped.

"Everything all right over there?" Cab called.

"We're okay," Noah called back.

"Oh, my goodness," Marta said, hurrying over. She peered up at the damp patch. Noah squeezed Olivia's hand and hurried to join her. Olivia followed close behind.

"That doesn't look good." Noah peered upward, too.

"I don't know what to do anymore," Marta said. "If the ceiling is going to come down, we'll have to close the place. That's dangerous!"

"Can't you call someone in to fix it?" Olivia asked.

"We don't have enough in petty cash to cover something like that. If I was younger, I'd climb on the roof myself, but—"

"I'll take a look," Noah said.

Cab and Caroline joined them. "Looks like the place needs a bit of work," the sheriff said.

"Noah's going up on the roof," Olivia told him. "Caroline, are you okay?"

Caroline nodded. "We're heading to the station."

"Want me to come?"

"That's okay. When we're all done, Cab's driving me to Billings. I'm going to stay with my sister and her husband for a while until everything gets straightened out. I should have done this a long time ago. I don't know what I was thinking."

"You never expected the man you loved to become a monster," Olivia told her. "It's not your fault."

"I feel like a fool."

Olivia hugged her. "I'm going to miss you. Can I come visit?"

"Definitely. Someday I'll get my life back, but until then thank you for everything you've done."

A half hour later, Olivia held the ladder as Noah climbed down after doing a thorough examination. "Well?" she asked.

"It needs more than a patch. I'm sorry. I know

that's not what you want to hear."

"It's not fair. This place means everything to Marta." Olivia tried to get a hold of her emotions, but there were too many problems to deal with at once.

"And to you, I think," Noah said softly. He leaned against the ladder and reached for her. "I am really sorry. I'm more than happy to organize a work party, but the library needs to cover the cost of the shingles."

"Where is Marta supposed to get the money for that?"

The strangest look came over Noah's face, and he bent forward and kissed her, catching her off guard. "I think I know."

"Where?" she asked again.

"Give me a week."

"To do what?"

"Trust me, okay?"

"But—"

"One week!" He kissed her again.

And refused to tell her anything more.

Chapter Ten

"WE'RE RAKING IT in," Jed gloated that night after dinner when he'd counted up the day's take from the tubing business. They were all gathered in the living room, and Noah kept looking at the clock, kicking himself for ever thinking Olivia had tried to take it again after they'd been together.

"Glad to hear it." Noah knew this was his chance. "Because I know exactly what to spend it on."

"Our bills," Stella said acidly. She was seated at a desk in one corner, going over their accounts, and from the amount of times she'd sighed in the last fifteen minutes, they couldn't be in good shape.

"No, not our bills," Noah contradicted her. "The library." He was seated in one of the easy chairs, where his father used to sit when he was alive.

Maya laughed. "The library?" Curled up on the couch, she was flipping through a magazine too fast to be reading any of the articles.

"It needs work. Bad. I was there today when part of the ceiling collapsed."

"What were you doing at the library?" Liam asked suspiciously. He was prowling the room near the back windows, looking out over the pastures every now and then.

"What do you think?" He wasn't going to admit he'd gone to find Olivia. "I went up on the roof, and it needs all new shingles. I want to raise money to help fix it."

"Why the hell would we do that?" Jed demanded.

Maya was the first to get it. "It will be our project, to help us win the Founder's Prize."

"The library needs a ton of work," Noah agreed. "Most of it we can do ourselves. We just need to raise the cost of the materials. It's an old building—it'll look great when we're done."

"That's pretty smart," Stella said. "We still need to pay our bills, though."

"We'll pay them."

"What about the letter-writing campaign?" Liam demanded.

"We can do both." Although Noah hoped Liam wouldn't have time to follow through with the letters. This library project could solve a number of problems if it kept his brother busy.

"I don't know," Jed began.

"I do," Noah said firmly. "The town's going to shut down this tubing thing any day now. Nothing about it is legal, so why don't we make money while we can—and have one final fundraising day as soon as we can pull it together? We'll have a barbecue, music and dancing, tubing all day. A big party. People will love it."

Jed was nodding. "And we'll win the Founder's

Prize."

Maybe. Maybe not. But Olivia would be happy.

That was all he cared about.

"THAT'S BRILLIANT," OLIVIA said into her phone when Noah told her about the fundraiser. She was sitting in her truck outside Crescent Hall, ready for a party planning date with the Hall women for the gala, but she was grateful Noah had called to fill her in.

"Can you stop Lance from doing anything drastic until I'm done?"

"I think so." She wasn't sure what to think about Lance's actions lately. He'd been keeping to himself, barely acknowledging her when they were in the same room, but he hadn't gone after Liam, and he hadn't touched the creek, even though that meant hauling well water out to a trough for the cattle every day. "I need a good excuse to keep him from taking matters into his own hands."

"Even if he knows we're raising money for the library?"

"I'll explain that to him, but I can't be sure."

"We've set the fundraiser for a week from Saturday. I promise as soon as it's over, I'll set things to right with Pittance Creek."

"Sounds good. My gala's the night before that. I hope the fundraiser goes great."

"Good luck with the gala."

"I'm going to need it." She didn't ask when she'd see him again. Not until both events were over, that was for sure. Both of them were much too busy.

Olivia knocked on the Halls' front door, hope and worry warring within her. On the one hand, she loved that Noah had taken on fundraising for the library with such verve. On the other, she wasn't sure Lance cared enough for the library to hold off when he'd already waited so long to get revenge for the way the Turners had diverted the water from Pittance Creek.

When Regan let her in, she was happy to set those thoughts aside and concentrate on the party preparations. Once again she was in awe of the women, who'd worked hard to make everything so easy on her.

Even more, she was taken with the sound of their children playing in the living room. She, Regan, Ella, Storm and Heather were working in the kitchen, with one of the women moving between the rooms to keep an eye on the younger kids. Now and then a child toddled into view—or belly crawled, as the case might be—and gave Olivia a once-over or a gummy grin.

"That's Lainey," Regan said when a baby cried from one of the bedrooms. She disappeared and came back some minutes later bearing a bundle of cooing baby. Olivia's heart melted on sight.

"Want to hold her?" Regan asked.

"Yes. Please." Olivia held out her arms, and Regan placed the baby in them. "Oh, aren't you sweet," Olivia gushed. Lainey really was, with light brown hair, blue eyes and a pert little nose. "Oh, I want one."

"Any prospects in sight?" Ella quizzed her. "Some cowboy we don't know about?"

Olivia hoped she wasn't blushing. "Not… really."

"That doesn't sound too convincing." Regan watched her with a smile on her face.

"It isn't going… too well. His family doesn't like me." She wished she hadn't said that last bit when Regan and Ella exchanged a look.

"So he's a Turner," Ella said.

"How'd you know that?"

"It's not rocket science. There was that photo of you and Noah that made its way around the internet. I wasn't sure if it was real or fake."

"It was real," Olivia told her shortly.

"Well, I for one believe in true love," Regan said staunchly. "I bet you and Noah find a way to work things out."

"Thanks." But Olivia wasn't sure of that at all.

Back at home, newly inspired by the Halls' tidy, cheerful home, Olivia decided it was time to start her project of spiffing up Thorn Hill. She decided to make two lists: one for tasks she could do right away, and one for bigger projects that required money, supplies or additional help. She had made it through the kitchen, living room and front entranceway when her phone rang. Olivia smiled to see it was Noah calling. "Hey, handsome," she greeted him.

"Can you get away?"

Her pulse picked up. "Now?"

"At the cabin."

"I'll be there as soon as I can." She decided she could finish her list another time.

"Can't wait."

Olivia hung up and ran lightly up the stairs to her room to get ready. She tucked her list in the drawer of her bedside table, surprised to find she was looking forward to crossing items off. She was ready for her life to change.

"Why can't everything be this easy?" Olivia said a half hour later when Noah took her in his arms. It had been no problem to sneak across Turner land to Camila's old cabin. All the lights in the main house had been blazing, leaving the pastures dark and quiet. Noah's embrace tightened around her, and he rested his chin on her head. When she looked up, he grinned down at her.

"Because then we'd all be lazy."

"I'd like to be lazy for once."

"Me, too." Noah kissed her, and Olivia wrapped her arms around his neck. She loved how Noah's mouth tasted under hers. How his hands felt on her skin. How he revved her up and turned her world upside down whenever he was near.

Olivia sighed when they parted again. "I want to be with you all the time." She bit her lip, hoping that hadn't sounded too needy, and gasped in relief when he lifted her. Her legs around his waist, she let him carry her to what once had been Camila's bedroom and nearly cheered when she realized Camila had left her bed behind.

Who could blame her? With Carl's money she'd decorated her new ranch house with lovely new furniture.

Noah tossed her on the bed, and Olivia shrieked, then laughed when he leaped after her. He rolled her over on top of him. "Have your way with me," he commanded and lay back as if ready to let her do all the work.

Olivia didn't believe it, and she was right. The moment she began to unbutton his shirt, his hands came up to help her out of her blouse. He struggled with her bra while she wrestled with the button of his jeans. Laughing, she finally gave up. "Get those off," she ordered him while stripping out of the rest of her clothes.

"I could watch you all day," Noah told her as she made short work of her jeans and panties.

"Oh yeah?" She climbed back on top of him as he shimmied out of his clothes, clinging to him as he rolled around to get them off.

"Yeah." Noah gripped her hips, lifted her a few inches and moved her to a more advantageous spot, growling with pleasure when she moved against him. "You're beautiful."

"Do you think so?" She thought he was beautiful, too. His body hardened by work, scarred here and there and rugged, just like she liked him. She bent to kiss him, letting her breasts graze his chest. Noah moaned again.

"I didn't ask you about protection before," he said.

"Too late now," she joked and shrieked again when Noah sat up quickly. "I'm kidding," she told him. "I'm on the pill, and I've been checked out."

"Scared me." He pulled her back down again. "But if you'd gotten pregnant, I'd have done the right thing. You know that, right?"

Olivia wasn't sure how to answer that, and Noah was already nudging against her, urging her to let him inside her again.

"Olivia?" His voice was husky.

"Yeah, I guess I know that, but I hope you know that's a chance I wouldn't take. Not without a husband and a plan."

He stilled. Sighed a moment later. "I didn't mean—"

"Didn't you?" She hated to ruin the moment, but this was important.

"Yeah, I guess I did. But not because I think you're reckless. I just want you to know *I'm* not."

"Except you were," she pointed out.

"Yeah. Except I was."

"Ironic, huh?" she couldn't help adding. She wriggled again, reminding him of how they were touching each other.

"You're not going to let this slide, are you?"

"No."

"Fine." Noah began to move again. "You're right. When we made love, I was the reckless one. You were the careful one."

"Thank you."

"And you know what?" he asked, flipping her over again so that now he was on top. "I think I'm going to be reckless all over again."

Olivia gasped as Noah slid inside her and moaned

when he slid back out. Hell, he felt amazing, and she was so ready for him, she thought she'd lose her mind right away.

She loved that he could laugh at himself. Could joke with her.

Could make her feel like this.

He captured her hands and lifted them over her head, stroked into her so strongly she arched her back with happiness. As he worked in and out of her, Olivia gave in to the pleasure.

Noah looked at her like he wanted to memorize her as they moved together. Olivia met him thrust for thrust. Kissed him until the taste of him filled her senses.

She was all sensation. Tightening. Aching. Longing—until she exploded in ecstasy. Wave after wave of glorious delight washed through her, making her cry out again and again until Noah slammed against her, grunting his release.

When they finally collapsed, breathing hard, Olivia laughing with the sheer wonder of it all, she wished she never had to leave. How could anyone object to her being with this man? He was obviously meant for her.

In a flash of clarity, she realized she was going about this all wrong. She kept waiting for permission to follow her heart—from people who would never give it to her.

Instead she needed to make a decision. Which was more important—to be a Cooper or to be with Noah?

She didn't need to make up her mind right now, but she would soon, no matter what happened between their families.

Chapter Eleven

"**I** WAS BEGINNING to think you'd run out on me," Noah said bluntly when he took Brandon's call the next morning. He was in the stable getting ready for a ride, but this was more important. He'd parted reluctantly from Olivia last night after spending a couple of hours with her. It was getting harder and harder to let her leave.

"I wasn't due for a meeting until today."

Noah's grip on his phone tightened. "But you'd been checking in more often." He stroked a hand down Warning's neck. Would he see Olivia tonight?

"Fat lot of good that was doing me."

"Let's meet." He needed to see Brandon face to face.

"I'll be at Linda's Diner at one." Brandon hung up before Noah could suggest they meet somewhere else. Somewhere Christie wasn't.

"Hell, Warning. Can't one thing go right?"

Warning flicked an ear as if it was a pointless question. Noah had to agree. Life seemed full of trouble these days, but as he hopped up into the saddle and set Warning walking down a trail, his spirits lifted. He couldn't help think back to his time with Olivia last night. How sexy she'd been. How it had felt to be inside her.

He travelled north on a meandering trail, and when he got to the edge of the Ridley property, he decided to keep going. He and his siblings had explored this area as kids, of course, but it had been years since he'd reconnoitered here. Alone with his thoughts, the only sounds the call of a bird and the distant lowing of cattle back on his own spread, Noah relaxed. This was a wonderful property, he had to admit some time later when he'd traversed much of it. A perfect extension of the Flying W. Or Thorn Hill.

As if he'd conjured up one of Thorn Hill's inhabitants with his thoughts, he spotted Steel Cooper on horseback several hundred yards away. Noah reined in Warning, considering his options, but it was too late to try to slip away, even if he'd wanted to. Steel had seen him.

Steel reined in, too, and when he realized Noah was heading his way, he came to meet him.

They paused when they were only a few feet apart, both of them scanning their surroundings as if they were simply out on a morning's ride together.

"It's good land," Steel finally said, surprising Noah, who'd been prepared for accusations.

"That it is."

"Heard you're raising money for the library."

"That's right. Least we can do. It's a shame the way it's falling apart."

Steel gave him a steady look, and Noah wondered if he knew his sister's part in the matter. "It is a shame."

"We'll get the water back where it belongs in the creek right after the fundraiser."

Steel nodded.

Noah wished he could read the other man's mind. He'd expected arguments. Demands they set the water to rights earlier than the weekend. Not this calm acceptance.

"It's going to get bad," Steel said suddenly. "You know that, right?"

Noah's stomach twisted. Bad? What did that mean?

"The drought. This isn't the usual kind. It goes deeper than that."

"How do you know?" Noah asked reluctantly.

Steel shrugged. Looked a little sheepish. "I feel it. It's in the smell of the wind."

Noah glanced at him curiously. He hadn't thought Steel had that kind of feeling in him. He wished he could suggest their families see the drought through together but doubted the Coopers would take to that idea.

"People are going to get hurt," Steel added.

Noah stilled. "Is that a threat?"

Steel flashed him a look of disgust. "If I was threatening you, you'd know it, Turner."

"Look, I—"

"Next Sunday. Creek back to normal, or there'll be trouble." Steel dug his heels into his mount's sides and galloped away.

Noah could only watch him, feeling he'd missed an opportunity. He turned Warning toward home, too.

OLIVIA WAS COMING out of the grocery store the next day when Lance flagged her down. He was marching angrily across the parking lot, his hair slipping into his eyes. He cocked his hat back, brushed his hair from his face and shook a fistful of newspaper at her.

"Did you see this?"

"No, what is it?" Olivia had to admit she rarely read the local paper these days. Everything was online, and the Chance Creek grapevine worked far faster than the printing press did for local gossip. She was surprised Lance was talking to her; he hadn't said more than two words since the day she'd watched him drive away from Caroline's house.

"Read it!" He pushed the paper into her hands, paced off and spun around to pace back.

Olivia realized he'd given her the letters to the editor page. She began to read the first one, and her fingers tightened around the pages.

Dear Editor,

I must say I'm sorely disappointed to hear of the changes coming to Chance Creek High. That school stands like a beacon in my mind to the best days of my life…

The letter went on, gushing about the good old days when the writer's life was full of studies and dances. It ended with a diatribe against brainwashing children with lessons on computers and how the school was headed for a bad end.

"What a crank," she said.

"There's more. Keep reading."

Olivia jumped to the next letter. It also lamented the proposed changes to the school and explained how Chance Creek High's old-fashioned values had made a lasting impression on the author's life. There was a third, a fourth, a fifth—

Olivia looked up. "I don't believe—"

"It's a setup," Lance exploded. "Those Turners did this. I know they did."

She shook her head. "It's just people afraid of change, that's all. We already won; the project is going ahead."

"It's not too late for them to shut it down," Lance pointed out. "What if they change everyone's mind? Huh? We need that property." He snatched the paper out of her hand. "I've been patient, like you asked me to be. The Turners are still stealing our water."

"Just until next Sunday. I told you they're helping the library. Marta needs that money, Lance."

"They aren't helping the library." His tone was scathing. "They're trying to win the prize. Stop being so damn naive."

Olivia watched him go, her stomach tightening into a knot, then dropped her groceries in the truck and veered off toward Linda's Diner. She needed a cup of tea before she went home.

Was Lance right?

Noah had been quick to volunteer to help raise

funds for the library. Was he doing it out of the goodness of his heart? Or to steal the Ridley property away from her family? Maybe she was naive. She hadn't even considered the second possibility, although it was staring her in the face. She couldn't believe the man who'd made love to her so passionately last night would do anything to hurt her, though. She had hated to leave the cabin and go home—and Noah hadn't wanted to let her leave, either.

Inside the small restaurant, she immediately spotted Noah and made her way over to him. She might as well ask the hard questions right now. She dimly recognized Brandon Sykes, one of Noah's parolees, sitting across from him, but she pressed on.

"Noah, I need to talk to—"

"Noah! Did you see my letter? They printed it!" Coach Latham rushed up to the table waving a paper, and Olivia stiffened. Coach Latham had written in? It must have been one of the ones she hadn't read. "Never had a letter in the paper before," he went on. "Wouldn't have ever done it if it wasn't for you!"

Olivia stilled and caught a flash of consternation in Noah's eyes.

Had he been involved in the letter-writing campaign, after all?

Olivia stepped back. Noah reached toward her, but she held out a hand to ward him off, going cold, then flushing hot as the reality of what he'd done hit her.

He was working against her. Against her family. Just when the Coopers had finally found a way to gain some positive traction here.

This is about the Ridley property, nothing else, a little voice in her mind said, but Olivia didn't care. Whatever it was about, it was underhanded and mean. And he'd done it while wooing her, while sweeping her off her feet—stealing away and making love to her—

He didn't care about her at all, did he? He just wanted his family to win.

He'd been pulling one over on her, and she should have seen it coming. Thirteen years ago Maya had pretended to be her best friend, right up until she'd discovered the evidence that put Olivia's father in jail. Now Noah was pulling the exact same move, and Olivia had fallen for it all over again.

Shame flared through her, heating her skin. How dare he? How dare he mess with her that way?

"Olivia!" Noah called after her, but she was already walking out.

Out the door. Onto the street. Out of his life.

Chapter Twelve

"QUIT WIGGLING," ELLA Hall told Olivia for the tenth time as she fussed with her hair, doing something complicated and stylish for the gala. The past week and a half had gone by in a blur, and Olivia felt like a wind-up doll, performing all her duties with an automatic eye on the details, fooling everyone—but at the end of it having no recollection of what she'd done. Her heart hurt as badly as it had the day she'd realized Noah was playing her. She'd ignored his texts and calls since then. He'd fooled her good, and she didn't need any more pain in her life.

She figured tonight would make or break the school project. Either they'd solidify support for the upgrade, thanks to Fulsom and his friends' commitment to it, or they'd lose ground. Meanwhile the letters to the editor were undermining their efforts.

The Turners had done their homework well, she thought bitterly. Letters against the upgrade outweighed the ones for it three to one, and that wasn't even counting the extra letters pinned to telephone poles downtown that appeared mysteriously each morning. Only in the last day or so had the tide begun to turn as those not beholden to the Turners realized the work they'd looked forward to at the high school might not happen if the naysayers had their way.

"Put the letters out of your mind," Ella told her. "Don't take it personally. This is business, and business can be cutthroat. Tonight it's your turn to do your worst."

"I was kind of hoping to do my *best*," Olivia told her.

Ella laughed. "Well, break a leg and all that."

"I'm nervous," Olivia admitted. "What if Fulsom and his cronies hate my family? Everyone else seems to."

"No, they don't. When Fulsom and his friends meet you, they'll think you're a charming young lady fighting the good fight for the next generation. They're going to be impressed that you got someone like Carl on your side."

"That was all Virginia," Olivia said. "She bribed him with a ranch."

"What does she think now that he married an almost honorary Turner?"

"She says Cooper blood is stronger and that Camila won't be able to help becoming one of us."

"But Carl isn't even a Cooper," Ella protested with a laugh.

"Evidently Cooper blood is contagious. You'd better watch out."

Ella just smiled. "I'm glad we've gotten to know each other," she said.

"Me, too," Olivia said, touched. "I'd never have gotten this all off the ground without you." If it hadn't been for Ella and the others, her shame and disappointment over Noah's betrayal would have crushed her. She hadn't told them what happened, but she'd let slip she wasn't seeing him anymore. They'd been tactful and kind, kept her occupied with plans and fussed over her until she felt a little better.

A little.

She wasn't sure she'd ever feel herself again.

"Sure you would. You sell yourself short a lot, you know that?" Ella surveyed her work and added one more hairpin. "In my experience women do that when something bad happened when they were young. They forget they're allowed to move forward and leave whatever it was behind."

Olivia wished wholeheartedly she could leave her trouble behind. But it seemed to be chasing her. Poisoning everything new and good she touched.

"I guess," she said to Ella. She couldn't believe the transformation Ella had worked on her. She wished she could make as big a change inside.

"If you need to talk—or need help with anything else, just ask," Ella said gently. "Whatever is going on, Olivia, you're not alone."

Her words struck too close to home because these days Olivia felt more alone than ever.

"Thanks," she said. "I'd better go check everything one last time."

"You look stunning."

"I don't even recognize myself." Olivia looked in the mirror one last time. She wore a deep blue Regency-style gown Ella had helped her pick out from the options Alice Reed, a local seamstress and costume designer, had shown her. The old-fashioned dress suited her, and she kept turning to see it from all angles.

"You're Olivia Cooper. The lady of the hour. One of Chance Creek's first-tier citizens," Ella proclaimed.

Hardly, Olivia thought. She wasn't a first-tier citizen. She was a Cooper.

And if she failed tonight she could lose everything.

"WHY ARE YOU being such a bear today?" Maya asked when Noah snapped at her for moving too slowly. She and Stella were helping him set up everything for the tubing fundraiser, which would begin at ten sharp the next morning, and they were both working hard. They didn't deserve to be the recipients of his ire.

But Liam was AWOL, and that steamed him—he needed another man to lug some of the heavy equipment out near the creek. Brandon hadn't shown up, either, even though he'd said he would. Noah had offered to pay him for two days' work—today to set up and tomorrow to help run the fundraiser. He'd thought Brandon would jump at the chance to earn a little cash. He could scarcely afford to part with it. Brandon was overdue by several hours.

He obviously wasn't that hard up.

Which begged the question: How was he making money these days?

At their last meeting, Brandon had admitted he still hadn't found work, but he didn't seem as worried as he had before. He said he'd been helping out his mom. There was something about him, something different.

Noah wasn't sure what to make of it.

He'd convinced several of Chance Creek's restaurants to sell food at the fundraiser and donate part of their receipts. The women at Fila's—including Camila—would be arriving early tomorrow to set up a food tent, and the folks from DelMonaco's were bringing their huge outdoor grill so they could sell hamburgers, hot dogs and barbecued chicken.

"I need to get this stage built," Noah answered his sister finally. "It's a two-man job."

His sisters exchanged a look. "We're not exactly helpless," Stella told him.

Noah took a deep breath. "I know. Hell, sorry. It's just—where the hell is Liam?" And Brandon, more to the point.

"Liam's done some good work this week," Stella chided him. "Maybe you need to give him a break."

Good work? He'd managed to screw up things between him and Olivia, Noah wanted to say. But his sisters wouldn't see that as a problem. Besides, he couldn't push all the blame onto Liam. After all, he'd helped convince the coach to write in.

When did he start playing fast and loose with the concepts of right and wrong? Brandon would have a field day if he could see his parole officer now. The letter-writing campaign was unacceptable, period.

Losing Olivia was like losing the sun. The world was a bleak, inhospitable place without her, and it was everything he could do to simply go through with his normal activities. He thought about her constantly. Dreamed about her. Somehow he had to make this right, but first he needed to pull off this fundraiser—

For Olivia's sake.

Would she ever forgive him? He wondered what she was doing now. Getting ready for the gala tonight?

He wished he could be there.

"I guess we'd better get to it."

"Sure thing, boss," Maya drawled.

He'd already loaded his truck with the wood they needed for the stage. Noah went back to get it, and by the time he'd driven out near the creek where Maya and Stella waited for him, he'd gotten himself in hand. Liam would turn up sooner or later, and the work would get done. He should be grateful Jed had left them alone today. He didn't think he could stand it if his uncle had decided to oversee the process.

"How many people do you think we'll get tomorrow?" Stella asked.

"I don't know." He hadn't exactly been thinking straight when he'd picked the day after the Coopers' gala for his fundraising event, but then they were targeting a different crowd. It would be grownups at the gala tonight. Families with young children at the Creek tomorrow. He hoped it would work out. "Hopefully enough to pay the library's bills."

"What gave you the inspiration to fix the library,

anyway? It's a great idea," she hurried to add. "Should balance the books a little between us and the Coopers."

Noah chose his words carefully. No need to mention Olivia. "I realized how bad it has gotten, and we needed a project we could handle. We can do a lot of the work the library needs ourselves once we have the supplies paid for. It'll be impressive when we're done without breaking the bank."

"My brother, the good Samaritan," Stella teased him.

"I'm doing my best."

He got to work framing the stage and refused to let his sisters bait him, although they kept trying. The afternoon waned, and when his stomach rumbled, Noah realized they'd worked through dinner.

"Guess that's good enough for now," he was saying when his phone buzzed. It was Camila's number, and he quickly answered it. "Hey, Camila. What's up? We're still on for tomorrow, right?" He didn't know what he'd do if she backed out of running the food court. She and Fila had volunteered to take charge of the vendors.

"Of course. We're all set," she answered. "But you've got a problem. Thought you'd want to know."

"What's that?"

Stella turned his way at the tone of his voice. Maya looked up from where she was packing away their tools.

"It's Liam. He's at Rafters with a bunch of his pals. They're drunk."

"Drunk?" It was barely seven o'clock.

"That's right. A friend told me. She thought I might

want to know, seeing as I'm with Carl."

"I don't follow."

"They're talking loud enough for everyone to hear. They're going to disrupt the gala, Noah. And that's not cool."

He couldn't blame her for being angry. It was Carl's reputation on the line, after all. He'd gotten the funding together for the high school's update—these were his friends and business peers attending the function.

"Hell. When does the thing start?"

"In less than an hour. You've got to stop them. I don't want trouble between us, but if they ruin tonight, I don't know how I'll forgive them."

"I understand completely. I'll take care of it," Noah promised her. He hung up.

"What's going on?" Stella asked.

"It's Liam. He's planning to ruin Olivia's gala." When his sisters didn't immediately react, Noah lost his cool. "Her *gala*. The party she's busted her butt to pull together. Hell, I get we're enemies, but that's going too far."

"If Fulsom and his people pull out, we're that much closer to winning," Stella pointed out, but he could tell she wasn't comfortable with the notion.

"Is that the way you want to win?" Noah demanded. "By humiliating Olivia—and Carl Whitfield—and all the ladies who run Westfield Manor? Heck, Ella Hall is helping to organize this shindig. I thought you were her friend."

Stella shut her eyes, color staining her cheeks. "I am.

God, this whole situation is bringing out the worst in me."

"In all of us," Maya said quietly.

"This isn't who I want to be," Noah told them. "Will you two help me stop Liam or not? He's probably already on his way there."

Stella and Maya exchanged a look. "Of course. But what are we going to do? If we confront him there, we'll just make a scene," Stella said.

"Wait—I've got an idea." Maya grinned impishly. "A good one."

"IT's BEAUTIFUL," REGAN Hall said.

"It is," Ella agreed.

They stood in the foyer with Olivia at Westfield Manor, ready to greet their guests. Musicians were tuning their instruments in the ballroom. The distant clatter of dishes in the kitchen announced the caterers had everything in hand.

Olivia tried to give off an air of composed satisfaction, but inside butterflies careened around her belly, and her palms were so sweaty she'd need to excuse herself to wipe them off before shaking anyone's hands.

"I can't believe how it all came together," she said. With the Hall women's help—and the women at Westfield, too—plus Carl's deep pockets to smooth the way, the party was set to be one of the swankiest affairs Chance Creek had ever seen.

About thirty guests were flying in with Fulsom. Other donors were coming from around the country.

The school board, teachers and staff had been invited, as well as other town dignitaries they needed to get on their side.

"Are you okay?" Ella asked, her concern clear.

"I think I'm going to faint," Olivia confessed.

"You won't faint. Just wait, the minute the first few guests arrive, everything will be fine. It's always worst right before the event begins," Ella assured her.

Right on cue the doorbell rang, and Olivia jumped.

"Go on. Open it," Regan whispered.

Olivia took a calming breath and did just that. She was relieved when it turned out to be a party of single teachers from the school who'd come together. Dressed in period costume, they clustered around her, chatting excitedly. Olivia knew most of them, and when she saw their awed reaction to the decorations in the beautiful ballroom, she relaxed a little. Soon the doorbell rang again, this time opening to several board members, followed by a couple of members of the Chamber of Commerce. Soon the ballroom was filled with talking, smiling and laughing people, all looking like they'd stepped out of the pages of a history book.

"See?" Ella said. "It's better already, isn't it?"

Olivia had to admit it was. In fact, the only thing missing was—

Noah.

Who was going to be missing from here on in, she reminded herself. He'd been fooling her. Acting like he cared while helping to recruit people to stop their school improvement project in its tracks.

She wasn't going to think about him tonight.

Soon she didn't have time to think about anything except caring for her guests, especially once Martin Fulsom, the billionaire helping to fund the project, showed up with a camera crew. She kept an eye on the waiters the caterers had brought and made sure everyone had a full glass and hors d'oeuvres to nibble on. When the orchestra struck up a lively tune, couples began to dance. Olivia spared a moment to wish Noah was here to dance with, then scolded herself. She had to forget him. Besides, she needed to tend to her guests.

As the ballroom filled, it grew warm, and Olivia made sure all the windows were open and even propped open the back door to make sure air was circulating. A half hour later she was hot, breathless and ready to sit down. She was threading through the crowd out of the ballroom, hoping to hide away in the kitchen for a moment of peace, when she heard raised voices.

Male voices.

Olivia pushed through another knot of people.

Liam Turner and several of his friends, conspicuous in their modern jeans and boots, were clustered near the orchestra.

"How'd they get in?" she hissed at Regan, who'd just come to investigate, too.

"I didn't open the door for them," Regan hissed back, going up on tiptoe to try to see what was happening.

"The back door. They must have slipped in. Those monsters—they're going to ruin everything."

"I'll find Mason," Regan told her, but Olivia knew there was no time to waste. The California guests had been having a good time, but if they saw what a hick town this could be, they'd pull their money and run.

"Must be fun to have enough money to ride rough-shod over a whole town," Liam yelled. Was he drunk?

He was definitely drunk.

A murmur of surprise ran through the crowd. Olivia shoved her way closer to him. "Sorry," she muttered. "Excuse me. Sorry."

"Read the paper," one of Liam's friends called out. "It's all right there in the letters section. We don't want these upgrades. Never did."

Olivia caught sight of two California guests exchanging a look. One of them drained his glass of champagne and looked around, as if seeking a way out.

"Liam!" Olivia finally reached him. "Get out of here, and take your thug friends with you!" She took hold of his arm, but he shrugged her off.

"Thug friends? Are you kidding me?" He raised his voice. "You Coopers are the thugs. Always have been."

His friends pushed back to clear a ring around them. Olivia knew everyone was looking.

"You're drunk," she said as calmly as she could. "I know you're trying to ruin this for me because you don't like my family, but I'm not interested in fighting you. I'm interested in helping this town."

"That's rich," Liam told her. "Last I heard you were only interested in breaking and entering. It's a wonder you don't have a rap sheet a mile long."

Another murmur ran through the crowd, and Olivia blinked back the sting of tears. She'd known it was too much to ask for this night to go right.

"There you are," Stella cried, suddenly appearing by Liam's side. "Oh, my gosh, when we saw you'd gotten out, we were so scared!" She spoke in the over-bright tone one might use with a senile relative or very small child. Olivia wasn't sure what was going on. By the look of it, neither was Liam.

He frowned down at his sister. "What are you—?"

"Sorry, everyone. We are *so* sorry. He likes to wander sometimes," Maya called out, taking Liam's other arm. "We try to keep an eye on him, but he's a wily one." She shook a finger at him.

Liam's face went a mottled purple color. "What the hell—?"

Noah broke through the crowd from the other side. "Nothing to see here, folks. Just a family matter. We'll get my brother out of your way. Come on, Liam. Let's go back home. You know you're not supposed to be out on your own."

Olivia bit back a surprised laugh as Noah and his sisters dragged a flabbergasted Liam out the back through the kitchen. His friends, as shocked as everyone else, melted away quickly, slipping out the back as well. Olivia followed them to make sure they all left, and when they did she closed and locked the back door.

She returned through a crowd of the out-of-town guests. "It's so sad," she murmured, loud enough for several of them to hear. "Before he hit his head he was destined for wonderful things."

"Ah," one of the female guests said and turned to pass on this information to another one. Soon the room was brimming with music and laughter again.

Olivia breathed a huge sigh of relief when Fulsom pushed his way to where the scene had taken place. He was a handsome older man with a loud voice that commanded attention. Like everyone else he was dressed in period costume and appeared as comfortable in the old-fashioned clothes as if he'd been born to them. "Wait, hold on," he was saying to no one in particular. "We didn't get that on film. Can we recreate it for the camera?"

Olivia slid away before he noticed her, trusting he wouldn't be able to make that happen.

"That was a close call," Regan said when they ran into each other again.

"Good thing Noah and his sisters came to help," Ella agreed.

It was. Olivia didn't know what to make of it—or the fact Stella and Maya had intervened, too. She and Maya hadn't seen eye to eye since Maya told the sheriff what she had seen in Olivia's barn. Olivia had always thought Stella seemed reasonable enough—but not when it came to Olivia's family. Too bad they were on opposite sides of this stupid feud.

But they hadn't been tonight. Both sisters had stepped up and helped her.

Olivia wondered what tomorrow would bring.

And what would go wrong next.

Chapter Thirteen

"**L**IAM'S COMING." STELLA pointed back toward the house, and Noah, carrying several inner tubes in his arms, paused to look, as shocked as she was at their brother's appearance. Liam had broken away from them as soon as they got out of the manor the previous evening, probably to return to the bar. They'd let him go, confident he wasn't about to go back to Olivia's gala after that humiliation. Noah hadn't heard him come home until two in the morning. He had expected Liam to sulk in his room or take off for a few days. Instead he was striding toward them.

Noah braced for an attack. He didn't have to wait long.

"I want answers," Liam began before he was within twenty feet of them. "What was that last night?"

"I could ask you the same thing. What did you think you were doing?" Noah stood his ground. Turners weren't troublemakers, and what Liam had tried to do at the gala was out of line whether or not they were feuding with the Coopers.

"I was saving our ranch. We can't let those Coopers get the Ridley property. Am I the only one who realizes that?"

"No, but we're not going to win that way. Olivia worked hard to set up that party. So did the Hall women and the people at Westfield. You wanted to trample over half the town so we get our way? What kind of a place are we going to live in when this is all over? You want everyone to hate us? You want to trade places with the Coopers?"

Liam balled his fists. "What does it matter what kind of a town it is if we're not even living in it anymore? If we've lost our ranch because you saved the Coopers' shot at the Ridley property—"

It was the same old argument, and Noah saw with blinding clarity it would go on and on unless he did something drastic.

"I love her," he burst out. "Okay? I love Olivia Cooper!"

Liam gaped at him. "Wh-what?"

"I love her," he said quietly. "I get that it's not convenient. And it's not what I'm supposed to do, but it's what I feel, and there's no changing it."

He thought Liam would yell at him some more, but his brother scraped his palm over his face and then lifted both hands in a gesture of defeat. "So, what? We just give up? Let them have everything?"

"No. We still fight for what we need, but we play to our strengths, not our weaknesses. I used to be proud of our family because we were the good guys. That's what I want to be. Don't you?"

"Thought that's what we were."

"Good guys don't ruin someone else's gala," Noah said. "They don't destroy someone's livelihood. A good recommendation from a man like Fulsom could put Westfield Manor on the map."

After a moment Liam nodded. "Yeah," he said quietly. "All right, you got me there. Was going to make an ass out of myself. Which you managed to do anyway," he added with a touch of bitterness.

Stella chuckled. "You should have seen your face."

"It's going to be hard to live that down," Liam muttered.

"I think it'll be easier if we donate a lot of money to the library at the end of today," Noah pointed out.

"And volunteer our time to do the renovations it needs," Maya added. "We're not giving up, Liam. We're going to fix the library, which will get us in the running for the Ridley property, at least. Then we'll see what else we can do. You going to help or not?"

He looked at her, then at Stella. "You two are fine with this? Our brother hooking up with a Cooper?"

"More than hooking up," Noah asserted. "I'm pretty serious about her."

"I guess I'm more of a romantic than I thought," Stella said softly. "I'm afraid you're going to get hurt," she told Noah. "But if Olivia loves you back, I can't stand in your way."

Noah couldn't tell what Maya was thinking.

"I guess I can live with it," she finally said. "But I'm not going to get all chummy with Steel and Lance." She shivered. "Those guys scare me."

"You don't need to get chummy with them," Noah said, but he noticed Stella had a funny look on her face. She caught him watching her.

"Have you ever noticed everyone's afraid of Steel, but no one knows why?" she asked.

Noah thought that over. She was right; he didn't know of anything Steel had actually done to anyone. He'd heard plenty of rumors, though.

"If Noah marries Olivia, she'll be a Turner," Maya mused. "Then we'll outnumber them."

Liam turned thoughtful. "Hey, that's a good point. That's one way to beat them." He grinned suddenly. "Never thought of that before."

"That mean you're going to go after Tory Cooper?" Stella teased him.

"I haven't seen that girl since she was a teenager." But he was still smiling. "Guess I'd have to hunt her down."

"That leaves you to marry Steel," Noah told Stella. "Better get right on that."

"Fat chance!" Stella laughed. "Can you think of two people less suited for each other?"

"Yeah—me and Lance," Maya quipped.

"Besides, if Maya and I hooked up with Steel and Lance, we'd be Coopers."

"You'd both better stay away from those guys," Liam warned.

"All right, back to work," Noah said before things got too out of hand. "That looks like Fila and Camila, right on time. Looks like they brought Ned and Carl to help. Good thing we stopped you last night, or none of them would have come."

"All right, enough preaching. What can I do?" Liam asked. "Those tables need setting up?"

Noah hid his relief. Liam was back on his side, despite the bombshell he'd dropped. "Yeah. We thought we'd group them over there where the food tents will be."

"Sounds good." But he hung back while their sisters moved away. Noah looked at him expectantly, and Liam leaned in to speak quietly. "I heard something down at Rafters last night. About Olivia. Some guy was in there, pretty drunk. Said she'd stolen his money and his girl. He was talking a lot of shit about what he wanted to do to her."

"Devon Host."

"You know about all that?"

"I know she helped Caroline Selwich get away from him. He hit her."

Liam whistled. "Sounds like he got what he deserved then. Could be trouble, though."

"Yeah." *Stole his money.* Noah pushed away his unease. As far as he knew, all Olivia had taken was jewelry and a photo album, both of which belonged to Caroline. She'd told him Devon had gotten Caroline to put him on the title of her house. Obviously, Caroline was afraid to go home. She'd just wanted a few of her things.

Stole his money.

Or was there more to that escapade than she'd let on? What else had she taken?

She'd run away from him when she'd seen him parking his truck.

"Thanks for letting me know," he said to Liam. "I'll look into it."

"Sure thing."

OLIVIA WAS SITTING at the kitchen table, picking at a toaster waffle and thumbing through the updates on her phone, when she came across a photo Carl had posted of Camila and Fila setting up their food tent for Noah's tubing fundraiser. Ned was clowning in the background. All of them looked like they were having loads of fun.

Olivia missed the days when Carl was just like another brother on her ranch. He'd evened things out around here in a way she hadn't appreciated until he was gone. He was well-read, a genius at business affairs but never too busy to chat with her. A man like him could have considered her a country bumpkin, but he'd never condescended to her. He'd treated her as if they'd come from the same background, and she'd gotten a glimpse of a wider world than she'd realized existed before.

She hovered her thumb over the photo, then clicked to like it. Why not? Carl and Camila had been nothing but kind toward her, and they weren't any part of this feud. They were there to support the library.

Which had been her idea in the first place.

If she was honest, it was killing her not to be taking part. Last night she'd been angry enough she hadn't cared, and she'd been far too busy with the gala to think much about it, but then Noah and his sisters had stopped Liam from ruining the evening, and she still didn't know what to make of that.

A text pinged, and she pulled it up. It was Riley Rudman, the proprietor of the bed-and-breakfast at Westfield Manor.

Mind if we take your guests to the tubing fundraiser? There's a hold-up with their flight.

Olivia's stomach sank. She'd assumed Fulsom's party was gone already. Many of them had stayed overnight at the manor. Others had stayed in town. Riley's husband, Boone, was supposed to oversee transporting them to the airport early this morning. She wasn't prepared to entertain them for another day. Olivia hesitated, but what could she say? She didn't know what she'd do with them otherwise.

Sure. But... isn't that a little rustic for them? Did they bring their swimsuits?

She meant it as a joke, but Riley texted back quickly, *Actually, they did. One of them overheard people talking about it last night, and they all want to go. You could come, too.*

I'd better not, Olivia texted back. *Have fun, though. And thanks so much!*

We'll get them to their plane when it's ready. Don't worry about a thing!

Olivia pushed her plate away. She couldn't help worry about the idea of a group of Silicon Valley types tubing down an irrigation canal. But Carl would be there, and he was the one who'd spearheaded the donor drive. He knew these people. He'd take care of it if things went awry.

Still, this fundraiser was supposed to help the library, which she loved, so when her phone pinged again, she grabbed it impatiently.

Your boy wants you bad, Camila had texted, adding a photo of Noah looking contemplatively at Pittance Creek.

Olivia wasn't in the mood for teasing. Not when she and Noah didn't have a chance anymore. How did Camila know about their relationship, anyway?

This day was going from bad to worse.

Her phone rang, and when she saw it was Camila calling, Olivia nearly didn't answer. She couldn't fathom what the woman was up to.

But she couldn't ignore her, either.

"Hello?" she said when she'd answered it.

"You need to get over here," Camila said without preamble. "We've got a crowd here, and it's nuts. We need more help."

"No one wants me there."

"Yes, they do." Camila's voice became more muffled. "Noah certainly does."

"What is it with you about Noah?" Camila's teasing was like sandpaper over a wound.

"Stella came to talk to me. She told me Noah's broken up over what happened between you. I think she was hoping I'd pass the message on."

"What message?"

"Noah made a big announcement to his family this morning. He said he loves you, and he's going to be with you no matter what they think."

Olivia's mouth opened, but no sound came out. She swallowed and tried again. "Stella told you that?"

"Uh-huh. And she said she's down with it."

Olivia blinked. "Down with it."

"Or something like that. You know what I mean. She's on your side. She said..." Camila paused. "She said she's never seen Noah look like that. And she knew she couldn't stand in your way. She wants him to be happy. Olivia, you've got to run with this if you care about him at all. I know what it's like when people don't want you to be with the man you love. It's hard to go against your friends, but—you only get one chance. Grab hold of it."

"I don't know..." Olivia gripped the phone so hard she was afraid it would shatter. "What if she's wrong?"

"What if she's right? Come help us with the fundraiser. What do you have to lose?"

Her pride, Olivia thought. Noah had betrayed her, after she'd reached out and helped his family gain a chance to win the Founder's Prize. Sure, she'd done it so the library would be saved, but still—

"Olivia, at least hear him out," Camila said.

Olivia took a breath and decided she could do that. She had nothing to lose at this point; she'd already given up on finding happiness.

"Even if you don't want to be with Noah, you still need to come. We're swamped!" Camila pressed. "Come on. You and Carl are still friends, right? Even if he married an honorary Turner?"

Olivia had to smile. "Yes, of course we're still

friends."

"Then get your butt over here."

"Fine. I'll be there as soon as I can."

"That's more like it."

Olivia pocketed her phone and turned to find Steel watching her.

"Where are you going?"

"To the Flying W. To help with the library fundraiser." Olivia lifted her chin. She wouldn't let Steel stop her, either.

He grabbed his truck keys from the set of hooks by the kitchen door.

"What are you doing?" she demanded.

"Driving you."

"OH, MY GOD." Maya straightened from where she'd bent to pick up a load of inner tubes to throw in the truck bed and drive back to the starting point. She and Noah had been in motion for more than an hour keeping up with the demand. "Will you look at that? What are *they* doing here?"

Olivia, Steel and Lance were striding toward them. Olivia was scanning the crowd of wet, happy tubers who were climbing out of the irrigation canal and heading back toward the start of the run. Noah dropped the pile of tubes he was carrying and went to meet her. When she spotted him, she faltered but kept coming.

"Olivia. Lance. Steel," Noah greeted them. Liam came to stand by his side, and Noah tensed, but his brother didn't say anything.

"What's going on?" Stella walked over from where she'd been talking to a group of kids.

"Camila called, said you could use a hand," Olivia said when she came near. "Steel decided to come with me. Lance, too."

"We could use help," Noah said.

"But we don't need any fighting." Stella looked Steel up and down.

He held her gaze. "We're not looking to fight."

"Lance? Does that go for you, too?" Maya asked.

Lance looked surprised she'd singled him out. "Uh… Yeah. I'm not here to fight." He flushed a little. Maya looked pleased she'd rattled him.

Stella turned to Liam. "Can you say the same thing?"

"I'm not going to start anything." Liam scowled.

"Are you sure?" Olivia asked him.

"Ah, hell," Liam said. "Guess I owe you an apology about last night. Got carried away."

After a moment Olivia nodded.

"I'm sorry, too," Noah told her, "about those letters—"

"No, that was my fault, too," Liam cut him off. "I had the idea. Jed helped me execute. We didn't give Noah much choice."

Olivia nodded again. "Water under the bridge," she said evenly. "What can we do to help?"

"Camila and Fila are pretty busy," Noah told her. Olivia wasn't meeting his eye. He wasn't forgiven yet, but at least she was here.

"Okay." She hurried off. A moment later Maya went back to collecting inner tubes, and Lance followed right behind, leaving Noah with Steel—and Stella.

Steel folded his arms over his chest. "You treat my sister right."

"I will. Promise." Noah understood suddenly that Steel was standing in for Olivia's father—and that he meant to take the job seriously. "I care about her—a lot. I won't let any harm come to her."

Steel held his gaze and nodded once, then turned to join the others loading the tubes into the truck.

"Come on, Steel," Stella said suddenly. "You can help us with the inner tubes."

Steel turned to her. Stella met his gaze. Held it.

Steel shrugged. "Lead the way."

Noah watched them go. Had Olivia's brother just given him permission to woo her?

Things were looking up.

IT HAD BEEN years since Olivia's time as a waitress in Idaho, and she'd forgotten how much fun a serving job could be. She kept the orders flowing between Fila and Camila, who were cooking up a storm, and the customers waiting to eat. Mia Matheson was working the register, so it was Olivia's job to run from counter to grill, and she talked to more residents of Chance Creek in a single hour than she had in the years she'd been back.

To her surprise, most people chatted unconcernedly with her, like they might do with anyone, and Olivia began to wonder if it had been her own attitude that had scared people away previously.

When Sylvia Atherton told her, "You should come join the quilting circle at Edna's Odds and Ends," the local fabric shop Olivia had never entered in her life, she thought she might faint.

"Pretty young thing like that doesn't want to quilt," Sylvia's friend Joyce told her. "She's too busy for handicrafts. Wait until she's old like us."

"I'm not old," Sylvia shushed her, "and Olivia can make up her own mind, can't you?"

"Um... sure," Olivia said. "I'll give it a try. Probably won't be any good at it, though."

"It's easier than you think." Sylvia picked up her order, and the two women went off happily.

Olivia looked around to see if anyone had overheard them, but no one seemed to be paying any attention. In fact, for once there was a lull between customers.

"I'm going to run to use the bathroom," she told Mia. "I'll be quick."

"You'd better be. Don't leave me alone with the hungry hordes."

Olivia hurried off, knowing Mia was right; she'd have to be quick if she didn't want customers piling up at the booth. She exchanged greetings with a half-dozen people as she headed toward the porta-potties set up in a nearby field and waved to Noah and Steel, who were helping to gather up inner tubes while Maya and Lance looked on.

Focusing on getting back to the food tent as soon as

she could, she quickened her pace but yelped when Devon Host stepped out from behind another booth to block her path.

Olivia tried to sidestep around him, suddenly cold though the day was hot. She'd figured Devon would be furious about the missing lottery ticket and cash, but how on earth had he known she—

He grabbed her arm, lifted his shirt and showed her the pistol tucked into his waistband.

Olivia's breath whooshed out of her lungs. He couldn't mean he'd use that thing in this kind of crowd. But even as she thought it, she knew he would. The man's jittery, brittle energy made it all too clear he was on something and didn't care what happened next.

"Let me go!" Olivia pulled back as he began to drag her forward.

"You'd better cooperate."

"Or what?" As if she didn't know. Devon shook his head, scanned the crowd, spotted Regan walking toward the creek, smiling and waving at everyone she knew, and pointed at her, cocked his finger and pretended to shoot. His gaze shifted to Ellie Donaldson, laughing with several other older women Olivia knew, and did it again.

Olivia got the message. If she didn't play ball with him, someone would get hurt.

Someone innocent.

And it would be her fault.

"What do you want?" she demanded as he dragged her toward the field past the porta-potties where people had parked their vehicles.

"What do you think I want? Where's Caroline? Where's my lottery ticket?"

Relief flooded Olivia. So he hadn't found Caroline yet. She hoped her friend's family continued to cover for her. "I don't know."

"Little bitch, you think I believe you? Caroline's always talking about you. I told her not to hang out with a Cooper. I was right; you're a bad influence." He shook her and kept going. Olivia stumbled as she went, trying to slow him down.

"I haven't spoken to Caroline in ages." That was stretching it, but they hadn't spoken in days.

"You're lying." He picked up his pace. "When I'm done with you, you'll regret you ever interfered."

Desperation seized Olivia, but she didn't know what to do. Devon clearly felt he had nothing to lose, and she worried he meant to take her and everyone else he could with him. If she ran, he'd shoot her. If she escaped, he'd shoot someone else. They were covering the ground too fast. If he got her into his truck—

"Devon," she begged. "Think what you're doing. You don't really care about Caroline. I know you don't."

"Fuck you. What do you know about it?"

She knew she'd seen Caroline's black eye, but she couldn't say that. "If it's money you want, take me to the bank. I'll give you everything I have."

"You don't have squat. You're a no-good Cooper. Stop wasting my time."

He was right about the money. She searched for another way to stop him.

"Olivia!"

Olivia winced as Noah called after her. She didn't want Noah interfering in this. Devon would shoot him, and she'd lose everything good she'd ever had—

"Who's that?"

"No one."

"Damn it." Devon stopped short. Olivia tried to keep moving. The last thing she wanted was a show-down between him and Noah.

"Devon, I swear—I'll get you money—"

But Devon had drawn his pistol. Pointed it toward Noah. "Fuck that. Fuck all of you do-gooders. I'm not taking this shit anymore—"

Chapter Fourteen

NOAH SAW THE gun. Dove to the ground as a shot winged over his head. He heard Olivia scream and scrambled to his knees in time to see Steel take Devon down with a move straight out of a football playbook. Olivia went down, too, Devon and Steel landing on top of her as the men fought over the pistol. Noah didn't remember gaining his feet, but half a second later he threw himself into the melee. Together, he and Steel wrested the pistol from Devon's hands.

Olivia cried out again as Steel punched Devon in the jaw and the man fell across her. Noah tossed the pistol to Steel and hauled Devon up before punching him a second time. When Devon landed on the ground, Noah straddled him, flipped him over and maneuvered his arms behind his back. "I need rope. Whatever you can find," he called out, and a moment later, Liam reached them and thrust a tangle of rope into his hands.

"The sheriff is on his way," Stella cried, running up to them. "Noah, you okay?"

"I'm fine," he told her gruffly. "Watch him," he said to Steel and hurried to Olivia's side. She was just pushing up from the ground into a sitting position.

"You all right? Did he hurt you?"

She shook her head. "I'm fine." But she was shaking as she stood, and Noah reached out to steady her, then pulled her into a rough embrace.

"Hell, I thought I was going to lose you."

"How did you even know——?"

"Steel and I were talking. We saw Devon grab you. Saw you stiffen when he said something. You're no coward. You wouldn't have gone with him if you'd thought you had a choice. We knew he was threatening you."

"I'm glad you got him."

"Steel was the one who made the plan. I distracted Devon so he could get close. Couldn't have done it without him."

Olivia's heart contracted. That was Steel, always looking after her. "Thank you," she told her brother.

He just nodded and dragged Devon to his feet.

"You're going to pay for this," Devon snarled at him. "All of you."

"I don't think so," Steel said.

"You're the one who's going to pay for threatening to kill my girlfriend," Noah said.

"Your girlfriend stole something that's mine."

Noah moved to protest, but Steel turned to Olivia. "What's he talking about?"

"I didn't steal anything." Olivia kept her gaze on Devon. "Caroline needed some things from her house. I went and got them." Steel didn't budge. Finally Olivia gave in. "Including a winning lottery ticket she'd purchased and the cash he cleaned out of her account. It's all hers, not Devon's. I didn't take a thing that belonged to him."

"Caroline's my common-law bride. What belongs to her belongs to me."

"No, she isn't—" Olivia started, but Noah spoke over her.

"Caroline took your last name?" he asked Devon.

"No—she's Caroline Selwich, not Caroline Host," Olivia answered when Devon didn't.

"She called you her husband?" Noah asked him.

"No," Olivia said again. "She only ever called him her boyfriend."

"Then you aren't husband and wife," Noah told Devon. "Not even common-law."

"We lived together for years," Devon snarled.

"That doesn't matter—not in Montana. There are particular steps you have to take, and it sounds like Caroline didn't take any of them. If she bought the ticket, it's hers."

"And beating her up doesn't give you the right to take it," Olivia added. "You should have seen her black eye," she said to Steel.

Steel's expression hardened, and when he lifted Devon closer, for the first time Devon's cockiness faltered. "Hey. Wait a minute—"

"Black eye, huh?" Steel said. "Like this?"

He struck Devon with his fist so hard the man flew several feet before hitting the ground. Steel went after him.

"Hey! Hold up!" Noah called out, rushing to pull him off. It took Liam and Lance as well to stop him from landing more punches. When a siren sounded in the distance, Steel settled down. Devon moaned where he lay.

"Why didn't you tell me about the lottery ticket? And the cash?" Noah asked Olivia when things were under control.

"I couldn't take a chance that you'd say we needed to let them figure it out in court. Caroline needed something to live on."

"Cab would have helped you—"

"When has a Chance Creek sheriff ever helped a Cooper? Law enforcement isn't on our side." She bit her lip and looked away.

Noah felt her words like a hit below the belt. He'd never truly realized what the world looked like from where Olivia stood. If she didn't think she could ask for help in even the most extreme circumstances, then how could she ever feel safe—or at peace?

"How come you didn't come to *me*?" Steel growled. "I would have taken care of it."

"And landed in jail like Dad? Maybe never made it out?" Olivia shook her head. "I handled it. Caroline's safe. She's going to have money to get her through. She's with people who will help her. I did what needed to be done because I know how to do that."

She looked from Noah to Steel. "I'm not made of sugar. I don't need a man to protect me—" She stopped. Closed her eyes. Noah could almost see her anger slipping away. "But thank you. Both of you. For being there when I did need you."

"Just what on God's green earth is going on around here?"

Noah straightened as Virginia marched up to them. She looked as mad as a wet hen.

This wasn't going to be good.

"That's what I want to know. Since when do you fraternize with the enemy on our land?" Jed asked, limping toward them, leaning heavily on his cane. He looked tired, and Noah wondered if the day had gotten to him. His uncle shouldn't be spending hours in the sun like this.

"We're saving the library," he said. "That's the whole point, right?"

"Coopers don't have any business with the library," Jed said. "Doubt they can even read."

"My girlfriend reads, don't you, Olivia?" Noah put his arm around her shoulder.

Jed's eyes widened, but it was Virginia who spoke.

"Girlfriend? What's he talking about?" she demanded of Olivia. "Coopers don't date Turners."

Jed rounded on her. "They did once upon a time."

"No need to cast that in my face. I've done my penance," Virginia snapped back.

"You didn't think it was such a hardship back when I used to kiss you good-night. Could hardly peel you off me." Jed limped nearer.

"I never kissed you!"

"Liar! You wore my ring for months. Would have

married me if—"

"If you weren't a reprobate and a dissembler and an all-around hooligan," Virginia cut him off. "You had me fooled for a time, Jed Turner, but I found out what you were about." She turned on Olivia. "You mark my words: this one will break your heart, too. Turners are Turners, and nothing can change that."

"You don't know anything about it," Jed told her. "Because you can never shut your mouth long enough to listen to someone else."

"That's because I don't want to hear what you have to say. You had your chance, and you lost it." Virginia humphed and marched away. "Olivia, Steel, Lance, come!"

"I'm not going anywhere," Olivia said. "I need to talk to Cab, and I don't want to go home. I want to help save the library."

"I'll make sure Virginia gets home. You got this, Turner?" Steel asked Noah, gesturing to Devon.

"Yeah, I got this," Noah said. "Go on."

"I'm staying, too." Lance shrugged when Steel frowned at him. "Want to see the bands later." But he glanced at Maya, who was hovering nearby.

Steel nodded. "I'll be back in an hour or so."

A small crowd had formed to watch the fun. "All right, everyone, show's over," Stella called out, "But another one is about to start on the stage. Everyone ready for some dancing?" Maya joined her in urging people toward the music, and moments later the crowd had dispersed.

"You sure you want to stay?" Noah asked Olivia, grateful to his sisters for diffusing the situation.

"I'm sure," she said. "I'm not letting Virginia call the shots."

"Good." Noah faced Jed. "I'm not letting anyone else boss me around, either. Olivia's part of my life now, whether you like it or not."

Jed was still watching Virginia walk away. When he turned around, Noah sucked in a breath at the raw pain he saw on his uncle's face. Jed glanced at Olivia and nodded.

"If you really love her, don't let anything stop you." He limped off without another word.

"What do you think happened between those two?" Olivia asked sadly.

"I don't know. But I don't want to make whatever mistake they did," Noah told her. "I want to be with you."

"I want to be with you, too."

"I'm going to ask you to marry me soon," he confessed. "You all right with that?"

"We haven't even dated yet," she pointed out.

"Fine. We'll date. Starting right now. I'll buy you lunch."

"Sounds good," she agreed. "After we talk to the sheriff," she added as the siren wound down and Cab's cruiser came into view, but when Noah bent to kiss her, she went up on tiptoe to meet him.

IT WAS NEARLY two in the morning when they gathered

again in the living room at the Flying W. The crowds were gone, Fulsom and his retinue had finally left for the airport, and everything that hadn't been packed up tonight would be dealt with in the morning.

"I never dreamed it would all go so well." Maya flopped back onto the couch. "How much did we raise?"

"Hold on. I've almost added it all up," Stella said.

Olivia waited, tucked into an overlarge easy chair next to Noah. Liam sat on the floor, his back to the couch. Steel and Lance prowled around the room looking too uncomfortable to stand still. Jed had gone to bed some time ago—thank goodness, as far as Olivia was concerned. He didn't like this truce between the families.

"Whatever it is, it will be a godsend," Marta said. She'd waited on Olivia's urging to see the outcome of the day's sales, although the librarian had pleaded too old to be up so late.

"We'll have exact figures in a day or two from our take from the food vendors, but judging from the estimates Camila gave me, and the entry fees we collected, I'd say we earned more than ten thousand dollars," Stella announced.

"Well," Marta said. "That's something!"

"That's not all, though," Stella said. "Carl Whitfield gave this to me earlier. Said it was something extra to throw in the pot from all the California guests. Olivia, it's addressed to you. I haven't opened it."

Olivia got up and crossed the room to take the envelope from Stella's hands. Good old Carl; he could always be counted on to help the town.

She tore open the envelope and pulled out a check, then swallowed hard when she took in the number of zeroes on it.

"Oh, my goodness. I—" She passed it quickly back to Stella, who sucked in a breath and then laughed.

"I think we'll get the job done with this," she said.

"What is it?" Liam demanded.

"Two hundred thousand dollars," Stella pronounced.

Marta gaped at her and placed a hand over her heart. "Are you pulling my leg?"

"Uh-uh." Stella read it again. "Two hundred thousand dollars. I think we're going to have the spiffiest library around."

"I think you're right," Marta said. "And Olivia, I think I'm going to be able to offer you that job you wanted."

"I can't believe it," Maya said. "We're going to win!"

Olivia, halfway across the room to hug Marta, stumbled as the truth of Maya's words crashed over her. With all that money, the Turners would be able to turn the library into something special. Would that be enough to win the Founder's Prize?

"Those California people certainly enjoyed themselves," Marta said, oblivious to the currents running through the room. "Never seen a bunch of grown-ups so pleased by something so simple."

"Carl always told me how many hours he worked at

a desk back in his Silicon Valley days. Maybe it's the same for them," Olivia said, still wrapped up in her thoughts. "Maybe they don't get to play outside enough." She'd only gotten glimpses of them through the day. They'd stuck together, but Marta was right; they did seem to have fun.

"I'll take ranching any day." Noah kept his gaze on her, obviously worried about her reaction to Maya's proclamation. As well he should be. The Turners and Coopers had worked together tonight. That didn't mean they would in the future, though.

"Well, I'm going to get these old bones home," Marta said. "That's more excitement than I've had in a lifetime. Thanks to all of you for saving our library. Chance Creek would have been the poorer without it."

Olivia and Noah walked her to the door. When Olivia hugged her on the way out, Marta paused. "I know it isn't any business of mine, but I want you to know I approve of what's going on between the two of you. You are not your parents, and what William and Enid did shouldn't keep you apart, no matter what anyone says."

Olivia froze, glancing from Marta to Noah.

"What William and Enid did?" Noah looked just as lost as she felt.

"Oh, heavens." Marta looked away. "What am I thinking? Loose lips…"

"What do you know, Marta?" Olivia demanded.

Marta sighed but continued reluctantly. "You know we have a computer system now for book loaning and returns, but it's only about five years old. Before that we checked out books the old-fashioned way."

Olivia remembered. She'd helped sometimes when she was young. The system included folks writing their names on a card held in a sleeve inside the cover of the book, and the librarian stamping both the card and the sleeve with the due date for its return. The patron took the book, and the library kept the card.

"That meant I saw the titles people checked out. I tried not to snoop, but I couldn't help but see them, you know."

"I know," Olivia said. She tried to hold her impatience in check.

"Your mother," Marta said to Noah, "checked out several books right before she left. One was called *The Best Revenge is a Life Well Lived*. It was about how to recover after being cheated on. Mary was very angry. I'll always remember what she said when she caught me reading the title. 'That's right—twenty-three years of marriage down the drain. One husband isn't enough for Enid Cooper. She wants mine, too!' She marched out of here before I could say a word. I never saw her again." Marta looked down. "I'm so sorry. I never should have brought it up."

"Don't be sorry," Noah said slowly. Olivia wondered how he could find his voice at all. She couldn't. Her mother and Noah's father? That made no sense. "My parents' marriage was rocky a long, long time."

Olivia looked up. "It was?"

"My parents always argued a lot. Still, it was a big

surprise when Mom took off. Always wondered what happened."

"But—" She couldn't see her mother taking up with William. "How long were they carrying on?" She needed to reevaluate everything she knew. Her mother had never breathed a word about William. Hadn't seemed affected at all when the man died several years ago. Something didn't add up.

"Mom took off right around the time your dad went to jail."

"So right after Maya spilled the beans—" Olivia stiffened. Hell, had she just said that out loud?

"Maya? Spilled the beans about what?"

Olivia opened the door and pushed Marta and Noah out onto the front stoop. She didn't want anyone else to hear what she had to say; the feud would flare up all over again.

"You have to swear not to tell a soul," she said. "Both of you."

Marta nodded instantly, Noah more reluctantly.

"The day I found the marijuana crop on the Ridley property, Maya was with me. Marta, this was years ago—back before my dad went to jail."

"I see," Marta said.

"I had to get Maya out of there before she saw what it was. I took her back to Thorn Hill, but Lance was hanging around, so I pulled her into our barn. She saw some pelts my dad had drying. She must have realized it was the wrong time of year for that. I'm pretty sure she's the one who told the sheriff my dad was poaching.

Then I told him the location of my dad's hunting cabin. He'd gone there for a weekend with the guys. They were supposed to be playing cards out there. He'd been doing that pretty regularly."

"Funny. My dad kept taking weekends with the guys, too, back then. We had extra chores when he was gone," Noah said.

Olivia shook her head. "Well, they weren't playing cards together," she quipped. "Sorry, but my dad never had anything good to say about yours. He definitely believed in upholding our side of the Cooper–Turner feud."

"Huh."

"What's that mean?"

"It's just... well, no one's supposed to know this." He went on when Olivia rolled her eyes. She was right; they were all telling secrets. He might as well tell his. "My dad took care of Thorn Hill after your dad went to jail. Paid the bills until he found a tenant, then kept an eye on the place. I found out when he died and the job fell to me."

Olivia blinked. "William watched over Thorn Hill? We were told there'd been a caretaker but not who it was. We all thought Dad sold the place. Mom signed away her rights to it, you know."

"I didn't know that." Noah thought that over. "If she was cheating with my dad, would Dale ask him to take care of the place? That seems mighty... open-minded."

"Unless he didn't know."

"I'm sorry to bring up old memories," Marta said again. She looked every bit her age, and Olivia realized she needed to be in bed.

"Don't worry about it. Noah and I would have shared all our stories eventually," Olivia told her. "Go home and sleep. I can't wait to start my new job."

"Can't wait to have you there. And to fix up the old place."

Marta took her leave. When she was gone, Olivia turned to Noah. "Marta's a sweetheart, but I think she's got that story wrong. I just can't see Mom being with your dad."

"Doesn't seem likely to me, either. Still can't figure out how Dad ended up taking care of Thorn Hill."

"It makes no sense," she agreed. She thought it over. "It's all such a mess. I hate that I'm the reason my dad went to jail."

"You aren't the reason." He drew her near. "He did what he did. You are not to blame in any of this, Olivia. Remember that. You tried to do the right thing. He's the one who messed up. My dad, too. He should have stayed home more. Tried to see eye to eye with my mom."

"If our parents did have an affair, would this be wrong?"

"Absolutely not." His arms tightened around her. "Even if they did, I don't think it could have been more than a short-term thing."

"My mom has to be the best actress in the world. I mentioned to her when your dad passed away. She didn't react at all."

"I guess we'll never know what happened."

"I could ask her," Olivia said doubtfully.

"Why stir up something so far in the past? Dad's gone. You've got your ranch back. Mom's got a new life. Enid is doing fine, too, isn't she?"

"I think so."

"Then let's leave it. That's what we Turners and Coopers need to learn to do—let the past go, and live in the present. Don't you think?"

"I guess so. I don't want to lose you," she confessed, pressing her cheek to his chest, hearing his heartbeat in the quiet of the night.

"You aren't going to lose me, I promise. Come on, let's call it a night."

"Do you mean—"

"You and me. Camila's old cabin."

Olivia grinned at him. "You're on."

THIS TIME WHEN Noah led Olivia into Camila's old cabin, he had an armload of bedding and a six-pack of beer, and Olivia's hands were full of leftovers Camila and Fila had offloaded on them earlier. They made up the bed, then spread out their food picnic-style on it. Noah offered her a beer, and Olivia took it. When they were both sitting cross-legged on the bed, they dug in.

Noah liked the companionable silence as they took the edge off their hunger.

"I can't believe Jed gave us his blessing," Olivia said finally.

"Not to mention Steel and Lance,"

"And Liam, Stella and Maya." She took a swig of her beer. "Do you think the peace will last?"

"I hope so." He paused. "I don't think we should count on it, though. Not unless Liam and Lance bury the hatchet."

"They didn't fight today," Olivia pointed out.

"Not today."

"You and Steel seem to be getting along."

She was right. Earlier this evening, once the tubing rides were done, he'd gone to see Olivia's brother by the creek. Working side by side in silence, they'd dug in the creek bed until less water ran into the Turners' irrigation channel and more flowed onward to fill the one where the Coopers watered their stock.

They'd faced each other in the dimness, the water rushing around them.

"Thank you," Noah had said. "For saving Olivia."

"Couldn't have done it without your help."

"And for helping with the fundraiser. We wouldn't even have a shot at the prize if it wasn't for Olivia's idea."

"Ideas aren't worth much without actions."

Noah had studied him, wondering how much there was he didn't know about Steel. Despite the mystery, he thought Steel could be counted on. The man wasn't quite the outlaw Noah had thought he might be. Which was a good thing, considering he would be family soon.

Family.

"We're even, then?" he had said at last.

"As long as there are no more tricks, no more letters or sabotage—" Steel had extended his hand, and Noah had clasped it firmly. "Then may the best family win."

Noah kissed the side of Olivia's head, glad to be with her tonight. "I'm not worried about what happens between our families. I'm just glad you're safe."

"I am, too. I'm glad Caroline's long gone and that so many witnesses saw Devon attack me. That's got to help her case."

"I'm sure it will." He kissed her again. He couldn't get enough of her. He was so thankful she was back in his arms. When he thought he might have lost her today—

"Noah, you're squeezing me."

"Sorry." He let her go.

"I'm going to miss Caroline. She's been my only real friend for a long time. First woman I've ever been able to trust since..." She cleared her throat. "Well, since Maya."

"That must have hurt when she betrayed you."

"It did."

He thought back. "Maya mooned around a long time after Mom left. I wonder if at least part of that was because she was missing you." He realized that all of them had suffered in silence when his family broke apart. He and his siblings had unanimously decided to stay at the Flying W instead of moving to Ohio with his mother, but he couldn't remember ever talking about it.

Now he wondered if they somehow collectively thought that if they acted as one she'd change her mind and stay in Chance Creek, too—or better yet, patch things up with their dad. He found he couldn't remember much about the day she'd left, as if the images and words they must have spoken had vanished from his mind.

He'd blocked it out.

Noah swallowed. He'd been more affected by his mother's defection than he'd realized. Were Liam, Stella and Maya scarred by his parents' split-up, too?

"Maya sicced the sheriff on us," Olivia said bullishly.

"She might not have realized the repercussions. She was just a kid—like you." Noah's chest tightened when he realized Maya really had been a kid back then. William had been busy running the ranch. She'd effectively raised herself.

"Maybe so. I sure didn't realize what I was doing when I went to the sheriff," Olivia mused. Her face was tight with remembered pain, and Noah wished he could ease it. He'd need to think more about Maya later. Right now Olivia needed his attention.

"You both tried to do what was right," he told her.

"And Dad ended up in jail."

Noah chose his words carefully. "You know poaching doesn't carry jail time." He didn't want to add to her misery, but he didn't want to keep secrets from her either.

She snorted. "Not unless you're a Cooper."

"That's not what happened." Gently, he relayed everything Mahoney had told him.

When he was finished, she looked resigned. "Gun

trafficking. I would have never thought it. I guess he really did deserve to be in jail. I'm beginning to think I didn't know my father at all—or my mother."

"We don't know what the circumstances were." Not that he could think of any good reason to smuggle weapons over the border.

"I feel like I've lost almost everyone I ever cared about," Olivia said tiredly.

"But you've got me," Noah said, tugging her closer. "And I'm not going anywhere."

"Do you promise? Because I don't think I could take it—"

Noah wrapped his arms around her. Knew he couldn't go on without asking. "Olivia Cooper, will you marry me?"

She stared at him. "Noah, don't—not if you—"

"I've never been more serious in my life. We had our date. Now I want more. I want you—forever. I want you to be my wife."

"Why?"

She looked so surprised Noah nearly laughed.

"Because you're you."

"What does that mean?"

Noah took both her hands. "It means you're brave and you're caring and you're reckless and you're maddening and you're wonderful, and I haven't been able to think about another woman since I saw you cuddling puppies in front of the hardware store."

Olivia smiled. "I forgot about that."

"I'll never forget it. That's the day I knew you were

going to become my wife."

"Really?"

"Really. I've been patiently stalking you ever since."

"Noah Turner, you are the strangest man I've ever met."

"Here's the thing. I want my life to change. I want to build up the Flying W, not let it fall apart. I want to forget this feud between our families and move forward, without carrying the past along. I want to be part of Chance Creek's renaissance, not part of the forces holding it back. I feel like I can do that if you'll be by my side. You make me better, Olivia."

Olivia's eyes filled. "You make me better, too. That's everything I want. A new future. A better one. I'm ready to work, Noah. To build something. Fix something. To grow up and get it together."

"Exactly." She understood him. "So will you marry me?"

She took a deep, rough breath, and Noah waited in agony until she finally nodded. "Yes, I'll marry you."

Noah swallowed. She'd said yes.

She'd said—

Noah kissed her with everything he had, but that wasn't enough, and when he moved to pull her down on the bed beside him, the food and drinks got in the way. Olivia gathered them up and set them aside. Noah pitched in, scooping things off the bed as quickly as he could.

"Where were we?" he asked when they were done. His hands went to the buttons on her shirt, and she lay on her back, allowing him to undress her. When he'd exposed her bra to view, she tugged on his T-shirt, and he pulled it up over his head. Tossing it aside, he pulled her to him, brushing kisses over her breasts before reaching around to undo the clasp on her bra. When he managed to peel it off her, Noah took a moment to drink her in.

"What did I ever do without you?" he asked her.

"I'm sure you were miserable every second," she teased.

"I was. I was missing you."

"Noah—"

"I mean it," he said, cupping a breast and running his thumb over her nipple. She sighed, and he did it again. "I knew something was missing. It was you. I need you, Olivia."

She leaned into his touch and reached to kiss him, already tugging at the button on her jeans. When they were both naked, Noah rolled over and pulled her on top of him. "I want to see you." He ran his hands up to caress her breasts. As she straddled him, he thought he'd never seen anyone so lovely. Olivia was fully herself and fully open to being with him. He couldn't ask for more.

She rose on her knees and sank down around him. As Noah pushed into her, he wondered if his life could get any better than this. He suddenly understood the power of sex in a visceral way: two people joining as one. An act so intimate and so binding with the right person.

Olivia was the right person. Noah was sure of that. He hoped to God she was as sure of him.

As she rocked above him, her breasts swaying with their movements, the heat building between them, Noah touched her cheek.

"Forever?" He hadn't known he needed to ask the question, but he thought Olivia understood.

"Forever," she agreed and then moved with him until her cries brought him over the edge. As his climax crashed through him, Noah held on to Olivia, giving himself over to the sensations—to what they'd built together.

Olivia collapsed on top of him, and he crushed her to his chest, breathing in her scent, kissing her hair, her face, then catching her mouth. He wrapped his arms around her, not wanting to let go.

A life with Olivia was worth fighting for. Worth standing up for.

He would make it his first priority.

Everything else had to wait in line.

SURROUNDED BY NOAH'S embrace, Olivia had never felt so safe. She knew to the bottom of her soul if she protested with a breath, he'd release her. Noah had no need to control her—let alone hurt her the way Devon had hurt Caroline. Every action he took showed just how much he cared.

He was right; she had him, and she had other friends in Chance Creek, too. The Hall women had rallied around her to make the gala a huge success.

Camila, Fila and Mia Matheson were friendly, too, and she'd done a great job at the food tent during the tubing fundraiser—she had a feeling they'd ask her to fill in again in the future.

Marta was one of her staunchest allies in town, and soon she'd have a new job. One she'd always wanted—a position that would earn her respect over time.

Maybe someday she'd go back to school, get a degree and be able to take over running the library when Marta was ready to retire. She wasn't ready to speak that desire out loud yet, but somehow it seemed possible in a way it never had before.

Maybe someday she'd patch things up with Maya.

Maybe.

Maya and Stella would be her sisters-in-law.

Crazy.

She and Noah talked and slept and woke to make love again in the middle of the night and then slept again. Now a streak of sunlight splashed across the bed, and she knew they'd need to get up soon.

She wished she could stay in Noah's arms, but they had work to do, jobs to go to, family to bicker with…

Life with Noah would be interesting, and she had a million questions about their marriage, but one in particular had lodged in her heart and made her stomach twist.

When Noah shifted, she turned in his arms to face him.

"Hey, beautiful," he said.

"Hey, yourself, handsome."

He surveyed her a moment. "You're thinking about something. What is it?"

He knew her so well already. She had a feeling it would be hard to hide things from him.

"Did you mean what you said? About getting married?"

"Hell, yeah." He pushed up on his elbow, fully awake. "Didn't you?"

"Of course, but—where are we going to live?" She held her breath.

Noah nodded and thought about it. "Where do you want to live?" he asked finally. "I mean, it's easy enough to go from one ranch to the other. We both have obligations to our families."

She supposed that wouldn't change, but they'd need a home. "Noah, I can't... I can't leave my family. Not now. Not when we're just pulling it together again."

She saw a flash of pain cross his face, but he quickly nodded again. "I can see that."

"Nothing against the Flying W. I know you love it—"

"But Thorn Hill needs all hands on deck," he finished for her.

"Exactly."

"The thing is... so does the Flying W." He thought some more. "How about this." He lifted one of her hands to his mouth and kissed it. "If you agree to take my name, I'll agree to live on your ranch. Doesn't really matter where I sleep at night. I'll be working both spreads."

Olivia's heart constricted. His offer was fiendishly clever, but she supposed she could make that compromise, especially if her husband-to-be meant to care for Thorn Hill the way he did his own home. "Okay," she said slowly. "I can agree to that."

"One more stipulation," he added.

"What?" she asked suspiciously.

"We go get your ring soon. I want this deal sealed for all to see."

Olivia smiled. "I guess I can live with that, too."

"Good. We're going to have to make a lot of these compromises, you know," he added.

"I know, but we're strong enough to handle that. We'll be fine," she told him.

"You bet we will."

WHEN NOAH WALKED into the diner that afternoon, Brandon was already at their usual table, waiting for him. For a moment Noah wondered if he'd lost track of time, but when he checked his phone he found it was just as he'd thought: the man was ten minutes early.

That was a change.

Brandon looked up and spotted him, then waved and broke into a broad grin. A mug of coffee stood on the table in front of him, and another stood in front of Noah's place, prepared just the way he liked it.

"What's all this?"

Brandon ducked his head. "I've got some news."

"Shoot."

"It has to do with Christie."

Noah figured he should have guessed that.

"I know you didn't want me hanging around her," Brandon hurried to add. "I get it, too. You didn't want me to drag her into something bad for her, but you underestimated her, you know. She pulled me up rather than the other way around. She gave me a reason to get up in the morning when I didn't have one. Hey, you still with me, man?"

Noah snapped to attention. "Yeah, sorry." He'd gotten lost thinking about himself and Olivia. His whole family had acted like Olivia would poison him just because she was a Cooper, but instead she'd proven she was the strong, caring woman he'd always known she would be. He should have given Brandon more credit. "It really does look like she's been good for you."

Brandon lit up. "You don't know the half of it."

Noah laughed. "Got something you'd like to share?"

"I finally got a job, for one thing." Noah started to congratulate him, but Brandon, caught up in his excitement, plowed on. "It was the darnedest thing. I thought about what you said, about giving my folks a break, and I asked my mom if she needed any help. She didn't, but she knew some other people who did. She started loaning me out to her friends. I did all kinds of things: errands, yard work, home repairs. A couple of days ago, Mom asked me to run and pick up snacks for her knitting circle. Most of her friends were in it, so I got to see everyone again. It was kind of embarrassing to walk into that frilly knitting place with a box of cupcakes, but those ladies were as happy as if I was delivering gold.

"Then Mom introduced me to a new member who'd just moved to town. We got to talking, and I asked what brought her to Chance Creek—turns out she's the wife of the new owner of the Simmons place. Hilltop Acres. When she asked what I did, I told her I was looking for work. She offered me a job on the spot as a hand on her new spread."

"Brandon, that's great!" Noah said. "Really, I'm impressed."

"Before you ask, yes—I told her I'd been in jail. Told her everything that happened, and how I wanted to make a new start. Mom vouched for me. So did all the other ladies I'd helped. The best part is the job comes with room and board on the ranch." He laughed. "That'll give the folks a little space."

Noah nodded. "Sounds like they'll have a lot of space. Hilltop Acres is pretty far out of town."

"I like it. Seems like a good place to get away from it all. Do some good hard thinking."

"What are you doing all that thinking about?" Noah spread his hands and clarified, "Not asking as your parole officer. Just curious what direction you're going to go with your life."

Instead of answering Brandon rummaged in his pockets for a few moments and brought out a brochure. Noah's eyebrows shot up when he saw it. "Firefighter training?"

"I realized it feels good to help people. I'm hoping I can do a lot more of that before my life is over."

"Sounds like a good way to give back."

"Anyway, that's not even the kicker," Brandon said. "Now that I've got a steady income, Christie and I are moving in together. We worked out a fair way to split expenses. Since she can bunk with me free of charge, she won't have to pay rent anymore, which means she can help cover some of the other bills. Together we'll be able to save some money. Maybe it's not our dream house, but by this time next year, we'll have enough for our wedding."

"You're getting married?"

Brandon called Christie over to their table. "Show Noah your ring."

She held out her hand to Noah, showing him a silver band with a modest diamond.

"It's a placeholder ring," Brandon explained. "One of these days I'll be able to buy her a real one."

Christine shushed him with a kiss. "I told you, this is the only one I'll ever need."

"Looks good on your finger," Noah told her.

Olivia entered the restaurant and joined them, giving Noah a kiss of her own. "Hey, guys—you having a party?"

"Brandon and Christie are getting married," Noah told her. "Coincidentally, we're off to pick out our ring right now," he added.

Brandon broke out into a wide grin. "Congratulations." He shook Noah's hand, then Olivia's. "Looks like things are looking up for all of us."

Noah couldn't help but agree.

A short time later he and Olivia pulled up out front

of Thayer's Jewelers. When they went inside, Rose Johnson greeted them with surprise. Noah couldn't blame her. A Turner and Cooper looking for an engagement ring? He was sure the news would be all over town soon.

"What kind of ring do you want?" Rose asked Olivia.

"Something simple," Olivia said.

"Something beautiful," Noah told Rose. "For my beautiful bride."

"Try on as many as you like." Rose pulled out some trays and set them on the counter. "Take your time, you two."

Olivia did just that, but there was one she kept coming back to, a beautiful square diamond on a white-gold band.

"Is that the one?" he asked.

"I... think so," she said. "I like it a lot. But... is it too expensive?"

"Absolutely not. This is an investment, like our marriage. An investment in our future. Together we're going to be so much more than we ever could be apart." He kissed her. "I'm going to do everything I can to make your life wonderful, you know that?"

She nodded, her eyes shining.

"That one is beautiful," Rose said, coming back to see. "Do you need to try on more?"

Olivia shook her head. "This is the one." She handed it to Rose, and Rose held it for a moment with her eyes closed. Noah held his breath. Local legend said that she could tell a lot about a couple's future by holding their ring.

Noah sighed in relief when Rose grinned. "I wouldn't have believed it if I hadn't felt it, but it looks like a Turner and a Cooper can have a long, happy future together. Congratulations, you two. I hope this is the end of the feud between your families."

"I hope so, too," Noah told her, but he wasn't counting on it. All he was counting on was the way he felt when he was with Olivia. She was his world now. To hell with everyone else.

SEVERAL DAYS LATER Olivia stood up from the fence she was mending when she heard footsteps behind her. "Hope you brought some beer," she called out, thinking it was Lance or Steel. When she turned, wiping her hands on her work jeans, however, she saw Noah approaching with a smile on his face.

"No beer, sorry," he said, "but I did bring you this." He planted a long, passionate kiss on her lips.

"An acceptable substitute," she said when they broke apart. "What are you doing here?"

"I'm here to help," he said. "Once we're married, this ranch will be my responsibility, too, which means I need to do my part."

She peeled off her work gloves and handed them over. "I'm not going to argue with that. Hope you like patching fences. We've fallen a little behind lately, so there's a lot to do."

Noah laughed as he knelt down, picked up Olivia's

tools and got to work. "Maybe that's why our families have been fighting so much lately. Good fences make good neighbors, right?"

Olivia groaned affably. She watched Noah work, resting for a little while, but she figured she shouldn't take too much advantage of his good nature. "Be back in a minute with another pair of gloves," she said and jogged off toward the barn. When she returned, she sighed when she spotted Virginia, Lance and Steel grouped around Noah.

"You fool," Virginia said when she spotted Olivia. "Don't you see this is all part of his plan? You turn your back on this Turner, and he's going to deliberately sabotage our fences."

"Even if it's not deliberate, he'll mess up the job all the same," Lance said. "Turners don't know a thing about ranching."

Olivia bit back the tirade she longed to unleash, figuring she'd better let Noah handle the situation. He carefully laid down the tools, showing more respect for the beat-up old things than her brothers ever did, then spread his hands. "If I'm doing it wrong, I'd be more than grateful if you'd point out my mistakes."

Lance grumbled and shoved his hands in his pockets. Olivia fought down her laughter. Clever of Noah to disarm her brother like that. Lance didn't know how to fight an opponent who refused to fight back.

"In that case, I don't know what to tell you," Noah said. "Except that you'd better get used to me pitching in around here, since I'm going to live here."

"Live here?" Lance said. "What the—"

"Would you rather I moved to the Flying W?" Olivia asked him.

Steel was watching Noah. "Is that right?" he asked. It wasn't a challenge, and it wasn't a welcome.

"That's right." Olivia said. She probably should have given her family a heads-up after she and Noah came to that decision, but if she was being honest, she'd been glad to put this conversation off for a while. Not to mention she'd wanted to have Noah here for support when she dropped the news.

"We'll all likely end up dead in our sleep." Virginia turned on Steel and Lance. "Are you Coopers or not? Why aren't you running this reprobate off our land?"

Steel scrubbed a hand over his face, and she was pretty sure he was holding back a laugh. Olivia relaxed. If Steel was all right with her living arrangements, everyone else would soon fall in line.

"If it makes you feel better," she told Virginia, flashing the ring Noah had bought her earlier that day, "I won't be calling myself a Cooper very much longer." She couldn't resist pushing her aunt's buttons. "Anyway, you won't have to worry about him sleeping under your roof. Noah and I are taking over Carl's old cabin."

Virginia glowered, but Lance suddenly stepped forward and extended a hand to Noah. "I guess I can live with that," he said, giving Noah's hand a reserved shake. "Welcome to the best ranch on God's green earth."

Olivia braced herself, wondering if, even now, Noah

could let the dig at his own spread slide. But he smiled warmly, and when he answered Liam, she could tell he was speaking to her. "It's a pleasure to be here."

Chapter Fifteen

"Y OU'RE SURE ABOUT this, then?" Liam asked three weeks later, standing behind Noah and looking over his shoulder at his reflection in the mirror.

"No. I don't know which tie to wear," Noah admitted. He usually wasn't so indecisive, but he was acutely aware that this day would set the tone for the rest of his life. "Let me see the skinny one again."

Liam passed him a tie he had tried on five times already. "You know that's not what I meant."

"I know. Go on, let it out," Noah told his brother. "I can tell there's something on your mind."

Liam sighed. "You know what I think of the Coopers. I know you don't want to hear any of that right now, and that's fine. If you think being with Olivia is the right decision, then I trust you. But you remember your promise?"

Noah finished putting on the tie and adjusted it slightly. It would do. "Which promise?"

"You said that no matter what happened between you and Olivia, you were going to stay on our side when it comes to the Founder's Prize. Just because you live on their ranch now doesn't mean you get to back their claim to it."

Noah nodded. "I don't think that will be a problem. I'm not touching that school upgrade, whether to help or hinder. And I was fixing the library for Olivia in the first place. If we happen to win the stupid prize in the process, that's fine by me." They'd been hard at work at it every spare moment. He'd arranged a work party and repaired the roof last week. Next they'd paint the exterior. Then they'd move inside and do more renovations.

Liam nodded. "Good enough."

"One more thing." Noah turned from the mirror to face his brother head on. "I'm not switching sides, but I'm not taking part in any funny business, either. Don't expect me to try and sabotage them from within or anything like that."

Again Liam nodded, this time reluctantly. "You always were the upright one. Dad would be proud, you know? Not saying I always condone the way you handle things, but I sure as hell respect it." He shoved his hands in his pockets. "Going to miss having you around the ranch."

"You'll see me every day," Noah assured him. "I'll live at Thorn Hill, but I'm going to work both ranches, as much as I can. And hey, maybe we'll have you all over for Thanksgiving."

Liam snorted. "Fat chance of that."

"You won't still be living on that fallow spread come Thanksgiving." Jed appeared in the doorway, arms crossed. "I wouldn't trust that new wife of yours to live on the Flying W, but the both of you can move onto the Ridley property after we win it in October. If you raise your children on Turner land, maybe they'll at least turn out all right."

Noah put on a pensive expression. "You know, by the time Olivia and I are having kids, we probably won't be raising them ourselves. We'll have robots to do that."

Liam guffawed, but Jed smacked Noah on the head with the flat of his hand. "Don't even joke about that." He paused. "Noah?"

"Yeah?"

"You look good, son."

A short time later they all piled into Liam's truck. While Liam drove them to the church, Noah thought about what his life was going to look like after today. He knew Jed thought he was abandoning his family, but Noah didn't see it that way. He was moving in with the love of his life and helping out on his neighbors' ranch while he was at it. After all, Olivia was his family now, too.

It would take some time to get used to waking up on the other side of Pittance Creek every day, but he was excited to see what challenges and surprises Thorn Hill held for him.

He glanced at the bag that rested under his feet and smiled to himself. He had a surprise of his own for the residents of Thorn Hill. It would be a surprise to his family, too, but they'd get over it.

As soon as Liam pulled into a parking space in front of the chapel, Noah got out and headed for the knot of

Coopers gathered around Lance's truck on the other side of the lot. Olivia hadn't put on her dress yet, so he thought he was in the clear to talk to her.

"I know it's a little early to open gifts," Noah said after greeting Olivia with a kiss. "But I don't want to make a scene later. Can we talk in private a minute?"

"Of course." She led him into the church, into a small room set aside for bridal party members to use. "What's up?"

"I wanted you to have this." He handed over the bag.

Olivia looked at the bag curiously, then opened it and pulled out the antique grandmother clock she'd tried to steal so many times. "Noah!" she gasped. "Are—are you sure?"

"Of course. Like you said, it belongs at Thorn Hill."

Olivia held the clock with a reverence she'd never shown while trying to pilfer it. "I've never noticed how loudly it ticks before."

Noah chuckled. "It hadn't been set in years. I started it again before I came here." It hadn't been easy to get it to work, either, but he'd done it in the end. While he'd tinkered with it, he'd thought about how much of his life he'd spent wishing time could run backward. Ever since his father passed away, he'd ached to return to that happy, stable existence.

Now he'd started to look forward to the future. With Olivia, he knew that no two moments would ever be the same. Each day would bring new challenges, new twists and turns as Olivia led him on spontaneous adventures.

He wouldn't have it any other way.

EVEN AFTER NOAH excused himself and returned to his family, Olivia cradled the clock in her hands, tracing its fine-grained surface with her fingers. When a shadow darkened the door again, she looked up to see Steel.

"He's a good man," he said.

"I know," Olivia said. "Is that your way of saying I have your blessing?"

"As long as you're sure you know what you're doing." He held up a hand when she started to respond. "I take that back. You know what you're doing. You wouldn't do it if you didn't."

Olivia shook her head. "I think you're giving me a lot more credit than I deserve. I rarely know what I'm doing. But in this case, yes. I've never been more sure about anything."

Steel nodded, then looked away. "I supposed you won't need me anymore now that you've got Noah around. Wish I could have done a better job protecting you."

"You did fine. Besides, I can take—"

"Care of yourself," he finished for her. "I know. Doesn't stop me from wanting you to have the life you deserve."

"I think that's happening."

"You're happy, huh?"

"I am." The realization swelled inside her. She was. She had Noah, her family, her ranch, her community.

What more could she want?

Olivia shifted the clock to the crook of one arm so she could poke him in the ribs with the other. "Now you'll need to find a new damsel to look out for."

"Bit of a stretch to call you a damsel," Steel said, but he seemed suddenly distracted. Olivia followed his gaze to see Noah and his family entering the chapel.

"I'd better get changed," Olivia said.

"What's the holdup?" Virginia groused as she joined them. "This heat is ungodly. Let's get on with it already. No wonder your mother decided not to come. Anyone would be a fool to sit in a church that isn't air-conditioned in conditions like this."

Olivia's heart gave a pang. She'd understood why Enid was staying away—sort of. Her mother hated Chance Creek and never wanted to come back. Olivia had thought she'd make an exception this once, but instead her mother had asked her to bring Noah for a visit later in the summer. Aunt Joan had come. It was good to see her again, but it wasn't the same.

"And here I thought you wanted to put off my wedding to Noah as long as possible," she answered Virginia lightly. She wasn't going to let any member of her family ruin her day. Noah's mom wouldn't be here, either. She'd had lots to say about him marrying a Cooper, none of it good, and Noah had told her to stay away.

"Nonsense," Virginia returned. "You think I would have allowed all this if it wasn't part of my plans?"

"Allowed?" Olivia scoffed.

"Think of it. We've got plenty of grunt work for Noah to take on. That means the Turners are down a pair of hands. Good luck keeping their ranch running and still stealing the Founder's Prize from us. At least one good thing will come of this hellish drought, if it keeps the Turners out of our hair."

Olivia started to point out again she'd be a Turner soon but elected to keep her mouth shut. Let Virginia justify it however she wanted. As long as they were all on the same page.

"And what have you got there?" Virginia asked. Before Olivia could stop her, she snatched the clock. "Did you really give this back to Turners just so you could steal it again yourself?"

"I didn't steal it," Olivia said. "Noah gave it to me."

Virginia pursed her lips. "Hmm. Very well. It's a little tardy of him to try and bribe me for permission to marry you an hour before the wedding. Lucky for the both of you, I was raised to be gracious. You have my blessing."

Olivia opened her mouth, then shut it again. No sense arguing. At the end of the day, the clock, and Noah, would find a new home at Thorn Hill.

Where they belonged.

She turned when Caroline tapped on the door and came in. "Let's get you ready. Everyone else out." She made shooing motions at Virginia and Steel.

"Come on, Virginia." Steel led Virginia away. Caroline closed the door behind them and quickly helped Olivia into her gown. Olivia had visited a salon in town to have her hair, makeup and nails done. Once the gown was on, all she needed was her veil.

"Have I said how glad I am that you're here?" she asked as Caroline secured it for her.

"Several times." Caroline laughed. "I'm glad, too. Thank you for everything."

Now that Devon was being held without bail, Caroline had felt comfortable coming home. She had hired a lawyer who was helping her to untangle Devon from all her financial doings, but that would take some months.

"I would do it all over again, you know that, right? You've been such a good friend when I really needed one," Olivia told her.

"Right back at you." Carline gave her a quick hug. "Now come on. Let's line up. But first I've got a surprise for you."

"A surprise?"

Caroline moved to the door, opened it a crack, stuck her head out and then flung it wide. "Ta-da!" She made a flourish with her hands.

Olivia shrieked when a pixie-faced brunette came through the door. "Tory! You made it!"

"How could I stay away when my little sister's getting married—to a Turner, no less."

"You're not mad?"

"Mad?" Tory looked like she'd deny it, but then she laughed. "I don't know what to be if I'm honest."

"But you came anyway."

"I did. You're my sister, after all."

Music swelled in the church as Tory reached out to

hug her. "That's your cue. Good luck, and I'll see you afterward." She slipped back out the door, and Ella, Olivia's second bridesmaid, came in.

"Everyone ready?"

Olivia, head spinning, turned to look in the mirror and smooth the full skirts of her gown. This was it. She was marrying Noah. Tory was here. She wasn't sure how her heart wasn't bursting from her chest. She was so full of happiness she could hardly breathe.

"Come on," Caroline said. "Let's go. Olivia? You okay?"

Olivia nodded, overcome with emotion. "I think so."

"Hold my hand. I'll make sure you get to the altar."

Olivia laughed. She squeezed Caroline's hand. "Thanks, but I've got this." She waved Caroline and Ella ahead of her and followed them out the door to the head of the long aisle that led to the altar where Noah stood. She already felt steadier, and with Noah's gaze on her, and with Caroline and Ella leading the way, she straightened her spine and began the journey toward him.

NOAH STOOD AT the altar next to Liam and Eli, his cousin and the one man in the world he always could count on, and waited for the wedding to start. His relatives sat on one side of the aisle, including Eli's siblings, who had arrived with him the previous day to attend the ceremony. Brandon and Christie sat with them. Deputy Mahoney was there, too. On the other side, as far away as possible, was Virginia, Lance and Steel. Marta from the library sat with them, and the rest of the pews were filled with people from town. Noah had worried that resentment at the tensions the two families had caused might prevent some people from coming, so he was happy to see the benches filled with well-wishers. Their union hadn't brought Jed and Virginia any closer together, but he'd noticed a bit of a thaw between his siblings and Olivia's, and he hoped any children he and Olivia had someday might help heal the rift between the Coopers and Turners further.

"Hey," Liam whispered, leaning close. "Isn't that Tory Cooper?" He jutted his chin at a cute brunette sitting near Virginia.

"I think you're right."

"Huh." Liam looked intrigued.

Noah forgot about Tory—and Liam—the moment the wedding march started. First Caroline and Ella stepped slowly through the door and made their way toward the altar. When Olivia emerged, Noah's breath caught. Dressed in a beautiful gown with a square neckline and beaded bodice, she looked like a queen, and Noah hoped like hell he was worthy of her. He found it hard to look away from her during the rest of the ceremony. Dimly, he was aware of himself reciting his vows, but his focus was on the beautiful, wonderful woman by his side. When, at Reverend Halpern's bidding, he cradled Olivia's face in his hands and kissed her, something shifted in his chest as if the armor encasing his heart had broken apart.

For the first time in years, Noah felt free. This was everything he'd always wanted—

And they didn't have to hide anymore.

OLIVIA NEVER WANTED to let go of Noah's hand again. While they waited for dinner to be served, their relatives came up to congratulate them, each greeting more awkward than the last. Underneath the table, she and Noah kept squeezing each other's hands. They were both hard-pressed not to laugh. Olivia didn't mind. She was positive she and Noah would see this through, no matter how bumpy the ride got. The rest of the Turners and Coopers would have to adapt.

Still, Olivia tensed when Jed rose from his seat and signaled he wanted to give a toast. Up until now, the wedding had progressed much more smoothly than she'd dared to expect, but looking around the room, she noticed she wasn't the only one cringing in anticipation of what Jed would say.

"We've all come here today to show our support despite wondering what these two young folks could be thinking. That's what people do for the ones they love," he began. Not too bad so far, Olivia thought with a private smile. "I want to do my part, so I'm offering this gift."

Instead of turning toward the bridal table where she sat with Noah, he headed for Virginia.

Uh-oh.

She shot a warning look at Noah. They needed to stop this right now. Noah half stood.

"Here you go." Jed put something into Virginia's hands—her umbrella, Olivia realized.

"How did you get that?" Olivia called out. She'd given the pieces back to Virginia the day she brought the clock back to the Flying W. Virginia had tossed them down on the kitchen table in anger. Olivia hadn't seen them since.

"You're not the only one who knows how to sneak into an unlocked house," Jed said with satisfaction.

"Thief!" Virginia squawked at him. "What did you do to it?"

"I had it repaired."

Virginia took it from him and held it at arm's length, eyeing it suspiciously. "Why would you do that?"

"Think of it as your consolation prize, now that my family has the Founder's Prize sewn up." He turned half-away from her and projected his voice, ensuring the whole room would hear him. "After my rafting business single-handedly saved the library for many future generations to enjoy, it seemed only fair to leave you Coopers with something."

Virginia stood up faster than Olivia would have thought her old joints could manage and brought Jed's gift down on his head. Tory lunged to grab it before Virginia could hit him again. Liam rushed from the Turner table, took his uncle by the arm and led him away. "Come on, Jed," he said loudly. "Let's go get some ice cream."

Virginia examined the umbrella again. "Strong," she said approvingly.

"You're welcome," Jed called back, following Liam willingly.

Noah sat down again. "Ice cream is Jed's kryptonite," he explained under his breath. Olivia filed that away for future use as he lifted her hand and kissed it. "Sorry for my ornery relatives."

"Sorry for mine. But there's not a thing Jed or Virginia, or anyone else, could do that would ruin this day for me," she assured him. "As long as I have you, that's all I need."

"Well, you have me, Olivia. For good." He raised his glass of champagne and toasted her. "To the future."

"To the future."

IT WAS LATE in the evening when Lance approached Maya. "Want to dance?" he asked off-handedly. "Song's pretty good."

"Oh, what the hell," Maya said. "It is a wedding after all."

To find out more, look for *The Cowboy's Hidden Bride*,
Volume 3 in the *Turners v. Coopers* series.

Be the first to know about Cora Seton's new releases!
Sign up for her newsletter here!
www.coraseton.com/sign-up-for-my-newsletter

Other books in the Turners v. Coopers Series:

The Cowboy's Secret Bride (Volume 1)
The Cowboy's Hidden Bride (Volume 3)
The Cowboy's Stolen Bride (Volume 4)
The Cowboy's Forbidden Bride (Volume 5)

Read on for an excerpt of
Issued to the Bride One Navy SEAL.

Four months ago

O N THE FIRST of February, General Augustus Reed
entered his office at USSOCOM at MacDill Air
Force Base in Tampa, Florida, placed his battered
leather briefcase on the floor, sat down at his wide,
wooden desk and pulled a sealed envelope from a
drawer. It bore the date written in his wife's beautiful
script, and the General ran his thumb over the words
before turning it over and opening the flap.

He pulled out a single page and began to read.

Dear Augustus,

It's time to think of our daughters' future, beginning with Cass.

The General nodded. Spot on, as usual; he'd been thinking about Cass a lot these days. Thinking about all the girls. They'd run yet another of his overseers off Two Willows, his wife's Montana ranch, several months ago, and he'd been forced to replace him with a man he didn't know. There was a long-standing feud between him and the girls over who should run the place, and the truth was, they were wearing him down. Ten overseers in eleven years; that had to be some kind of a record, and no ranch could function well under those circumstances. Still, he'd be damned if he was going to put a passel of rebellious daughters in charge, even if they were adults now. It took a man's steady hand to run such a large spread.

Unfortunately, it was beginning to come clear that Bob Finchley didn't possess that steady hand. Winter in Chance Creek was always a tricky time, but in the months since Finchley had taken the helm, they'd lost far too many cattle. The General's spies in the area reported the ranch was looking run-down, and his daughters hadn't been seen much in town. The worst were the rumors about Cass and Finchley—that they were dating. The General didn't like that at all—not if the man couldn't run the ranch competently—and he'd asked for confirmation, but so far it hadn't come. Finchley always had a rational explanation for the loss of cattle, and he never said a word about Cass, but the General knew something wasn't right and he was already looking for the man's replacement.

Our daughter runs a tight ship, and I'm sure she's been invaluable on the ranch.

He had to admit what Amelia wrote was true. Cass was an organizational wizard. She kept her sisters, the house and the family accounts in line, and not for the first time he wondered if he should have encouraged Cass to join the Army back when she had expressed interest. She'd mentioned the possibility once or twice as a teenager, but he'd discouraged her. Not that he didn't think she'd make a good soldier; she'd have made a fine one. It was the thought of his five daughters scattered to the wind that had guided his hand. He couldn't stomach that. He needed his family in one place, and he'd done what it took to keep her home. That wasn't much: a suggestion her sisters needed her to watch over them until they were of age, a mention of tasks undone on the ranch, a hint she and the others would inherit one day and shouldn't she watch over her inheritance? It had done the trick.

Maybe he'd been wrong.

But if Cass had gone, wouldn't the rest of them have followed her?

He'd been able to stop sending guardians for the girls when Cass turned twenty-one five years ago, much to everyone's relief. His daughters had liked those about as little as they liked the overseers. He'd hoped when he dispensed of the guardians, the girls would feel they had enough independence, but that wasn't the case; they still wanted control of the ranch.

Cass is a loving soul with a heart as big as Montana, but she's cautious, too. I'll wager she's beginning to think there isn't a man alive she can trust with it.

The General sighed. His girls hadn't confided in him in years—especially about matters of the heart—something he was glad Amelia couldn't know. The truth was his daughters had spent far too much time as teenagers hatching plots to cast off guardians and overseers to have much of a social life. They'd been obsessed with being independent, and there were stretches of time when they'd managed it—and managed to run the show with no one the wiser for months. In order to pull that off, they'd kept to themselves as much as possible. He'd only recently begun to hear rumblings about men and boyfriends. Unfortunately, none of the girls were picking hardworking men who might make a future at Two Willows; they were picking flashy, fly-by-night troublemakers.

Like Bob Finchley.

He couldn't understand it. He wanted that man out of there. Now. Trouble was, when your daughters ran off so many overseers it made it hard to get a new one to sign on. He had yet to find a suitable replacement.

Without a career off the ranch, Cass won't get out much. She might not ever meet the man who's right for her. I want you to step in. Send her a man, Augustus. A good man.

A good man. Those weren't easy to come by in this world. The right man for Cass would need to be strong to hold his own in a relationship with her. He'd need to be fair and true, or he wouldn't be worthy of her. He'd need some experience ranching.

A lot of experience ranching.

The General stopped to ponder that. He'd read something recently about a man with a lot of experience ranching. A good man who'd gotten into a spot of trouble. He remembered thinking he ought to get a second chance—with a stern warning not to screw up again. A Navy SEAL, wasn't it? He'd look up the document when he was done.

He returned to the letter.

> *Now here's the hard part, darling. You can't order him to marry Cass any more than you can order Cass to marry him. You're a cunning old codger when you want to be, and it'll take all your deviousness to pull this off. Set the stage. Introduce the players.*
>
> *Let fate do the rest.*
>
> *I love you and I always will,*
> *Amelia*

Set the stage. Introduce the players.

The General read through the letter a second time, folded it carefully, slid it back into the envelope and added it to the stack in his deep, right-hand bottom drawer. He steepled his hands and considered his options. Amelia was right; he needed to do something to make sure his daughters married well. But they'd rebelled against him for years, so he couldn't simply assign them husbands, as much as he'd like to. They'd never allow the interference.

But if he made them think they'd chosen the right men themselves…

He nodded. That was the way to go about it.

In fact…

The General chuckled. Sometime in the next six months, his daughters would stage another rebellion and evict Bob Finchley from the ranch. He could just about guarantee it, even if Cass was currently dating the man. Sooner or later he'd go too far trying to boss them around, and Cass and the others would flip their lids.

When they did, he'd be ready for them with a replacement they'd never be able to shake. One trained to combat enemy forces by good ol' Uncle Sam himself. A soldier in the Special Forces might do it. Or maybe even a Navy SEAL…

This wasn't the work of a moment, though. He'd need time to put the players in place. Cass wasn't the only one who'd need a man—a good man—to share her life.

Five daughters.

Five husbands.

Amelia would approve.

The General opened the bottom left-hand drawer of his desk, and mentally counted the remaining envelopes that sat unopened in another stack, all dated in his wife's beautiful script. Ten years ago, after Amelia passed away, Cass had forwarded him a plain brown box filled with envelopes she'd received from the family lawyer. The stack in this drawer had dwindled compared to the opened ones in the other drawer.

What on earth would he do when there were none left?

End of Excerpt

The Cowboys of Chance Creek Series:

The Cowboy Inherits a Bride (Volume 0)
The Cowboy's E-Mail Order Bride (Volume 1)
The Cowboy Wins a Bride (Volume 2)
The Cowboy Imports a Bride (Volume 3)
The Cowgirl Ropes a Billionaire (Volume 4)
The Sheriff Catches a Bride (Volume 5)
The Cowboy Lassos a Bride (Volume 6)
The Cowboy Rescues a Bride (Volume 7)
The Cowboy Earns a Bride (Volume 8)
The Cowboy's Christmas Bride (Volume 9)

The Heroes of Chance Creek Series:

The Navy SEAL's E-Mail Order Bride (Volume 1)
The Soldier's E-Mail Order Bride (Volume 2)
The Marine's E-Mail Order Bride (Volume 3)
The Navy SEAL's Christmas Bride (Volume 4)
The Airman's E-Mail Order Bride (Volume 5)

The SEALs of Chance Creek Series:

A SEAL's Oath
A SEAL's Vow
A SEAL's Pledge
A SEAL's Consent
A SEAL's Purpose
A SEAL's Resolve
A SEAL's Devotion
A SEAL's Desire
A SEAL's Struggle
A SEAL's Triumph

The Brides of Chance Creek Series:

Issued to the Bride One Navy SEAL
Issued to the Bride One Airman
Issued to the Bride One Sniper
Issued to the Bride One Marine
Issued to the Bride One Soldier

The Turners v. Coopers Series:

The Cowboy's Secret Bride (Volume 1)
The Cowboy's Outlaw Bride (Volume 2)
The Cowboy's Hidden Bride (Volume 3)
The Cowboy's Stolen Bride (Volume 4)
The Cowboy's Forbidden Bride (Volume 5)

About the Author

NYT and USA Today bestselling author Cora Seton loves cowboys, hiking, gardening, bike-riding, and lazing around with a good book. Mother of four, wife to a computer programmer/backyard farmer, she recently moved to Victoria and looks forward to a brand new chapter in her life. Like the characters in her Chance Creek series, Cora enjoys old-fashioned pursuits and modern technology, spending mornings in her garden, and afternoons writing the latest Chance Creek romance novel. Visit **www.coraseton.com** to read about new releases, contests and other cool events!

Blog:

www.coraseton.com

Facebook:

www.facebook.com/coraseton

Twitter:

www.twitter.com/coraseton

Newsletter:

www.coraseton.com/sign-up-for-my-newsletter